My Way and the High Way

My Way and the High Way

A novel

Jaide Marie McGee

Artists support artists, not AI

Cover design, chapter icon, page break design, title page artwork by Ryan Snyder

Cover photography by Iryna Wilcox

Author photograph by Didi von Boch

This story is for all those who reported to me when I was a new manager trying to shatter the glass ceiling.

My bad.

1

Your plane is taxiing down the runway. Everything outside is exactly as you would expect. Cars look like cars and people look like people. You can even make out the garish design of some cheap plastic suitcase waiting its turn to be loaded on another plane. While the plane picks up pace, you remain confident. You know exactly what is going to happen. The plane will lift off the ground, and you'll start to feel pressure pushing you down into your seat followed by a temporary weightlessness until the plane levels out. High enough in the air, flying starts to feel like being driven around in a taxi.

But you're not on the ground.

When you look out the window, people don't look like people, and cars don't look like cars. They look like toys until you can't even make them out at all. Mountains are sprawling enough to be seen, but they appear to flatten from above. It's all getting lost in the clouds. Your understanding your surroundings goes right out the tiny, shared window.

You stop trying to make sense of what you're seeing and push in some earbuds. Your head is filled with sounds of your favorite podcast. You relax (to the extent possible while flying through the sky in a metal tube filled with the recycled breaths of strangers).

Out of nowhere, the smooth glide is interrupted as if the plane has challenged a giant pothole to a game of chicken. You glance discreetly through the window, unwilling to be the first to panic. You're reminded there is no road. No pothole. Only sky. Sky that looks the same as the rest of the sky with wisps of white against the baby blue.

The reassuring voice of the pilot announces some temporary turbulence. You realize that it wasn't the sudden rough ride that pulled your focus from your self-help podcast, it was a subtle chime you barely registered. The sound of the seatbelt sign, which turned on moments *before* the slight downward chop of the plane put your heart in your throat.

It can only mean one thing.

The pilot knew this patch of sky was different. They realized changes in the feel of the movement of the plane or in the sky itself. Things you did not discern. You're immediately grateful that you're safe with this omniscient pilot.

I'm not saying you don't need airplane mechanics and luggage handlers to keep things moving on the ground. But when you get to 10,000 feet or whatever and everything on the ground gets two dimensional and distant, you're happy to surrender control to the pilot.

For an experience pilot, the higher up you get, the more similar everything becomes. Sure, a pilot has to learn some buttons for new planes or silly little rules for different airports. But at the end of the day, the sky is the sky is the sky.

Which is exactly why you need experienced executives running companies. A great Chief Executive Officer doesn't have to have *industry* experience. They have *executive* experience. It doesn't matter if the company produces cars or hats or thingamajigs. It's all just another widget when viewed from the top.

A CEO can run a company that sells or does *anything*. If the CEO is fantastic, then the product will be too.

In this case, that *anything* we sell is cannabis, and that CEO is me. Today is the official press release announcing my appointment to the role, but I've known for a long time.

I've been consulting for the CEO of the Wellness Enterprise of Exceptional Dispensaries for the last few years. I've become a close personal confidant and basically like family. A consigliere if you will, just with less crime. Not *zero* crime though because cannabis is still federally illegal.

I may not know much, or anything, about cannabis. But I *am* still the best choice to fill his shoes. Everyone knew I was next in line. Except one man whose delusion is only outweighed by his hubris and his big head. Not a metaphor for his ego. Man just has a giant head.

It's about time W.E.E.D. had a woman in the cockpit *and* someone that's under fifty. If there was one thing I'd learned about consulting for Joe, the previous CEO, it was that old dudes like that are resistant to change. They hate new ideas. I was always a little baffled at how someone like him came to be the founder of a cannabis company when he was already past retirement age.

Founder being a generous word for it. These big companies are backed by a lot of money while masquerading as a 'start-up'. A bunch of elderly men with too much money get together and decide to start a company. Doesn't matter if they have a good or unique idea because they have enough money to push the competition out of the way.

They get in a big financial circle jerk and vote the one with biggest dick to be the founder. Or would it be the biggest balls? No guarantee those would belong to the same man. Either way, whether they pulled out the ruler or the scale, W.E.E.D. decided Joe Caldarelli would be the 'founder' and CEO and everyone else would be investors or on the board. Since none of them needed future jobs, titles were irrelevant. Everything was about the money. Joe did also get praised for 'being a visionary' as if he were the first to introduce the concept of selling weed.

Joe didn't seem to care about being in the spotlight. But he also didn't step down when the company went public like he should have. It never made sense to me. Except that none of the other dinosaurs wanted someone younger in charge.

The optics of that were too risky. God forbid anyone assume a pothead is running our cannabis company. Most of the stoners do work at the entry level; retail or cultivation facilities. Executives are more likely to take a microdosed gummy at night to fall asleep then take a handful of amphetamines in the morning to get the day started.

Knock. Knock.

I just barely arrived, who knows I'm here? I didn't even get out a full "Who is..." before the door to Joe's office – my office – opens abruptly and a giant head pops in, followed by a lanky body. Only one person I know enters the room headfirst.

"Tony?" I say, his name holding the place of the question: *what do you think you're doing?*

"Checking to see if I left anything in here," he said. Straight to his wants. Didn't even say 'howdy'.

"It's been a *week*, enough time to clear out." Looking around the office, it was giant, but mostly empty. Joe had simple style. While the two mahogany bookcases, mahogany desk and dark brown leather chair were massive, they weren't cluttered. He had it arranged so that sitting in the chair put your back to the window, the high back blocking the "view" for any guests.

"I spent several months in here."

"*Two* months," I corrected.

"*Almost* three," he negotiated.

"Maybe it was one and a half," I countered.

He took five steps forward, halving the distance between the door and the desk, putting his weight on his right foot, a peculiar stride I'd become accustomed to. "I didn't come in here to argue." Says the guy who lost the argument. "I wanted to check if I left any... files. In the desk."

I scoffed. "I've never seen *you* keep a paper copy of anything. I'm sure Tiffany has them."

"My agent cards might be tucked away in—"

"I gave them to Tiffany."

Tony took two steps closer. Was he trying to intimidate me? "Sometimes I leave extra shoes or shirts, for urgent meetings."

Urgent meetings on the golf course.

"It's a desk, not a wardrobe and I gave *everything* from the closet to Tiffany." I ended my sentence with too soft of a period, like I was going to say more. I resisted the urge to fill the silence, to ask him what else he needed. *He's* the one that entered *my* office, uninvited. Least he can do is be the one to unburden us from this awkward show down.

"I…" he took a deep breath. "I wanted to say goodbye."

"What are you talking about?" I asked. Was he quitting? My heart did a jig, but my head was rooted firmly in reality. "You're the COO. We're going to see each other all the time. No need to say goodbye."

"Not to you," he chuckled a little. I felt my face blush. "I wanted to say goodbye to the office."

Trying to avoid embarrassment, I pulled out of nowhere, "It *is* a pretty nice view." The view is mediocre. I keep rescuing him from his uncomfortable choices, burdening myself with making the conversation run smoothly. "The view isn't going anywhere. We'll have lots of meetings in here."

"You're going to change this place," he said, like it was a bad thing.

I offered testily, "Change is progress. A lot about this place needs to change. You'd do well to get with the times."

He breathed heavily, forcing the air out through slightly pursed lips. "Jesus, Vanessa. Can you stop busting my balls for five minutes? This office, it's going to change from how my... how Joe left it. I saw him more in *this office* the last ten years than I did anywhere else."

Oh. I guess this means *I'm* the jerk. Not sarcastically but factually: I am the jerk. Time to back track. "I'm sorry, Tony. I know it was hard for you when he died. Joe was like a father to me these last few years and I…" Yikes. This is a bad apology. It's not about *you*, Vanessa. "I can't understand how hard it was for you to lose your father so suddenly. I don't want to make his passing any more difficult for you."

He had been looking at me, staring straight through me. He shifted his eyes down. "Thanks." I felt my posture soften some. You don't realize how stiff you've been until you unclench your ass.

"I'm in no huge hurry to redecorate," I said, only because I don't know where to start. This is the biggest office I had ever had, but I'm not going to admit it to Tony. "If there's anything of Joe's you want to take feel free. It'll be here at least another week. He really liked this…" I looked around for ideas. "This desk lamp and this pen holder," I lied, unprompted. "You can take whatever. I'm fairly sure Collin already helped himself to the whiskey cabinet, saw him in here yesterday when I stopped by." Tony's eyes widened in concern. Looks like I continue to be the jerk. I started to flip through Joe's little rotating contact thingy to avoid eye contact. I felt even more awkward as I apologized. "Sorry, I should have told you, I know he's supposed to be on the wagon right now. It didn't feel right to interfere. It was your dad's whiskey too, maybe he'll offer to share." *A Rolodex… that's what it's called!*

Tony laughed genuinely. "Share? Collin? He got chicken pox as a kid and didn't come in the same room as me for three weeks. Didn't want me catch them. So he wouldn't have to share Mother's special attention."

Now he's talking about his mom? Happy to cut the tension between us but I'm not ready to hear about the mommy issues of the Caldarelli boys. And I don't want to gossip about Collin. He's my friend and he's been kind to me. I laughed politely then came to my own rescue with an abrupt change of topic. "Let's not let the last month affect our working relationship. I know we can have a great run of things if we work together. If there's anything you need from me, let me know."

I guess the moment wasn't as tender as I thought because he turned to leave and was facing the door when he said simply, "You too." He took three steps towards the door.

It wasn't a large opening, but I barged through it anyway. "There is *one* thing I need from you." Can the back of someone's head look irritated? Because Tony's did. "The desk key."

He turned around and paused, feigning a thoughtful face. "For the middle drawer? Never found it," he shrugged.

"No, the top right side," I fiddled with it some as if to say *see, huh? Doesn't open and I'm not crazy.* "I didn't even realize this middle part was a drawer, probably the same key if you have it."

"Probably nothing in the middle drawer. Dad didn't keep a lot of paperwork. I wouldn't bother with a key." From across the room I can see him furrowing his brow and pinching his mouth into a tight resistant smile, fighting the urge to frown outright. "The right drawer is stuck, not locked. I shut it too hard. Then couldn't get it open. I'll send someone to pry it open and clear Dad's stuff out for you." He turned away again and threw me a "Good luck." He slipped out of my office and closed the door silently behind him. It didn't latch so it popped back open. I don't care enough to walk all the way over there.

That was weird. Did we *almost* have a civil conversation? It seemed like it was going that way. Tony never joked. He did enjoy bad-mouthing Collin, though. Not like I was ever going to be the guy's friend, messaging gifs in the chat during calls with the board and going out on his boat on the weekends. Could possibly stand chatting with him about the future of W.E.E.D. over coffee though. One day.

At least, that's what I *was* thinking. Until he said 'Dad didn't keep a lot of paperwork.' Bullshit. Joe *hoarded* paperwork, hardly kept anything digital. Barely used his computer. True that he wouldn't keep it here in the desk. Tiffany would file it away for him or pass it off to some lucky person in accounting or human resources. Joe loved paper, just not cluttering up *his* space.

Regular paperwork wouldn't make Tony weird. I need to see it.

This right drawer can't be that hard to open. I'll just give it a little more force now that I know it's stuck and I'm not just breaking it. Or I'll break it if I have to. I'll be damned if *Tony's* going to send someone to take *my* stuff.

Using both my hands, I grunt, "Urg—" as I pull. Didn't even jostle.

I pull out the drawer below it. Maybe something is wedged in keeping the drawer from opening. The lower drawer was empty. I get down on my hands and knees and try to see the underside of the top drawer, looking for anything that's stuck. I see the drawer is lopsided in the back, sagging down off its track. I reach as far back as I can, straining my knees as I lean forward.

"Oh-oh-oh!" I say to myself, a warning that some idiot is hurting my body. I sigh and push back slightly, putting the pressure on my haunches and off my knees.

What am I doing?

The CEO of the company, down on her knees under a desk, waiting for anyone to walk in. All I'd need is for there to be a man in that chair for the rumors to be true. The one that says I got this job on my knees.

Using the desk, I pull myself up. I will not allow myself to be caught in such an undignified position for the unknown contents of this drawer. I stride across the room towards the door with my head held high.

I'm also not going to let Tony send someone to open it and take everything before I get to see inside. Whatever's in there belongs to the CEO. That's me, not Tony. I push the office door all the way closed and lock it. Can't have Mr. Bobblehead poking in.

Back at the desk, I scoot the chair in, angling it slightly. Joe's old-fashioned chair didn't have wheels. Atrocious for desk work, perfect for this task. I kick off my black heels and put my left foot on the center drawer, planting my right foot firmly on the ground. Let's put these thick thighs to work. I reach out my hands and grasp the handle of the top right drawer. Pleased with myself for the forethought to lock the door and avoid the bad PR of "CEO flashes executive assistant her panties". Let me get through my first ninety days before flashing anyone.

I pull once, hard. Nothing. Picturing how it sagged off the track, I apply downward pressure, trying to lift it onto the track and pull again. It moved. But I may have completely broken the track based on some of the sounds I heard.

I want a standing desk anyway.

This time I pull as hard as I can, up and towards me, while pushing with my left leg and precariously adding my right leg to the mix by putting it just below the top drawer. The drawer yanks open, stopping less than halfway as it predictably collides with my right knee cap.

"Ow," I say, as nonchalantly as possible. Wouldn't want to embarrass me in front of myself. I immediately forget the pain, as multiple things rattle and roll to the back of the drawer.

I put my feet on the ground and lean forward, pulling the drawer out further to investigate. I pick up one of the translucent orange bottles with the opaque white top, immediately identifiable. I read the label of one.

Tony Caldarelli.

The next, Tony Caldarelli.

All of them have the same warning: Misuse may lead to abuse.

All possess the same details, same medication, same instructions, except: The doctor's name. Only one reason to go to multiple doctors for the same opioid. So none of them know how much you're taking. Or selling.

Goddammit. I'm not a jerk, I'm a sucker. Tony had me feeling bad for him, like I usurped his role as CEO right after the death of his father. "Here, take this lamp to remember your daddy by," I mocked myself out loud.

I was trying so hard to be nice to him and he was just trying to break into my office and get *his* drugs. Good to know the COO isn't getting high off *our* supply.

"Tiffany, I need some coffee!" I called through the closed door. "Please.

2

She was organized and methodical and her desk reflected it. But every shift, it would accumulate odds and ends. And by the end of the day, it was piled with other people's messes. Tiffany didn't appreciate everyone using her desk like a junk drawer. But she was powerless to stop them.

As the Executive Assistant, her time and her desk space were monopolized by The Executives. They were always 'too busy' to file things on their own. They would leave the weekly Executive Committee meeting carrying copies of the meeting packet and give them to Tiffany to handle. She would take them because she couldn't *not* take them. She didn't know what to do with them. At least five copies of the packet made it to her each week, all the same. She meticulously made files with the date and the meeting name. Then she'd record the name of the executive at the top before filing away in the copy and filing room. She used the special cerulean folders she ordered to find them easily. It took her a few months to realize that no one would ever be asking to see those files.

The pages had a shorter life span than a mayfly. They'd be born in the copy room, spend their life in the meeting, and make it back to copy room to be put to rest. It contributed to her melancholy; pointlessly printing then filing the same pages week after week.

It must serve *some* purpose.

Six months in, she discovered that they were a veritable gold mine. Not for the frivolous charts and graphs but for the handwritten notes of each executive. She didn't understand what a 'KPI' was or remember what 'EBITDA' stood for. The acronym obsession of the executives was tedious and she only retained what she had to. This often made the meeting packets inscrutable. But she *did* know how to read people. The executives had no inkling of what they were giving away with their handwritten musings.

She deduced that half of them were dazzled by the sultry voice and silky hair of the Chief Marketing Officer, Maya. She identified by their doodles on the financial pages that the Chief Financial Officer, Phil, bored them to tears. She could also tell when they hated each other. This was the most valuable information; the most volatile. As Joe's Executive Assistant, Tiffany was privy to most things. She attended all *other* meetings, to take notes for Joe when he couldn't be there. During these meetings, the executives, who were bad at hiding their anger, would express their frustration with their teams. But they were forced to play things closer to their chest when it came to the other executives.

Not in the Executive Committee meeting, the only meeting she wasn't allowed to attend. Those were no holds barred and she longed to be a fly on the wall. But with the notes, ramblings, and scribblings from the meeting packets; she had everything she needed. She could have caused pandemonium. But Tiffany never overplayed her hand. She only used small manipulations to make her day easier.

One week, she discovers in the Chief Technology Officer Derrick's notes that he is furious with Phil over budget cuts to IT. So, when Derrick wants her to do a coffee run: she tells him she's busy making copies *all day* for Phil's financial presentation. The following day, Phil has to make his own copies because *someone* complained to Joe that Phil was dominating Tiffany's time. Next time Derrick asks her to do a coffee run, she makes sure to casually tell Phil the cost.

The week after, Joe declares coffee runs to be outside of the budget.

She ran into Phil and Derrick in the break room. She watched Phil's face as he poured the last drop of coffee into his *Freak in the Sheets* Excel mug, right in front of Derrick. She saw Derrick smirk when Phil dribbled hot coffee down the front of his pants from the too-full mug. The subsequent week, Tiffany didn't have to make copies *or* do a coffee run.

That was child's play though. She challenged herself by trying to bait Maya into a tiff with Tara, the Chief Human Resources Officer. Tara's notes said that departments needed to be more aware of lunch break times, citing marketing as the worst offenders. Thinking Maya would be defensive, Tiffany mentioned her frustration at being "hounded over lunch breaks" to Maya one day. It was plausible. Maya defended Tara with "She's just doing her job. The lunch break rules are designed to protect hourly workers, *like you.*" Maya's accent often put the emphasis on odd words when she spoke, but the "*like you*" part felt rather pointed.

Either the only two women on the executive team were allies or they simply were too smart to get involved in the drama. This taught Tiffany a valuable lesson. Don't bother watering if the seed wasn't already planted.

That's why she loved poking the Caldarelli brothers. These quintessential spoiled rich kids, were now allowed to run amok in daddy's company. Collin and Tony did whatever they wanted as long as it didn't undermine Joe.

Collin's goal was to find every feasible way to travel and party on the company's dime. And when that wasn't possible, he took some of his unlimited paid time off to take his wife (or girlfriend) on romantic getaways.

Tony's driving motivation was convincing everyone he was single handedly responsible for the success of the country's best and biggest cannabis company. He managed to self-aggrandize enough to believe every win of W.E.E.D was his, he wasn't content if there were ANY failures.

As far as multi-state operators went, the Wellness Enterprise of Exceptional Dispensaries performed near the middle of the pack. Tiffany didn't know much about the market, but everyone in the company knew Tony was not happy about the declining stock price.

What only a handful of people knew was that Tony blamed Collin almost entirely. Money insulated the brothers from most of life's unpleasantries. Except for each other. Daddy Joe didn't let his boys fight in plain view. He knew that would expose chinks in his armor. They were *required* to make nice in front of the rest of the company. Thanks to her access to their notes, Tiffany saw through this façade.

The best part was that no one knew that *she knew* as much as she did. While everyone else showed her their cards, she could easily arrange for her own winning hand.

Collin's notes were simple to understand. When he was bored, he'd doodle on the meeting packet page. Usually on the four pages used for the financials. Things he liked had a symbol. Plus signs, check marks, and smiley faces were most common. Dollar signs seemed to be reserved for truly special ideas, ones that he thought would get him a bonus. Tiffany thought of it as a code that only an idiot could love, since everyone could easily decipher it. On two separate occasions he'd drawn a pair of breasts on the pages for marketing. That likely had more to do with Maya's low-cut tops than it did the printed content. What the cretin thought while handing those packets to Tiffany for filing, she would never know.

Like all cavemen fascinated by boobies, Collin was most easily manipulated through anger. A few times, the quarter end financial results made him furious, the low numbers meant he wouldn't get bonused. All the other times, it was Tony who really seemed to push his buttons. Collin's biggest button? The one that required him to do work. Tiffany assumed that Chief Revenue Officer was an important role, but had no idea what Collin did. Tony assigned him to pivotal projects, and blamed the CRO for failed initiatives.

Collin would enthusiastically scratch out entire words and phrases he didn't like, like a kid who hates bananas smashing one his mom packed in his lunch rather than returning home with it whole. Everyone in the room had to see him furiously scribbling. No doubt he didn't care if they knew when he was upset.

Tony's method was different. Not as immature, more intelligent, equally angry. Collin's packets were reminiscent of a toddler's temper tantrum. Tony's were a crock pot of rage. It took Tiffany longer to find out exactly what made Tony tick, and it all boiled down to what made Tony ticked off.

Tony's main triggers were missing deadlines and failing to meet performance goals. Collin's specialties. Tony prepared for things to fail, and he loved tracking everything meticulously. He wrote copious notes, she'd seen him furiously scrawling them through the glass doors of the conference room. Unfortunately, those were on his tablet which never left his side. There was *some* information on his weekly packet.

There was never any indication when he was pleased, if he ever was. He seemed to exist on a scale of mildly irked or about to go berserk. There was a range of indications. A single underline, an exclamation point or a question mark meant something like "I told them this would happen." Marketing got attention for a low performing ad campaign. The IT department would get it when website outages affected sales. Combining or doubling up the symbols (an underline and a question mark, a question mark and an exclamation point, a double underline, six question marks, etc.) meant he was furious. If he was truly apoplectic, out came the yellow highlighter.

The CFO got the yellow treatment for missed revenue or net income goals. Small targets of rage. But Collin's page could probably glow in the dark. Missed target after missed target, Collin's failures incensed Tony.

Most people weren't bothered by Collin's antics. He screwed up all the time, it *was* kind of his role. They all pretended to like Collin, but they tired of his antics and lackadaisical work ethic. He did play the part of lovable goofball at every work event very well. Until the shots started. Guaranteed for every after-hours event. He shifted from good time guy to wild thing. Joe never put his foot down on the behavior. Collin, in his mid-forties; was clearly the *baby*.

This explained part of Tony's anger. Tiffany, too, was an elder sibling and knew the frustrations. Her kid brother was only ten; unlikely she'd ever have to work with the little brat. Tony not only had to work with Collin, he had to clean up his messes. This must be the origin story of the highlighter. The subtlety the first few times he pulled it out. The eventual realization Collin must have had: Highlighter = Collin did bad. Or was it more of a Pavlov's dog situation? Collin didn't know *why* but when the highlighter came out, he started sweating and clenching his jaw.

She wished she could be there. See the look on all their faces. Fear, discomfort, maybe even a genuine smile from the observers. Then she'd look to Tony, where she'd see nothing. He only plastered different expressions on his face when required. Usually, he didn't bother much.

That's why everyone liked Collin more. He was obnoxious, sometimes funny. He was human. To most he probably seemed harmless. But Tiffany had learned the hard way how quickly the moment could turn with alcoholics. She'd been around when the switch flipped with her stepdad.

Tony, on the other hand, could wipe everything from his face. He was the opposite of overly emotional. He could turn his icy blue eyes off until there was nothing behind them. She'd seen during meetings his intense focus and drive. She was transfixed.

Tiffany may have gotten herself out of busy work, but she was willing to do *real* work. More ambitious than anyone she knew her age.

When she was six, she started ballet. She was born with the desired build. Her grandfather paid for private classes. He would pay any amount of money for the chance at a trophy. He would drag his rich friends to watch her perform. Pointing and saying, "That's *my* granddaughter," like he owned her: that *was* the trophy. These things meant she was lucky. But more importantly, she was dedicated. By age eleven, she was on pointe. Her instructor believed she could become a professional someday.

Her mother had given up on her own dream of dancing when she had Tiffany at sixteen. It became Tiffany's job to do what her mom could not. But as in every other way, she failed her mom. She fell when ice skating on a date. It led to three months of resting; led to six years of becoming hopelessly dependent on weed; led to the only job that would let her smoke on the clock trimming plants; led to her cushy office job.

Her grandpa had helped, but Joe loved promoting company loyalists.

She quit smoking three months into the desk job realizing that Joe, the fossil, was much sharper than he should have been at eighty. He was a grade A asshole, but damned if she didn't want to be him one day. She couldn't afford to be foggy minded in the mornings. Which meant quitting smoking. She hadn't been willing to quit for ballet because ballet wasn't *hers*. She was willing to quit for this job. Step one to being on the path to becoming the CEO.

The next steps weren't as clear. How would she close the gap from being the struggling daughter of a teen mom to running a big company? She didn't know. But she didn't know how to dance when she started, until one day she did.

She was so proud of herself for quitting weed with no help that she rode that momentum for a few months. But, like all highs, it didn't last. She hit a low when she realized her job was not the opportunity she had been promised.

The hours were long, which didn't affect her non-existent social life. She had no friends and had cut off her toxic family years earlier. The pay was good. But all she did was get coffee, make copies, file papers, fight to keep her desk clear. She believed here was nothing *executive* about her assistant role.

Until Tony showed her otherwise. He'd flirt with her and chat about Joe's day. What meetings, with whom, can he see her notes? She kept him at arm's length, another creepy old guy trying to get into her pants. She wasn't ballerina thin anymore but she had her mother's angular face and her bio-dad's long thick dark hair, which old men commented on regularly. Which was fine as long as they didn't say anything gross about her father's Vietnamese background. They always did.

Tony never talked about her appearance. He said she was intelligent, organized, and clever. The flattery proved her job wasn't as unimportant as it seemed. She let him in, planning to take what she could. She'd tell him whatever he asked about Joe; in return finding out what Tony thought mattered.

He was smart enough to keep everything *he* did secret; in his tablet.

His tablet that he 'left behind' during his last visit. She guessed his unlock code immediately: his mother's birthday; which she knew because Joe had her send flowers. Unfortunately, he had everything further locked in secure folders which were harder to open.

Except for his porn. Tame stuff really, saved indiscreetly like only old guys would do. She was glad it wasn't incest porn or something. Tiffany did like Tony, but his mommy issues had her weirded out. She didn't care about the porn, but she fully planned to pretend to be hurt anyway, to try to get a rise out of him. It was hard to get almost any emotion out of *him*.

Speak of the devil.

"Good morning, Tony," Tiffany said as he approached Vanessa's office door. She kept her tone cold.

"Good morning, Tiff." Tony was as dry as ever. The flirting lilt gone after many months of assumed *victory*. He went to walk past her.

"Had fun last night," she said curtly.

He looked around uncertainly, "Y-yeah."

Oooh a quiver. He was unusually unnerved.

"You forgot your tablet," Tiffany teased.

"I've been looking," he said, giving nothing away. "Glad it was in good hands."

"Your *girlfriend's* hands." She drove home the word. He hated when she said *girlfriend*, but pretended to like it. Today, no reaction. She pressed, "You know I would never snoop, but if it just so happened I did, what would you say about what I saw? In your *secure* folders?" *There it is!* Some life in his eyes after all. Poor old fella, probably embarrassed that his office fling discovered he liked giant asses. She felt a twinge of regret recognizing that was not like her.

"Not here. Just give it to me." She got up and went to walk past him. He grabbed her upper left arm hard and pulled her back. "Now," he hissed.

"Ow, what the fuck, Tony?" she whispered, with real pain in her voice. He let her go immediately. She brushed past him, bent down, and opened her blue faux leather laptop bag which was leaning on the floor against a small bookcase. She put his tablet on top of the bookcase. "There."

His face went blank. He noted where the tablet was set. He turned to the office door, took a few steps and knocked before immediately entering. He'd been in the habit of knocking while the office belonged to Joe, and in the habit of entering right after once it became his. She decided he could find out the hard way it was already occupied.

He'd never grabbed her like that before. She knew he kept a seething rage simmering on the backburner. If it was going to boil over, she needed to get away from him.

She *could* learn more from Tony. She valued that he pushed her to be better. Unlike the boy she dated for years who barely became a man, encouraging her to lie around smoking all day. She learned her lesson when she pried that leech off. Every relationship had to end, preferably before it sucked all the blood out of her. She was starting to feel anemic.

She blanched, thinking of what more time with him could do to her.

She was glad that when he came out of the office, she wasn't closer to the door. His face was red but became pink in the few steps between the door and the small bookcase where she was still standing. Like microwaved soup having been blown on, he was still molten lava under the surface.

He put his hand out, she flinched, and he grabbed the tablet next to her. "Let's talk about this on Wednesday. I'll pick you up for a nice dinner."

"Okay." She relaxed. He always went all out for their dinners, usually picking somewhere fancy where people minded their business. That would end things on a high note.

"In the meantime, please don't tell anyone about this," he held up the tablet. "As long as it's not too much to ask of my *girlfriend*." He gave her the word girlfriend like a gift. Immediately, he switched back to COO. "Can you please pick up Frank's care package before then? I plan to see him on Friday."

She nodded. He walked away.

Yes, one more nice evening to end things with a manipulative asshole. Then she can turn over a new leaf. Dive back into the job.

This new CEO could change everything. Women supporting women! She walked over to her desk with her head a little higher. Joe had locked her *out*; Vanessa was the *in* she needed.

She started, on edge, hearing Vanessa's door click closed behind her.

Tiffany knew little about Vanessa. She knew she was young for a CEO. She knew she had run her own business and that Joe trusted her.

And she wasn't Tony. Tony was savvy and had experience. But he did everything with his daddy's help and with the ease of being a man. It *was* amazing to watch Tony betray absolutely no emotions on his face. But he didn't have to worry that people would ridicule him for having a 'resting bitch face'. Vanessa would know the struggles only women experience.

Tiffany allowed herself to get excited. Vanessa could be the missing piece she needed to complete her ambitious puzzle. The Badass Boss Bitch of today here to usher in the next generation of BBB's. She could elevate Tiffany beyond fetching coffee and making copies. She could invite her in to the important meetings to *say* something not just take notes.

She heard a loud bang in Vanessa's office. Should she rush in? Offer help? No... that's not what a strong BBB of today would want. She'd want the same treatment as a man. Until she asked for help, Tiffany was on standby for the important tasks.

"Tiffany, I need some coffee!" Vanessa called through the closed door. "Please," was an afterthought.

There goes that hope. She had outlasted Joe and Tony's regimes, she would outlast Vanessa. *She's not going to get rid of me that easily.* Tiffany thought. Even if she is a *fucking bitch.*

3

N ot today," I groan, seeing the beige drips on my white and gold blazer. My hands didn't *feel* unsteady. But the drips, like blood at a crime scene, were evidence that they were. My head throbbed on the right side. A pain I could trace from my temple all the way down to my jaw. I rubbed at the muscle below my cheek, feeling it jump lightly away from my fingers because my jaw was clenched.

On Wednesdays we wear coffee stains to meetings. My calendar was full of meetings. Clicking through the attendees list of each, I saw Collin would be at some of them. At least there would be *one* friendly face. He was so supportive when I got the job. He took me out drinking to celebrate a couple of weeks ago and it was a blast. But his brother was pissed when I had to call him and help get Collin under control when three in the morning rolled around and he started trying to score an eight ball while crying about his dad. I just wanted to go home.

It's partially my fault he needs to take a break from drinking.

"Tiffany," I said through the cracked door. "Come here." Her little desk was just outside of my office, so I expected a quick reply. Clicking through the calendar, I didn't see many words I recognized, aside from 'meeting'. Acronyms I'd never heard of. What is an 'EC'?

After receiving no response from Tiffany, I stood up. I grabbed yesterday's coffee mug, I'll run this to the break room after she fills me in on the meetings. "Tiffany, I was...." I stopped, realizing I was talking to no one. I set the mug down on her desk, not wanting to wander around looking for her with it. I walked around the pony wall that guarded my office, Tiffany's workspace, and access to our bathroom.

She might be in the file room.

I'd been here dozens of times to meet with Joe on other business, but I usually went straight to his – *my* office. The rest of the office was an indistinct blur. Joe probably designed it, knowing him and his need to be involved in every little thing. He'd positioned it so that no one came near his office unless they were going to it, making his office the furthest from the stair landing. A mob boss who always sits at the back of the restaurant. I imagine he built his office first, then said, 'fill in the gaps'. Not surprising that this little world revolved around him, and now me. I didn't have long to contemplate it on the several steps to the file room where I spotted Tiffany.

She was standing at a large copier in the file room. She hadn't heard me over the sound of it printing, collating, stapling packets. Or over her companion. "Tiffany, could I get your help with something? Whenever you're done chatting with *Tony*," I added pointedly.

"I was making copies," Tiffany defended. "For *your* meetings. And I'm done with Tony." She walked away, but a subtext lingered. I'm too busy to read between the lines right now.

"Vanessa, how have you been?" Tony asked. He'd spent the last forty-eight hours avoiding me and he had never asked me how I was doing. He obviously wanted to distract me from whatever they were discussing.

"Fine," I said with little conviction, then immediately, "Great actually." Because fine wasn't good enough.

"That's good." He leaned against the cabinets next to the copier, easing off his left foot. A relaxed pose that someone with a stick up their ass would have to rehearse. I wonder when Tony found the time. "Big day today. Meetings day. None more vital than Executive Committee. Sets the tone for the rest of the meetings."

Oh, *EC* was *Executive Committee.* The first meeting.

"Of course," I said. I'm not stupid, I know meetings are important.

Tony walked towards me. Very stiff, which was more natural for him. He looked down at me. "Tough that you're expected to run Executive Committee with two days on the job."

"It's my third day," I raised him.

"Your third day *ever* in this industry," he anted up. "It's a complicated industry, Nessa." He used Joey's nickname for me, either to endear or enrage me. "I've been running the EC for a while now. If you're nervous" – his eyes flicked to my coffee stained blazer– "I wouldn't mind taking the lead today." He gathered up the completed packets and offered them to me. His sincere smile was maddening.

I wanted to snatch the papers from him, shout 'No mine!' and hiss until he was forced to leave. But I am not a toddler so I took the packets slowly. "Yes," I was biting my cheek to help temper my anger. "I think that's the correct approach." Now to turn it into my idea. "I'm glad you agree that the team needs to see a cooperative transition."

"Well, yes, exactly what I meant." Tony tried to turn it back into his idea. If he had been shaken, he didn't show it.

"It's a great way for me to observe your management skills and how you interact with your *peers.*" I offered the packets back to him. He took them and walked away.

The paper cut was worth the confirmation, Tony was indeed like James Bond's Martini. Shaken.

My feet suddenly felt light in my four-inch heels, making me realize they have been bothering me today. Maybe I should switch to the more practical two-inch slingbacks Mom suggested. I wanted to impress my first week. Practical shoes were never impressive.

Exhibit A. As I approached Tiffany, I could see her practical black flats peeking out from her extended standing desk. Why would a woman in her early twenties have such orthopedic looking shoes?

"Pull up my calendar?" She didn't respond but as I rounded her desk I could see on her monitor that she was doing as I asked. "It looks pretty full today."

"It's Wednesday," Tiffany said as if that was an answer.

"Right. Can you explain what each meeting is? Of course, I know EC is Executive Committee. What's Mswot?" I said, sounding it out.

"That's M-S-W-O-T. Marketing's Strength Weakness Opportunity and Threat meeting," Tiffany answered. She said it so matter-of-fact, I pretended I understood.

"And who attends?" I inquired.

"It'll be Maya taking point. Sometimes, she has Brayden lead the MER, But the MSWOT is only once per quarter, so she leads it," Tiffany said.

"And the M-E-R is..." I left her an opening, and she left me hanging.

Mercifully, she eventually filled the gap. "It's not today. It's the Marketing Event Recap and it only happens the Wednesday after the MMME." I raised my eyebrows indicating a need for further explanation, and she sighed. "The Major Monthly Marketing Event. It's usually on a Friday or Saturday. Except 420 is whatever day of the week. You have about a month until that happens." She huffed again. "420 is like THE cannabis holiday in April that—"

"I know what it is," I snapped. I knew enough to not put up with her crappy attitude. It had been nothing but attitude for the last two days. "Can you just write this all down for me? You seem to know so much."

Tiffany softened at my compliment. "Yes, I do. I worked hard to get it all into the calendar." She turned to her screen and clicked through the meetings. "If you click on each meeting, you can see a list of the attendees, a description, and I included a link to the drive where I drop the prior week's notes. I'll show you."

"That's okay," I'm not going to read a novel about the meetings... "You go ahead and write it all down in one place for me." My voice was as sweet as I could manage.

She paused, irritated. "It *is* in one place," she said, deliberately. "If you just click on each—"

"Tiffany, stop," I rubbed lightly at my temple, trying not to convey my pain. "This may have worked for Joe, or Tony, but it does not work for me," I said clearly.

"*It* didn't work for Joe. *I* did. He never checked his calendar. I would go and tell him exactly when and where. And I would take notes for him and summarize the prior week. I knew more about every meeting than he did. You can't expect to come in and figure it all out in two days," she argued. "I might as well be the CEO," she said quietly.

A bold thing to whisper.

"Let's start with the agenda for EC, and last week's meeting notes then." I was unable to hide my self-consciousness around my limited experience in the job.

"I..." she shrunk herself some. "I wasn't allowed to go to that meeting."

"Oh, that makes sense to me. Since you are the assistant and I am CEO." I was being petty. I knew it and it wasn't my finest moment.

"Ahem," said a disembodied voice. Tara, the Chief Human Resources Officer, had gotten surprisingly close to us without me noticing, the monitor on the standing desk just the right height to disguise her arrival.

"Sorry to interrupt. Tiffany, I wanted to make sure you got my updated section before the packets were printed."

"Yes, I did," Tiffany was short. I recognized her hard swallow. The type of swallow that helped hold back tears.

"Thank you, I'm so grateful to you, Tiffany," Tara praised, exaggeratedly. "Vanessa, I was just about to head to EC, shall we walk together?" It was like I was about to be reprimanded by my mother.

"No, I'll be right there," I said, sweetly. Tara turned and walked away. The meeting room was near Tiffany's desk, she must have heard us from there.

"Did you want me to come to EC? I can take notes," Tiffany offered. Her change in tone seemed real but so had her *almost* tears. Nothing had felt more real than her disdain for me when I had asked her to do her job.

The disproportionate power dynamic made me feel like an ass, but now was not the time to back down. A man in this position would not. "No. I want you working on the meeting list I asked for. I'll see you at the M-WOTS meeting."

"M-S-W-O-T," she corrected, without missing a beat. Her glare told me I had made the right decision. No negative energy necessary for my first big meeting. I went around her desk and headed straight to the meeting. The meeting room hardly seemed like a private space for important confidential conversations. It was centrally located and surrounded by glass walls, like the office television put on mute. I stepped inside for the first time and realized my office is bigger.

Almost everyone beat me to the meeting. There were eight chairs and six of us. Looking at the attendees reminded me how *uneven* these settings were between men and women. Tara, Maya, and I were all dressed in our best professional. Maya's hair, makeup, and nails might even be considered glam. Her ribbed lavender dress was form-fitting but zipped up enough to cover most of her cleavage. Tara was immaculate; not a hair out of place, her lips lined in a perfect neutral, her glasses fashionable. Her matching beige pencil skirt and blazer covered a cream top that was buttoned to her neck. The men were one step up from wearing their Football Sunday best: jeans, blue polos, *sneakers*. They were dressed like they had the right to be there; the women like they were lucky enough to have the privilege.

Tony broke the mold with his perfectly tailored navy-blue suit with no tie. He was usually in stark contrast to Collin's t-shirt and jeans. But the *Oxy* to Tony's *Moron* wasn't there. "Collin?" I asked the group.

Only Tara attempted to answer, "Possibly running late," she guessed.

"As usual," Tony added, adding nothing. He was seated at one end of the oblong table. Everyone else was seated on the two long sides. It felt like they were watching me decide whether to take the chair at the other head of the table opposite Tony, or sit next to him like his Girl Friday.

I opt for the seat next to him, in support *not* subservience. I look at my phone. "It is two minutes past, let's get started. Tony?" Making it clear he was following my direction.

"Right," Tony said, sliding an obnoxiously yellow legal pad with a pen on top to me. "So you may take notes, and observe, like we discussed."

Son of a bitch.

The EC meeting flew by. We skipped Collin's section which cut out a chunk of time. Everyone took turns reading their section out loud. Tony grilled them, but otherwise no one said anything. Between each person's turn, they all worked on their laptops.

One thing is clear. Tony does not have one eighth of an ounce of charisma. He is smart. In the business world he's basically a genius, thanks only to his powers of manipulation. But no one in the Caldarelli family ever talks about *why* he was fired from his big corporate lawyer job. I think I've cracked the case: he's a giant uninspiring dud.

This is exactly why *I'm the CEO*. But maybe there is a place for him here. Afterall, this pilot still needs a co-pilot. I can do all the important pilot tasks, but he can keep us on course if I have to pee. If he works well with me, I'll let him push the button for the landing gear. You know, co-pilot stuff. As long as he stops trying to push me out of the plane.

The next meeting passed by just as quickly, and was much more interesting. Tiffany stepped in for this one, as did Brayden and another person from marketing whose name was either Emily or Anna Lee. I didn't ask her to repeat herself, because her shyness was so painful it hurt me. Maybe marketing wasn't the place for this very slight young woman to hide behind her wavy blonde curtain of hair. She was silent for the remainder of the meeting.

Tony and Maya also stayed for this meeting. Maya did the presentation of our *Strengths Weaknesses Opportunities and Threats* around the upcoming *420* holiday. It felt like a college class prompt where each *SW* and *T* were shoehorned in, Maya did have some brilliant points when talking Opportunities. I found myself being dazzled by her glistening hair and confident cadence. Maya was undoubtedly in the right department. I asked some questions but I mostly nodded knowingly on things I'll have to look up later *incognito*, lest anyone discover this cannabis CEO didn't know the significance of *420*. Yesterday, I looked up the poorly worded question 'what is an eighth of cannabis an eighth *of*?' Turns out it's an eighth *of an ounce*. Then I had to look up how to erase my search history.

Maya paused and looked at me. She's looking for my approval.

My turn to say something smart.

"Everything you've proposed makes sense. I just need to know if it's going to make dollars and cents." No one has to know how long I planned to say that. "What are your revenue projections?"

Maya looked uncertain for the first time since the meeting had started. "Well... they're very strong." She smiled widely.

"What's strong? The margins?" Tony pressed.

"Mmm hmm," Maya affirmed.

"I find that unlikely. How are we going to add all these promos and discounts and still maintain margins? Are the vendors absorbing it or crediting us back?" Tony dug in.

Maya looked clueless. "Let me guess, Collin was supposed to prepare those details?" Tony smiled widely.

"Yes, but—" Maya started.

"But he didn't show up." Tony looked awfully satisfied for a man who hadn't gotten any answers. Perhaps he'd gotten exactly what he was looking for.

"Tiffany," I said. "Go see if he's in his office." I pointed across the hallway, to Collin's door. She went to check.

"Yeah well, he'd better be dead," Tony grumbled. He earned the glare I gave him. "What? It's not *me* skipping out the first time you're in charge. It's disrespectful. To you."

He was right. Collin was a flake and everyone knew it. But the feeling I got about Executive Committee was that everyone treated it with deadly seriousness. You could miss anything else, but not that meeting. Collin specifically chose NOT to come to my first EC meeting. I thought we were friends. We always snuck off and joked about Tony's big head at family gatherings. He said he was *proud* of me and that he rooted for me to get the job.

But here Tony was, keeping the plane steady while Collin hadn't even bothered to catch the flight.

I left the meeting room and headed straight for Collin's office.

Tiffany intercepted me. "I knocked already."

Ignoring her, I reached for the handle and opened the door. It was unlocked. It was like waiting for a public restroom only to find the person at the front of the line never did their job of making sure there was no one inside. Their bashful little face when they realized it was their fault you all almost peed your pants.

Except, there *was* someone inside and my heightened emotions switched from anger to terror when I saw him. I gasped, "Collin?"

4

ollin!" I rushed to him. His head was down on his desk, and he wasn't responding.

I panicked, grabbing him by the shoulder and pushing his torso upright in his chair. His head flopped unnaturally, and his body pushed into me, wanting to slump back on his desk. My heart sunk. Tony rushed up next to me to help. I looked into his blue eyes, grasping for a parachute and finding only the vast and empty sky there. My eyes turned from them quickly when I saw movement to my left. It was Collin, finally straightening himself up, his head still awkwardly lolling about, like a newborn who didn't have neck strength. But his eyes were fluttering open.

Tony suddenly grabbed him by the face and said, "Hey! Hey Collin!" snapping and trying to draw his eye.

"Wh-what?" Collin responded, confused but taking back control of his head and then his upper body as he sat back in his chair. I stepped back to give him space. He shook his head like there was water in his ears. I scanned the room for whatever was responsible.

A tall thin bottle with about an inch of murky mahogany colored liquid in it sat on Collin's desk, within arm's reach of him. I turned my whole head towards it, unable to look at Collin. He is *lucky* his last name is Caldarelli.

Immediately after me, Tony saw the now mostly drunk bottle of his father's whiskey and moved to hide it from view. He was on the opposite side of the desk and had to circumvent Collin's chair to get there, but most everyone was staring at Collin and Tony's awkwardness was observed only by me. Why he would cover for Collin, whom he hated, was beyond me. Must be a brothers thing.

It didn't matter. I'd seen it. I wasn't about to be gaslit. The room was in a frenzy as Tony asked Tiffany to get Tara. But Tiffany was frozen, eyes wide and locked onto Collin. Maya called for help.

I can hear them discussing their concern around me, but I'm focused on confirming my suspicion. Near Collin's hand is his coffee mug. I grab it, the motion bringing Collin out of his dazed state. His eyes follow the mug as I bring it to my face. I can smell the remaining whiskey coffee mixture before it gets close to my nose. I set the mug down.

Though his eyes can't make perfect contact with mine, I can still read them. My naturally honey brown eyes have crystalized. I will not rescue him.

"No," he says, looking at the mug. He shakes his head. "No, Nessa, I didn't," he pleads.

Tara appears and rushes in. "Is everyone all right, what's going on?"

Others had gathered by the opening of the small office.

Someone mumbled a response. Tara saw Collin's disorientation herself and asked, "Has anyone called for an ambulance?" As the CEO, the right thing to do would be to calm everyone down. Reassure them that Collin was going to be fine. Get Collin a ride home and deal with the consequences later.

But I don't wanna.

Tony was talking Tara out of calling paramedics. Which I appreciated. But he was treating her like a hysterical woman. From her perspective, her reaction was understandable. A man, mid-forties, passes out early morning for 'no reason'. It was obvious to everyone he wasn't just napping. It didn't help that just a couple of months earlier a dead man had been found the exact same way.

It was Tiffany who had found Joe in their shared bathroom. Imagine the shock of walking in on your boss on the toilet. The terror when you realize you're apologizing to a dead man.

"Tiffany," I said. No response. "Tiffany!" I was louder than I intended but I got her attention. I turned to leave. On my way out, I spotted something familiar on Collin's wrought iron bookcase. I snatched them quickly before anyone could see.

Tiffany followed behind me.

"Go refresh the meeting room," I instructed. I hope she felt my intention. I offered her a parachute to land safely in a field far away from this. She accepted the distraction and moved in front of me, making a beeline for the meeting room.

"Tara?" I called out, refusing to look back. "Don't forget, HR meeting in ten."

The frenzied room behind me calmed and I knew she had heard me.

I kept walking straight past the meeting room, towards my office. Instead of going in, I veered to the left, entering my private bathroom.

Technically, anyone *could* use this bathroom, but no one other than Joe and Tiffany ever did. Once inside, I locked the door. The room had only one toilet, and that toilet had an additional door with a lock, able to be shut off from the rest of the bathroom. Third day on the job and I still hadn't been in here. I had this feeling that I'd walk in and see Joe.

It would feel strange to sit in the same spot where he died.

It wasn't exactly the same spot though. Tony had it completely redone, I'd been told. Tony's taste was exactly like his father's, boring and minimalist. Occasionally, Joe liked absurd things like his enormous desk. But otherwise, his taste was lightly-buttered-whole-wheat-toast.

The bathroom was the same. Black doors, gray flooring. black trim on white walls. I bet if I asked about the mosaic tiling that covered one entire wall in shades of gray, Tony would say it was $20,000 a square foot or some nonsense. It didn't look expensive. It only mattered that it was.

Looking around the sterile room, I feel like I'm going to be sick. I want to wad up a stack of these expensive cloth like paper towels, cram them in the drain of this sleek floating sink, fill it with cold water and dunk my whole head in.

However, since I have an HR meeting in − I look at my phone − seven minutes, I'd rather not look like a wet dog. I came in here to check my face and reset myself for the rest of the meeting day. A bit of a mess, even after only a couple of hours. Some stress sweat has been going on, even before I discovered Collin. I grabbed a paper towel and dabbed lightly at the shiny oily skin on my forehead. Not ideal, acceptable in a pinch. I wet the towel, using a small corner to dab at my mascara, where the sweat had caused it to bleed into the fine lines that led from my under eyes.

I took off my blazer, with the world's most obvious coffee stains and hung it on the hook behind the door. I wet the paper towel and took a quick pass under my boobs before taking it to my armpits. It felt good but I realized too late the towel was much wetter than intended. Just a few minutes left before the meeting, I started fanning with my hands rapidly under each arm.

"Ha!" I laughed out loud, startled by my own exclamation. If only the office could see me now, I looked like a monkey. Joe's stupid fucking monkey. Here to clean up the mess caused by two of his sons. Left all to me because Joe had to go and kill himself.

The HR meeting dragged on forever. It wasn't Tara's fault. My head was throbbing and I was distracted. Distraction typically speeds things up. Like when your mind wanders while driving home. You know you did it, but somehow you pull up to your house five minutes after you started your hour drive home. No memory of using your blinker or driving the speed limit.

I was the opposite kind of distracted. The type where you have an indica gummy and put a frozen pizza in the oven. You sit on the couch and binge watch a show and write your debut album in your head. You remember the pizza a few hours later but when you're positive you've burned it to hell, you rush to the oven to see the timer still has seven minutes left.

That was *this* meeting. I'm sure the 'rolling overtime wage change' was a huge deal for our facility in Nevada, and the unionization of our competitor's dispensary in Arizona was probably a concern, but I couldn't help thinking there were much bigger problems for me to deal with.

I was also distracted by how distracted Tiffany was. I kept pausing Tara to say "Did you get that down, Tiffany?" Which would make Tiffany snap back into focus. Tara was irritated by this, but it was *Joe* that had hired such a poor note-taker as an assistant. I knew she might have been disoriented by the morning's events; but what she needed was a leader who wasn't going to let her fail. And a smidgen of tough love to face down the day.

After the meeting, Tara approached me when Tony got up to use the restroom. "Would you mind if I stopped by your office later today?" she asked.

"I wouldn't mind at all. Tiffany?" I asked. "When's my last meeting today?"

"I don't know," Tiffany said, dully.

"You can go look on your computer," I hinted. Poor girl was struggling.

"Don't worry about that, Tiffany," Tara inserted. "*I* can check your calendar from my end and I'll pop on over when your last one's done."

"Sounds great!" I said enthusiastically. Not that I love the idea of *another* meeting to end meetings day. But there was a reason Tara waited until Tony left the room. *This* is the meeting I've been hoping for. The one where the executives share their grievances with the prior regime. Where they can tell me, under safety of anonymity, how bad Tony and Joe were for the company. They would begin to confide in me how happy they are that I, *a woman*, am finally here to get everything in order. Finally, a chance to see what only I can bring to the table.

Until then, I guess I'll listen to Derrick talk about firewalls.

A very unproductive meeting with the IT department pushed right up against an even more tedious meeting with Phil. They blurred together and I probably wouldn't have been able to distinguish them but for the procession that would occur at the end of each where everyone filed out and the participants of the next meeting filed in.

Phil's meeting was a once-monthly meeting called 'Review of W.EE.D.'s EV/EBITDA.' I considered asking Tiffany what it meant, but her demeanor had become even more frigid. I went to the bathroom between meetings to look it up on my phone instead.

I sat with my back straight and my hands on the conference table in front of me, armed with the knowledge that we would be discussing 'W.E.E.D's Enterprise Value divided by Earnings Before Interest, Taxes, Depreciation and Amortization'.

If Phil was any good had his job, I'd know what that means by the end of the meeting.

He began the meeting trying to set up the projector. Every other executive had simply come in, plugged their laptop in and started their presentation. While he struggled, I looked at his team. Most execs had brought one or two younger people; Phil had brought an entourage of four.

They'd been introduced by Phil exactly as, "Jorge: financial analysis, Eric: cash management, Ali: cost accounting, Jenny: Controller."

Like the other executives, Phil found comfort in surrounding himself with younger people. Whether it was the industry or the fact that everything now ran on computers, the environment makes him seem every bit his age. His glasses had a thick silver frame. His salmon polo shirt was tucked into his jeans too tightly, emphasizing his round belly. The rest of him was rail thin. His hair could only be described as 'tax accountant'. I'd never understood why balding men kept growing hair on the sides. It made the spreading bald spot at the top an obvious and lonely island of nothing. Just be boldly bald. Way sexier.

I'd guess Phil is mid-sixties, but he seemed about ninety by the time Jenny finally stepped in to plug the laptop into the projector and open the slide deck. She was in her late twenties and carried herself with a professional and serious calm, unlike her similarly aged male co-workers.

Finally, Phil started talking. Speaking directly to Tony, he said, "I've been asked by the board to work with the M&A consultants" – damn another acronym to look up – "to determine how we can best position our market cap for consideration in possible acquisition. Our EBITDA is declining, but that's a norm across the board for MSOs, right now. We may have plateaued on this, though Jenny does have some color to add."

I looked towards Jenny, who seemed like she was about to speak, but heard Phil continue... He droned on as if he had memorized it. "However, after further discussion with Eric, I believe our more immediate concern will be focused on the cash position and, specifically, our debt service. On this slide, you'll see that an upcoming balloon payment to our private lender Angelo Giaimo exceeds our debt service of the past three years combined. Next slide, Jenny."

Phil filled two hours easily. The meeting was only scheduled for an hour. But the next meeting was supposed to be run by Collin who hadn't left his office since the morning. I assumed he wasn't going to bother and let Phil continue. Like a gas, his bloated presentation expanded to fill the new container.

Jenny regularly chimed in with corrections which Phil would refer to as 'updates' when it was obvious he had made a mistake. Tony interrupted constantly. I couldn't tell if Phil and Tony were on the same side of the heated conversation or not. Eventually I zoned out. I had moved my hands to my lap to discreetly search terminology on my phone and occasionally wander through social media.

I see movement all around me and I refocus. Everyone is leaving. Tony isn't moving. I woefully remember the final meeting of the day is supposed to be a debrief with me and him.

I realize I've been holding the keys I took from Collin's office in my hands, rubbing the small ivory chess piece, a king, feeling the carved initials *JC* with my thumb. I didn't want Tony to see, so I surreptitiously put them in my blazer pocket.

I make eye contact with the man who would be my co-pilot if I let him. His blue eyes were deep set, like Joey's but not as bright. His body was slim which he tried to cover up in a suit tailored to make him look more filled out. But I had seen him in a swimming suit at family gatherings where he couldn't hide. His face was narrow and long and he did not have a strong jaw line or a five o'clock shadow. His hair was dark with only gray flecks. With a lot more salt than pepper, he would have looked just like Joe.

His self-assuredness made me want to let Tony keep taking the lead until I was ready. But if I stepped up and took control and I flew this business one iota differently, would he just hijack the whole thing?

"How was your first meeting day?" Tony began, once everyone else had left.

I chose my words carefully. "Very informative." I knew he itched for more.

"I felt it went well," he led. I gave him nothing. A pause dragged on so long it became a full stop. He'd talked at every meeting. All. Day. Long. Why stop him now? "You should have seen the mess before I took over. There were no slide decks, no one brought laptops. Very ineffective use of time. We can have more meetings because everyone can bring their work with them. The new format works very well."

"The *interim* format," I corrected. "It's a good jumping off place."

"Hmm." He was dissatisfied with anything but groveling praise. He licked his thin lips. "I will say, Phil's meeting got away from you."

"Criticizing my methods?"

"Not criticism. Of you at least. Just fair warning that Phil pushes boundaries if you let him. He thinks everything he does is the most important. Dad couldn't bring himself to fire him because of how long they worked together. But you would be well within your right to deal with him. I'd fully support you."

"I'm not going to fire Phil for ranting for two hours," I said. Tony talked just as much if not more.

"I didn't say that. A word to the wise, you should keep an eye on him. He was gunning for the CEO position." That seemed like genuine advice, but I never knew with Tony what was just manipulation. "I didn't really have anything else to debrief on. I have plans this evening, I'm going to head out early." He closed his laptop and started to gather himself.

"That will be fine, for today," I permitted. *The COO reports to the CEO.* He stacked everything on top of his laptop and stood abruptly, leaving without another word. There was nothing he could say to win.

I picked up the legal pad I had used for the Executive Committee notes and walked back towards my office. Tiffany was coming my direction. Her left arm in her light sweater, struggling to get her other arm in while holding her purse.

"Leaving for the day?" I asked, suspiciously recalling the subtext from her and Tony in the copy room.

"It's on your calendar," she snapped, straightening.

"Do you always leave early on Wednesdays?" I watched her tense again. "I hope you're doing something fun?"

"A date," Tiffany was terse, but she gave a tight little smile that I thought might be real. She kept walking, getting her right arm in the sweater as she did.

"Have a great time," I called. Subtext: *With Tony.*

5

I wish I could say I'm relieved to be back in my office instead of the glass meeting room. That room was an exposed fishbowl. The whole staff would pass by throughout the day. Taking slow steps to walk by, checking who was in the room. Sometimes they would wait nearby, clearly needing to see someone but not daring to tap-tap-tap on our glass bowl.

The worst part was knowing they *couldn't* see the projector screen. They weren't spies trying to steal company secrets or checking to see if a layoffs were on the horizon. They were looking at us. It felt like putting on a performance for the entire office for the *entire* day. Being in my office sitting in my too big chair should've been a vast improvement. But how I feel now is the same I felt all day.

Alone.

My short meeting with Tony gave me extra time by myself. I looked at my phone to see it was another twenty minutes before Tara would be coming. I pulled up my contacts, clicking on Joey's name and seeing his little profile picture. It made me smile. I called him. The phone rang twice, I hung up when the third ring started. He was a two-ring guy. He either picked up by then or he wasn't answering.

He was traveling this week. As an independent business consultant, he often picked his hours and his projects. I didn't want him to go this week, but Joey said timing was everything for this project.

A text comes through from him.

In mtg.

Rather than cry, I called my backup plan.

"Hello?" A woman's voice answers in a singsong tone.

"Mom?" I ask, even though I had called her.

"Hi honey! How are you? How's the new job?"

My eyes welled with tears. "So good. Really good," I lied very well. "I... you should just *see* this office. It's so big. And there's a view of... outside. Plus, I have this executive assistant" — who hates me — "and a private bathroom." — where my predecessor killed himself — "and I am just so.. you know.... So," I struggled to find the right words.

"Happy?" she guessed, incorrectly.

I decided to be honest. "No. I am so alone." And then everything poured out of me, except for the actual tears. I told her about Collin and Tiffany and Tony and EBITDA's and firewalls. I managed to summarize the longest day of my life in one giant run-on sentence. Then I crashed into wall of silence.

Mom blew some air out forcefully and broke down the wall. "I'm so sorry to hear that. I wish I was there so I could give you a hug." If she had left it there, she wouldn't be my mom. "This would be a lot for anyone to handle. Didn't I tell you this was too much? Too big of a step up for you? You're so ambitious and so talented, Vanessa. But you don't need such a demanding job. Joey makes so much money, you shouldn't even have to work."

I rolled my eyes. "I can't do this with you again. We've gone over this. I need *my own* thing and this is an amazing opportunity. You just want me to be some housewife. We aren't even married yet." I immediately felt defensive.

"I know, but you don't have to pick the hardest job. Why don't you come back to work for me... *with* me this time. I have some great clients for you," she enticed.

I scoffed. It was silly to call her. "No, mom. I am the CEO of a multi-state, public cannabis company. How many women do you think can say that?"

"Maybe there's a reason," she said. I laughed outright. My tears turning to angry ones. "Not that *you* can't or shouldn't. You know I'm a feminist and I believe women *can* do anything men can do. But do really want to go work on an oil rig or fight fires?" She reasoned.

"Sitting in a board room isn't like that. There *are* women who work on oil rigs and fight fires. I just happen to be good at this instead of those things," I argued.

"Don't take this the wrong way, sweetie, but do you really think that?" Her voice had softened so I knew she was speaking from the heart, even if her words were stabbing me in mine.

Knock. Knock.

Tara was here early.

"Gotta go, mom. I'm at *work*," I pressed the last word through the phone, making sure she heard it before I hung up.

"Come in," I called to Tara. Only she couldn't hear me because it was Collin at my door. He let himself in, technically invited. That's how the vampires get you. Invited in on a technicality.

"Uh, do you have a few minutes?" he asked, his eyelids hanging lazily.

"Two minutes," I remained seated while he stepped closer. This was on my terms, he wasn't going to suck the life out of me.

"That's all I'm asking. I just want to say I'm sorry. Really, from the bottom of my heart." He touched his chest as if to prove it. "I would never miss that meeting. I swear to you, I have no idea what happened."

"One: you *did* miss that meeting. Two: which is it? Are you sorry, or did you do nothing wrong?" I asked.

"I didn't say that. I should not have had that whiskey. But I didn't even have much."

"I saw the bottle, Collin. It was mostly empty."

"It was old, it was Pop's. It was nasty too. I didn't even finish what I poured. I'm more of a tequila guy," he joked. He was a big joker because he was a big kid. He looked like a Tony impersonator; like Elvis impersonating *himself* in the later years. Bloated in the face and stomach from too much alcohol. It was easier to remain angry while looking in his eyes because, unlike Tony, Collin did not have Joey's blue eyes. His were a chestnut brown. He wore one of our company's black graphic T's depicting a floating hand offering a joint saying *Smoke 'em if you got 'em*. He paired this with jeans and bright red shoes that I knew cost a fortune.

"Is it funny to you how you embarrassed me? How you showed everyone that you don't take me seriously?" my voice is shaking, but I can't get it under control.

"No one thinks that. They just think *I'm* a screw up."

"You would never do this if Joe or Tony were in charge."

"I'm telling you, I had no idea that would happen. One drink? Knocking me out? I used to chug a water bottle filled with tequila before swim meets." His second attempt at humor belly flopped, succeeding only in pissing me off. He recalibrated. "I do respect you. I stayed all day today getting sobered up enough to come apologize. I still don't feel right, but I just needed you to know I'm sorry."

"Noted," I said curtly.

He changed course again. "Joey is lucky to have you. And I'll be lucky to have you as a little sister. I'll do better tomorrow and every day after that. I promise, Nessa." He turned to leave.

"Collin?" He looked back at me, and his face brightened. His hopes were up. Good. "Fuck you."

He turned and left in such a hurry that he almost collided with Tara. "Oh!" she exclaimed. "Is everything..." she cut herself off when she looked to his face and Collin disappeared. She slipped into my office and closed the door gently behind her. "Is he all right?" she asked.

"No," I stated. Tara furrowed her brow. "He says he'll be better tomorrow."

"I hope so. He had me worried today," she said. Tara's face was kind and wise. She was also beautiful, an unspoken requirement for women in executive roles. Her short mahogany brown hair was complimentary to her diamond face. Her nails were perfectly manicured, and her makeup was done expertly to look like light make-up. When I first met her, I'd gaged her age as early forties. But her outfits were matronly. A perfectly matching blazer with a skirt, and a blouse that went up to her neck gave away her age. She also spoke with wisdom and authority that only came with time and experience. Maybe mid-fifties?

"Me too," I begrudgingly admitted. Ten percent worried, ninety percent burning with a white hot fury. "Please, have a seat." She did. "You wanted to talk about Tony?"

"Tony? I didn't say that," Tara said, confused.

I covered, "Not Tony specifically. The state of the business. Perhaps some changes you were hoping for after the end of the prior... regime." I smiled to let her know my word choice was playful and that she could get comfortable. "Everything you say to me about Joe or Tony will be kept in confidence. I want to encourage you to speak your—"

"If I may," Tara politely interrupted. "I am not here to discuss Tony or Joe. I am here in my role as the Chief Human Resources Officer." She was still friendly but there was a stiffening in her posture when she said her title. "This week I have observed several of your interactions with Tiffany. She is your executive assistant, and it is your prerogative to request tasks of her. But your manner of instruction is teetering on the edge of aggressive and certainly un*professional*."

I had to ask, "She complained?"

"No, she hasn't. And it's possible that she wouldn't. Thanks to social media, a lot of younger people these days have a distaste for corporations and see rude managers as par for the course. They have their limits, but they also don't trust Human Resources departments. Rather than complain to me, they'll sew seeds of discontent amongst each other. Tiffany is a hard worker and may not seem sensitive. But it was obvious that your tone today rubbed her the wrong way. And the Collin incident shook her up."

"I know that," I heard the defensiveness in my voice and tried to lower my voice to combat the high pitch that came when my guard went up. "I saw she was emotional. I gave her a bit of tough love to get her head back in the game."

"I see. And this morning when she was explaining the calendar system to you, was that also tough love?" Tara asked. I was impressed by the evenness in her voice, despite her accusations.

I gathered my thoughts. "I understand that women in your generation are used to asking women in leadership to tone it down and be more complacent. I know Tony and Joe. There is no way I was any more demanding of Tiffany than either of them would be. So, woman to woman, if I were a man would we even be having this conversation?"

Her face didn't move. There was not a single micro expression. She was either Botox-ed or exceptionally good. "Women in my generation know we must work together if we want to be successful in these types of settings. Would I have said something to a man? Yes, I would. And I did. The difference is, I thought you would listen. I didn't want to make a big deal of it but it seems you are... unaware... that Tiffany is Frank's granddaughter."

My brief, uncomfortable laugh bought me some time as I searched for the meaning of this in my head. "Frank who?" It immediately dawned on me. "Oh, *Frank* Frank." Tiffany Miller. Frank Miller, from the board.

"Yes. Tiffany is estranged from her family, but I don't think that means you're protected from complaints. If you were Frank and your only granddaughter came crying to you about her mean boss, who do you think Grandpa's going to blame?" she said.

"Did you come in here to threaten me? You're going to report me to Frank?" I asked, as calmly as I could.

Tara stood up. "I would not threaten you. I came here as a *professional* courtesy. I know that Joe was a huge advocate of yours. And for whatever reason, Frank made sure you — not Tony — got this job. But, woman to woman, before you go burning bridges ready to rest on your laurels, you may want to ask yourself what it is that makes you so darn special." 10/10, she stuck the landing with a perfect dismount. Exiting and closing the door just as softly as when she entered.

I stretched my arms across the desk in front of me, it was so big I couldn't reach the other side. I groaned and put my head straight down on it.

"Fuck." I said out loud, my voice muffled even to me as I spoke into the desk. I know this place has been a boy's club, but do the women have to be against me too? What happened to women supporting women?

No use wallowing, time to get ahead of this. I reached my right arm down to my pocket, bringing my phone back up by my face. I lazily roll my head to the side so I could see the screen. I open up the text messages, starting a new one.

I typed, formulating the message as I went.

Hey, girl.

Delete.

Good evening, Tiffany.
I know we got off on the wrong foot. I was

Delete.

I know today was hard. But sometimes more is required of us even when we aren't feeling up for the challenge. We just have to work through

No, stop. Less is more. Delete everything. Start over.

Hey, Tiff. I don't like how things went today. Can we talk? Woman to woman?

Perfect, don't leave myself time to over think. Send.

As my text whooshes away into the world, I lift my head up. Damage control is under way, but I need to go. My head is throbbing and my neck is tense.

Wait, why are there two mugs on my desk? One is my personal mug. A beautiful ocean inspired hand made one, extra-large. The other is an average size plain black mug, the office mugs. The same type that Collin had his Irish coffee in this morning.

But it wouldn't be *that* mug. No, it's *my mug* from yesterday, which I left on...

Damn! That passive aggressive little bitch. She brought it back to my desk instead of taking it to the break room?

I realize the mug is in my hand and I just want to.... I threw it at the wall as hard as I could. It fell to the ground, already shattered into pieces.

Just one more mess *for me* to clean up.

Tomorrow.

6

Yesterday had shaken me to the core. I doubt myself more and more lately. But Joey doesn't. He always believes in me. He thinks that I'm smart and capable and an amazing businesswoman. He values that I know what I want and how to get it. He's the only man that was attracted to me for *those* reasons first and my curves second.

Men often approach me because I'm attractive yet *obtainable*. Insulting when it's said that way but if I say it myself it takes the edge off. Mom always told me not to call *myself* beautiful because it was unbecoming. Other people could call me beautiful. According to her, I wasn't pretty enough for them to overlook a big ego.

If I told people this, they would say my mom is cruel. I know that's not true because she also says I look exactly like her when she was my age, and I do. Anything she says about my appearance, she also says to herself.

When she talks to me, I imagine it's like her using a time machine to talk to her younger self. "Don't squint like that, you'll get more wrinkles," she says, as she puts on her glasses, which obscure her crow's feet. Or "You should start Pilates, like me," when I complain that my thick thighs keep ripping my leggings. Or my favorite "I cut out [random food] the last thirty days. I don't even miss it!" She'd then give her tummy a little pat.

It might not upset me *if* all those things were the miracle she claimed. But I know she uses Botox and weight loss injections. To each their own but maybe don't lie about it to your daughter who has the same genetics. I was a teenager when my mom was my age and I won't easily forget the way she looked at her body which later became *my* body.

Mom was concerned I'd never find a man if I didn't change my appearance. But I found plenty of men, starting in my teens all the way through my twenties. Some long term. None of them *complimented* my flabby arms or my fupa, but every time I left the room their eyes would follow my ass. Except for Larry, who I dated for over two years. He took me to a semi-romantic restaurant on the Sacramento River two days before my thirtieth birthday. Half a bottle into the date he said, "I always pictured my future wife would be dainty. I want someone I can carry over the threshold." He dumped me before dessert, my favorite part of a meal.

I had no idea that two days later I would meet the man I would spend the rest of my life with.

My friends, Lindsey and Courtney, had taken me to some nightclub in Union Square, San Francisco. It wasn't our first stop and Lindsey was leading the charge, so I don't know which club. Just that it was loud and dark and playing (sometimes) familiar music on a never-ending stream where songs didn't finish, they just melded into the next one. I was having a fun time, and it wasn't too crowded.

It was my birthday and I'd had a birthday shot with every drink order. Courtney must've had two each time she bought a round because the only thing keeping her from falling down on the dance floor was the forty-year-old sweaty dude she was grinding. His face was red and puffy from dancing and drinking. He was an attractive enough older guy wearing far too many clothes. His suit jacket had been discarded somewhere and Courtney was living her Skater Girl fantasy wearing his loose tie. Courtney's blonde hair stood out, glowing in the neon lights. She was all dolled up for our night out. The man was clearly interested in her as he kept pulling her slender frame towards him by the hips.

Courtney, the smallest of our group, looked even shorter next to him.

Lindsey said something to me but I shook my head and pointed at my ears. She shouted slowly using her lips to help me read, "Who is that?"

Looking back at Courtney then turning Lindsey I shrugged my shoulders, mouthing, "I don't know."

Lindsey shook her head. "No, him!" she grabbed me by the chin, too hard, as drunk people do, and pointed my face at the bar. The rest of the club had purple and green lasers plus the occasional smoke screen blurring everything, the bar had dim lighting for anyone standing directly around it.

At the bar, scanning the club slowly, was a man in an either gray or tan three piece suit. He was good-looking for an older man. I could see he was tall and his suit jacket was tight on his arms. His perfectly tailored suit jacket was open revealing he had a *dad bod*. He looked like a B-list actor playing a businessman that accidentally wandered into a club. Drunk me thought he looked like an A-list actor.

As I was unashamedly staring at him, he approached us. I grabbed Lindsey's hand and squeezed it for reassurance, she squeezed back harder.

A tap on my shoulder had me turn around. Courtney had appeared behind me, slipping her arm around my waist, holding on to the hand of her new friend. The man from the bar reached us then.

Courtney's friend let go of her hand, quickly hugged the man from the bar with a firm pat on the back then swung around to face the semicircle us ladies had formed. Pointing at each of us in turn he counted, "One, two, three," pointing at the other man he said, "Four," then at himself, "Five, six. Six tequila shots! Be right back!" He yelled.

The man from the bar looked exasperated, but Mr. Tequila Shots was long gone. Courtney turned to me and started speaking excitedly about her dance partner, I didn't catch most of it due to my intoxication plus the noise. She kept wrapped around my waist to get close enough for me to hear her and to hold on to me. I caught the part where she said, "He lives in Sac!" But that was about it. I kept looking, casually at the new man. Lindsey had his ear. She must have been interested in him because she kept playing with her long wavy balayage blonde hair. She was the tallest amongst us women, but even she had to look up to him, blinking at him through her thick fake eyelashes.

The man was staring at me.

Mr. Tequila Shots came back miraculously carrying all six shots, pushing the glasses together in his hands. He encouraged everyone to grab one. He feigned ignorance when the shots outnumbered the people and while we all took ours, he took one in each hand and poured them both into his mouth at the same time. He slammed his empty glasses down on the table next to us. He grabbed Lindsey and Courtney, heading straight back to the dance floor with a blonde on each arm.

The other man and I were left alone with no buffer. He tried to talk to me some but his deep voice combined with the bass of the music and got swallowed up. I eventually heard: "Do you... to..... k?"

"Do you want to fuck?" I shouted at him, alarmed and offended.

He froze, looked confused, then he started laughing. He kept trying to explain but couldn't get any words out. When he saw I was angry he composed himself and said slowly and clearly. "*Talk.*" He pointed at the bar. I followed him. It was quieter by the bar.

"Hi," he said. "I'm Joey. And that guy on the dance floor is my idiot brother, Collin."

"Joey? What are you, twelve?" I teased, quickly hoping he'd take it as the flirty joking I had intended but had always been criticized for.

"My father's name is Joe, so Joey avoids confusion. Only Pops gets to call me Joe," he smiled down at me. Him saying *Pops* made me scrutinize his appearance; he was practically my dad's age. "What's your name, gorgeous?"

"Vanessa," I tried on my most demure smile, though the tequila stretched it into a full toothy grin.

"Vanessa, what are you, a sea witch?" he asked, I was immediately relieved my comedic gamble had worked.

"I didn't take you for a Little Mermaid fan, do you have a wife and kids?" I asked, only half joking.

"You're the one who asked me if I wanted to fuck," he taunted.

"Touché," I said, Frenchly. "What did you want to talk about?"

"What do I have to do to convince you to leave here with me?" He abruptly stopped, and put his hands up, daring to play innocent. "Not like that at all. I heard from your friend back there that you're calling the shots, birthday girl. Look, Collin's an adult. But I've got another day loaded with business meetings tomorrow and I need him a hundred percent."

"Best you're gonna get at this point is seventy percent," I looked over at him, on the dance floor just in time to see him spin and dip Courtney, then grab his back in pain as soon as she looked away.

"Sixty percent," I said. A deep voice echoed me, and I realized Joey and I had made the same joke. I made the horrible mistake of making eye contact with him. Fireworks of green and purple exploded in his intense blue eyes and I lost myself.

"What do you want me to do?" I was prepared to do so many things.

"I know Collin. He's not going to leave behind three beautiful ladies to go back to a hotel room with his brother. If you come back with us, he'll have a nightcap or three and pass out on the couch. Then, I won't be out all night looking for him." He sounded so logical.

"What's in it for me?"

"You get out of this noisy, miserable place. You can enjoy some high-end booze in a swanky suite. And perhaps some repartee with a handsome man who knows he's much too old for you," he said through a sly smile. "What do say birthday girl? I can tell in your eyes this place isn't for you."

The funny part was, I didn't want to leave. I wasn't a nightclub and bars girl, but I was having fun that night doing something new. But once Joey said it, I wanted nothing more than to leave this place and go anywhere he said.

I said, "Yes," believing Joey knew something I didn't. He knew me better than I knew myself.

And that's what the last five years have been like. Joey always knows what to do. He never tried to take away my independence, but I listened to him anyway. He saw something special in me.

Before you go thinking that was our 'meet cute', you should know we've only been dating for three years. It started out strictly platonic; we worked together in business. We stayed up all that first night talking strategy, and he brought me into his company as a business consultant. I've never felt so valued and respected by a man for my mind.

Which is what led me here, to the office of Joey's dead father, both in the long term and the short term. Because it was his text this morning that encouraged me to get out of bed. I read it again.

> *Good morning, my Nessa.*
> *Sorry I couldn't talk yesterday. Meetings all day, you know how it goes. Can't wait to get home to see you tomorrow. I want to take you out for a nice dinner. Let's go back to my place for dessert. Wear a skirt. I'm going to put you up on the bar top and slide your panties off. I'll kiss your thighs lightly and my fingers—*

BZZZ

I almost threw my phone in shock when it started vibrating with a call. My thighs tingled, they knew what the rest of the message said. I immediately felt embarrassed when I saw who was calling. *Frank Miller.*

"Good morning, this is Vanessa," I answered professionally.

"Frank," the man croaked through the phone. "For Vanessa."

"... Yes, this is she," I responded, confused because he had called my *cell phone*. Probably couldn't hear me through his forest of ear hair.

"Glad I caught you on your mobile, I trust you have enough minutes," he laughed. His laugh was a smoker's laugh, though I'd never known the man to smoke. Maybe it was more like an evil millionaire's laugh, the kind you earn from being a trophy hunter like Frank. "I tried your office but there was no answer." Men like him always expect you to answer unasked questions.

"There's no direct line here, it has to be sent through Tiff—" I caught myself. "My assistant didn't make it in for the day yet. You're welcome to call my cell directly as you *always* have."

"Nonsense. I want this to be official. Can't have anyone accusing us of nepotism," said the man who's unqualified, ungrateful granddaughter had her desk right outside the CEO's office.

"Of course not," I said. The silence drew on until I finally remembered my line. "I just want to thank you from the bottom of my heart, Frank. Such an amazing opportunity. The board respects you. I know you were the deciding vote to make me—" (subtitle: Not Tony) "—the CEO."

"It's what Joe would have wanted," Frank acknowledged. "But this is not a call for pleasure." Easy for him to say now that I've given his ego a little chubby. "This is a call for business. Strap in young lady. It might be your first week, but the cannabis business waits for no one to catch up," I could hear his bony finger waggling at me through the phone. "Joe was a very dear friend of mine. I had a lot of trust in him. But I can't say he ran the company perfectly. As the treasurer, I should be involved in every large cash decision. I predicted our declining position more than five years ago." Here we go. Guess he prefers the way he strokes his own ego. "I told Joe to consider getting some additional investors. He didn't want to dilute the stock. Which is reasonable. But only leaves us the option of a private loan since we're in the Cannabis business and banks still won't touch us. The Wellness Enterprise of Exceptional Dispensaries' great strength has always been its low cost of capital which has allowed us to expand rapidly while keeping M&A costs in check. Now... there are other ways—"

Here was where I started to tune him out. Frank had a way with words: the long way. I'm told he had come up with the company name and despised the shortened version: W.E.E.D. Frank's goal always seemed to be to keep someone listening for as long as possible. Eventually, he would get to the point, I just had to ride it out while his words passed over me in gentle waves.

"—In my experience, we always have the chance to re-negotiate—"

Since Frank wasn't calling to lecture me about Tiffany, I could afford to be distracted. I flipped through Joe's Rolodex but quickly got bored. Now is as good a time as any to clean out my purse.

"—seventeen percent is just unheard of—"

I gathered all the loose coins and shoved them into my coin purse. Pack of gum: keep. Smoothie receipt: trash. Ruby Woo lipstick: keep. But is it my shade? I'll think about it. Pink Nude lipstick: classic. Keep for sure.

"—We did value the quick access to capital—"

A third lipstick? I barely wear lipstick, no wonder my purse is so heavy. Lip Balm: *don't mind if I do*. I cover my dry lips with balm. Feeling something sticky on my hand, I say "Ew, gross."

"Sorry, I didn't catch you. Come again?" Frank said.

"Nothing!" I covered quickly. A discerning person would have deduced that I wasn't listening. Frank continued without skipping a beat. I put myself on mute.

"My main concern, as I'm sure you'll agree—"

I grab a wipe from my purse to clean my hand and some of the lip gloss explosion. So much for my new sleek, black,

Celine purse. I don't bother taking out the four pill bottles. I already knew what they were. I had looked them up, thinking they might be weight loss pills. Tony had dropped about seventy pounds recently. It would be fun to rub it in his face that I knew his secret. But they turned out to be hydrocodone which felt like too heavy of a topic to be fun to tease him over. I'm not ready to decide what to do with the bottles. At the bottom of the bag, I wrap my hands around the forgotten keys from yesterday.

"—trending to the negative—"

A sticky pink smudge is on the ivory chess piece; I use my hand wipe to delicately clean it. Not sure if it's actually ironic or just Alanis Morsette *Ironic*, but Frank was the one who had the piece made for Joe. A tedious story I heard in entirety before I learned to tune Frank out.

"—as the treasurer, I'd be remiss—"

He'd had one made for everyone on the board plus Joe, all of them kings, white ones. Not sure Frank knows how chess works. He did have a bit of a chuckle when he said he'd made some for their sons too and the pieces were all very *fitting*. Even then, I thought about the fact that he didn't mention daughters or wives and what pieces they would be. Evidently, Frank had forgotten how powerful queens were in chess.

"—I've called their offices, but—"

Looking at the keys reminded me: the middle desk drawer. Three of the keys were small enough to be the one. I tried one, no luck.

"—It's no picayune matter—"

Did Frank just make up a word? Ignoring him, I tried the second key and immediately knew it worked. "Yes!" I exclaimed, sliding the drawer open. It was deep but it didn't go far back and didn't hold much. There was a black box, also locked, and a small brown leather book. A quick flip of the pages told me it was handwritten and mostly full. The spine wasn't that worn so it must have been written quickly and probably not read much to keep the spine so inflexible.

"—Which is why I need you to arrange a meeting," Frank concluded.

"Uh-yes." I was stupidly caught off guard. "I can absolutely make that happen for you. Let me just—"

"Hello? Are you there? Can you handle the scheduling?" He sounded irritated. I imagined his white wizard eyebrows furrowing, the man was really exceptionally hairy. Clearly, he wasn't listening.

I got louder. "Yes, I said I can make that—"

"Hello, have I lost you?"

Thinking it might be my service I look at my phone. Still muted. Idiot. I unmute and put it on speaker, setting my phone on the desk to keep my hands free.

"Hello, can you hear me?" I asked.

"Yes, I can, now," he responded, louder than necessary.

"Weird, must be *your* phone because I could hear you fine. I was saying, I'm happy to schedule whatever you'd like." With my hands free I pulled out the locked box. It was heavier than it looked for the size. It was about as wide and long as a small laptop, but much deeper. I tried one of the other small keys.

"Good. It's about time I have a conversation with this Mr. Giaimo. Have you talked to him recently?" Frank asked.

"Joey and I just had dinner with Angelo last week," I offered, distracted as I popped open the box.

"Joey? Joe's son?" Frank pressed.

Lifting the object from the box, I only vaguely registered I had said something I shouldn't have. "Joey? No, Joe. Sorry, must be your connection."

"Dinner with Joe, *last week*?" Frank was perplexed.

"Frank I've got to go. Thursdays around here are meetings day. I'm jam packed," I lied easily, making myself sound rushed.

"I need your assurance that you'll arrange—"

I cut him off, a trick I'd have to retain for the future. "Frank, I appreciate your vote of confidence in me as CEO.

Your continued trust is invaluable. I'll be in touch." I touched the red button.

The CEO gets to decide what's most important. Not the treasurer.

Right now, what's most important is the gun in my hands. And answering why the dead CEO had gambled on a handful of pills when a bullet to the head would have been so much more dramatic.

If there is one thing that is always true about men in power; they are such *drama queens*.

7

He looked at the large face of his yellow gold watch. It clearly showed the big hand was halfway between the I and II. *More than five minutes late.* He ran his finger lightly around the edge of the watch, releasing a couple of hairs that had been pinched in the metal band. He lamented the fact that his heirloom classic watch sat at home while he wore this much more expensive, less comfortable one. But it was important to communicate one's status.

It was not the watch that prompted the waiters at Il Migliore to roll out the red carpet upon his arrival. They knew Joey's face. Frustratingly, they never remembered his *name* and which one of the brothers he was. They all knew Joe. They all respected Joe. He had been coming there for decades.

Anywhere Joe had been first, Joey was in his shadow. His little brothers were in Joey's shadow, but anywhere their dad was, they were in the darkness together. Joe's footprint was shrinking. Joey had been given his father's name but had been forced to relinquish it to the older man and take on the less sophisticated version. After more than fifty years, Joe's hold on the name was dead. Joey was finding new paths not marred by his father's previous steps everywhere. The crisp, untouched snow. Now that Joe wouldn't be taking any more muddy steps, Joey could go *just about* anywhere with a clean slate.

But none of those other places had the world's best gnocchi.

Vanessa appeared at the table, out of breath. Joey stood up to greet her "Nessa, my love," he pecked her on the lips. "I'm glad you made it. It's unlike you to be late." He helped her out of her cashmere coat, putting it on the back of her chair which he pulled out for her in one smooth motion.

She squeezed into the chair, looking up at him. "I'm sorry, I thought I told you I wouldn't be off work until seven. I didn't realize you made the reservation for seven." Her eyes followed him back to his chair.

"That's all right, I've taken the liberty of getting us a bottle of wine." Joey carefully lifted the bottle and tipped it, pouring steadily into Vanessa's glass.

"It's... red."

"It's a *Syrah*," he corrected. She tended to over simplify, to distill important elements. This was why she struggled to appreciate the finer things. Like the cashmere coat he got her that she casually wore everywhere.

"Sorry, a *Syrah*," she repeated with near perfect pronunciation. "I usually get the clams though."

"A good opportunity to try something new. The gnocchi would pair perfectly," he suggested helpfully.

"You're right," she said, because he was. "I've had a long day, so I was feeling a little stuck in my mind. But I *should* try the gnocchi, maybe I'll like it, this time." She paused and took a small sip of her glass. She hadn't bothered to open up the wine with a gentle swirling as he'd taught her. Consequently, she made a subtle face and quickly had a sip of water to rinse the harsh tannin taste. Joey smiled knowingly to himself. "I knew this job was going to be a challenge, but I thought there would be more of a ramp up while I got my footing. It's just been this constant battle. There's no one there to support me. Tony spent the whole week trying to be the CEO. My assistant didn't show up for work yesterday and no one could reach her today. And I really don't know how to tell you this but Collin…" she trailed off when Joey's eyes looked behind her.

He was watching the server as she approached the table. She was pretty. Long auburn hair which she had put up loosely into a high pony. Joey preferred Vanessa to wear hers down. The server wore the same black button up as every other server in the classy but dated restaurant. Except, she had stopped buttoning hers four buttons from the top.

"Have we decided?" the server asked. She'd already greeted the table and delivered the wine earlier. No need to bother acknowledging Vanessa. She looked to Joey for the answer, knowing he would have it. When Joey was around, people deferred to him. Vanessa was used to it by now.

"We'll each have the gnocchi. House salad, dressing on the side," Joey made it clear there wouldn't need to be any follow up. Though he had watched her approach, he did not look at the server now.

"Excellent choice, we'll have it out shortly," the server seemed unsure of what to do with her hands. It was clear to Joey that she was new here, having come from a different restaurant where she'd been allowed to write down customers' orders. She stood at the table, committing the simple order to memory. She awkwardly offered, "May I pour you some more?"

Joey put two fingers on the base of his wine glass and slid it towards her. Vanessa reached for Joey's hand, now out in the open while the server poured the wine and walked away.

"Joey, I tried to call you on Wednesday to talk about—"

"I was traveling for work," he asserted. "You know this."

"I do. I'm sorry. I'm just trying to tell you that Collin started drinking again."

"Again *again*, you mean. Can't say I'm surprised. This is his cycle."

"I know, but it's been more lately. After your dad died Collin went on a bad bender. Then that time you had to pick him up…"

"I had to pick you *both* up," he reminded her.

"I could have gotten myself home. Collin wouldn't listen to me."

"That's Collin for you."

She looked down at their hands, running her index finger along his.

"His drinking is bad. I walked into his office and he was passed out. He looked dead. It pissed me off, but it really scared me too. This time when he quit, I thought it would stick. That last time he knew he messed up with you. I thought you'd want to know."

"I *do* know. He's *my* brother. It's *my* family," his words were intense, but his deep voice was dropped low enough to avoid any eavesdropping. Vanessa's eyes fell to the table.

"I thought you wanted me to be part of your family."

He squeezed her hand. "I do.... you are. But your first week on the job and all I'm hearing about is how bad my brothers made it for you and how I couldn't be there for you? That's going to make any man defensive."

"I didn't mean it that way, my darling. You make things so much better when you're here, that's all." She straightened. "I'm a big girl, I can handle silly workplace problems by myself. Enough about that. What about you? Did you make any progress on the latest project?"

"No," he took his hand away from hers to pick up his wine. "We haven't agreed on the terms."

"You spent five days in LA and you don't have a contract yet?"

He took a drink and took his time to answer. "It's complicated."

"You haven't had a new contract since the last one we worked together."

He stared at her. They were both silent until he spoke. "I got contracts long before you ever got involved. Do you think it was *your* masterful negotiation that landed them?"

"No!" she laughed uncomfortably. "I would never say that. You were always the mastermind."

He nodded in agreement. "Then it doesn't make a difference if I don't have a contract right now."

"Of course not!" she agreed eagerly. "I was just being nosy."

He leaned forward and she leaned towards him. "That's you, my Nessa," he tapped her on the nose. "My needy busybody." She laughed without parting her lips and looked away. "But I understand. You're curious about me and I love that about you. I know there's some part of you that wants to know where my next big paycheck is coming from."

"A small part," she admitted.

"I hope you know, I'm always going to take care of you. Like I did when you worked for me. And I built your little career and I connected you with a whole world of upper class people." He picked up her right hand, holding it with both of his hands. "I got you this job, at the helm of a multi-million dollar company." She squeezed his hand, and he kissed her hand softly. "Soon, you won't have to work at all."

"I don't mind working," she said. "I've always worked. I was working when you met me, in a job I got for myself."

"You were working for yourself."

"I owned my own business. I was the CEO."

He paused, and clicked his tongue. "You can do whatever you'd like. But there's a big difference between *wanting* to work and having to."

"I make an incredible salary now, it would be hard to replace that!"

"Who knows how long a cannabis company can really keep raking it in? That oil is going to run dry soon enough."

"You said—"

"What I have in the pipeline by the end of this year will set us up for life. That plus my inheritance. But that could take years to get."

"Hmm." She withdrew her hand. "I don't feel like I can count on that."

"I know there is a lot going on, but I'm confident I'll get what's owed to me. I know what I'm doing."

"I'm not talking about you. I'm talking about *us*. We aren't even married. We don't live together. How do I know what will be there in a few years?"

"That's what this is about? That we aren't married? Do you want me to apologize for planning my father's funeral instead of our wedding?" She shook her head emphatically. "You *know* you're welcome at my house anytime. I'm not going to take away your place from you. It would gut me if I crushed your independent spirit just to come live with me."

"But when we're married?"

"Yes, then, of course we'd live together. We'll need to buy a new house, a bigger house, so you can have your space. My house is just a Bachelor pad. Nessa, I love you. You're my princess, I'll do anything for you. But don't ask me to give up any part of you. I don't want you to change." she smiled at him. "There she is, the happy woman I fell in love with. My future wife."

Joey's plate of gnocchi was nearly gone.

Vanessa had taken a few bites of hers, pushing the food around her plate like a picky little eater who preferred chicken nuggets. He smiled to himself, she never did like Il Migliore's red sauce. Her palate needed some refining.

The server approached. "How is everything?" she asked Joey. "Ex-cell-ent," he drew the word out. "My compliments to the chef."

"Great! How are we feeling about dessert?"

"Yes, I think I'd like—" Vanessa started.

At the same time, Joey said, "No, we're fine."

"I'm sorry, I interrupted you, go ahead," Vanessa offered.

"I was saying, I think we've had quite enough rich indulgences for the evening. This'll be all." Joey dismissed the server.

Joey worked on his last couple of bites. They had eaten in near silence. Vanessa couldn't help but bring up work again.

"Got a call yesterday from Frank," she said.

Joey froze, a piece of bread dipped in red sauce most of the way to his mouth, "And?"

"You know Frank! Could hardly get a word in." Joey chewed on the bread and nodded his head. "He just kept going on about financial stuff. He was all 'as the treasurer… cost of capital… I disagreed with how Joe did things,'" she mimicked Frank's dull tone, and slow cadence. "Blah blah blah."

"Oh." Joey was as interested in what she was saying as she had been with what Frank was saying.

"He did briefly mention Angelo. I was hardly listening. You won't believe what was—"

"What did he say about Angelo?" Joey asked. She was trying to point at the *A* she got in English while covering the *C* she got in math with her finger. But Joey, the ever-aware dad, wasn't letting her bad report card get past him.

"Nothing really. Frank just wants to meet with him," she looked down sheepishly.

"You explained that he's private right? That he'll only meet with you? Like we talked about." The last part wasn't a question. Joey wanted to remind Vanessa that she had agreed to it.

"I told him we already met with him," she said like ripping off the Band-Aid.

"*We?* As in with me?" Ouch. The Band-Aid had ripped out some hair.

"What's the big deal?" she shrugged.

"You know what—" he started loudly. Then he looked around and brought himself down to a whisper. "If Frank knows that I know Angelo, he'll know it was me who brought him in as a financer."

Vanessa felt her confidence grow in light of the audience; recognizing how much Joey did not want to perform.

"I'm already the CEO. I don't need credit for finding this *financer* anymore. Everyone already thinks highly of me. Worst case scenario, they find out you and I are together. They'll assume that's how you know Angelo." She sat back in her chair, relaxing into the idea that her honest mistake could lead to the engagement announcement she hoped for. "They're going to find out anyway when I become Mrs. Caldarelli," her tone had become light and flirty.

He was shaking his head. "You can't go and do stuff without talking to me first. You're screwing this up."

"Hey now," she said, playfully. "I'm the CEO of W.E.E.D. I can't sit around waiting for my *fiancé* to weigh in on everything I do. Remember, I got this job because I'm smart and capable and all the old guys love my voluptuous figure. I'd be in this role with or without you, mister big man."

He rolled his neck back, sighing a bit as it cracked audibly. "You have no idea what you're doing." His tone was so deadly serious that the wine in her giggled its way to the surface. She fought back against the involuntary reaction, forcing her eyes down. She stopped making any sounds then. It had been his eyes that had told her to stop. This was not like their usual lighthearted banter. He saw her fear and decided that he didn't want it. "Vanessa, my love," he reached for her hand but she pulled it away.

If she wants to throw a tantrum, fine.

His phone, which always sat on the table when they ate, began to ring. He looked at it. "Shit," he said to himself. "I'll call you tomorrow." He stood.

"But what about...." she was silenced by one single finger, admonishing her, a warning to stay quiet.

"Uncle Frank!" he said jovially into the phone. "I was just meaning to call you." He began putting his jacket on, turning away from her just as the server returned.

She placed the check in front of Vanessa and left without acknowledging her.

Vanessa was alone, clutching her purse.

8

There is a version of Vanessa that would have been crushed by her first week as CEO of W.E.E.D. She would have cried herself to sleep on Friday. She would have tried to call Joey all day on Saturday and be too concerned to sleep that night. She would have drunk herself to sleep on Sunday knowing that no sleep was worse than a hangover for Monday morning.

She is the default version of me: Vanessa Standard. In ninety-nine alternate universes I would have crawled into my second week like a pathetic worm. But not in this one. This me is the one that prevails. Because this me is the one that found Joe's book.

I drove home from the restaurant on Friday in a blur. Don't worry, I wasn't buzzed. I stayed late at Il Migliore. I decided to treat myself to tiramisu. But I *was* upset. I slammed on my brakes too hard and the box of gnocchi in red sauce on my passenger seat fell on my purse.

I got home and went to clean up my (thankfully black) bag, I saw Joe's handwritten book inside. I had been planning to give it to Joey, a piece of his dead dad. After the way he bailed on our date night, I felt like being petty. I'm not an asshole; I *will* give it to him one day. Once I'm done with it.

I spent the weekend reading; instead of watching the latest season of some reality television and sipping frosé in a ridiculously hot bath while rethinking my life. Though that is a perfectly valid way to spend one's weekend.

I stayed up late reading it, I haven't been so engrossed by a book in years. Cracking open the hard leather cover felt like reading Joe's diary, a peak into his private life. Except it was entirely work-oriented. The first page had the title *Joe's First Ninety Days*. It was a silly title. Partly because of its usage of third person *Joe's* instead of *My* took away the memoir feeling and instead made it sound like a children's picture book. *Joe's Big Adventure* or *Joe's Day at the Zoo*; both had similar vibes.

It was an odd choice from Joe. Everyone who knew Joe said he wasn't quite himself the last year or so. Not as present, maybe groggy. This might not have been that weird for him. I had known him for a few years but since he always seemed old to me, this was a natural progression. Old man became really old man, then died.

Technically he killed himself, perhaps seeing it as the inevitable. Joe seemed like one of those guys that would live forever, unwilling to let go of their house to move into a care facility, refusing to retire and let someone else step into their role. Death gave him no choice. Maybe that's why he killed himself, to take that part into his control.

Joe's book was slow and boring. But it was the *idea* that had me captivated. Normally, the advice that rich people give is *never* the advice that got them there. *Work hard* or *save every penny you can* was useless advice. No one has ever saved their way to being rich or stayed late at the office and gotten promoted. That's just the rich people's cover story. What they tell the rest of us to keep us where we are. It *is* lonely at the top, because it has to be. If everyone is at the top, there's no bottom to prop it up. And Joe, my dead future father-in-law was no exception.

He occasionally gave me advice when he was alive. But he saw me as an extension of him. My success was his success. Joey said that's why Joe wanted *me* to be the CEO of W.E.E.D. To continue his legacy.

But I was only getting a glimpse into his *real* plans.

Thus, when I realized the journal was no diary, but instead a personal roadmap to Joe's own success, I started reading and couldn't put it down. Well, sort of reading. More like looking to for inspiration. The book was a real skimmer. Joe wrote like he spoke: laboriously. His speech pattern wasn't particularly slow, but he used so many fluffy words to get there. Worst of all, while on the scenic route, he'd throw in tons of twenty-five cent-words (now known as ten dollar words thanks to inflation). Hence the skimming. I settled on making my own Cliff notes version and through it my road map to success. I was completely absorbed all weekend.

I did find a couple of hours to spare on Sunday, for Joey. When I didn't reach out to him Saturday (like ninety-nine percent of all Vanessas would have) he finally stopped by Sunday morning. He brought my favorite bagels and tempted me away from my work. The power shift was palpable when, naked and relaxed, I suddenly turned to him. "I need to get back to work."

Joey chuckled until I sat up, reaching for my shirt. He touched my shoulder. "I thought we would decompress together before the week starts."

"I don't have time today," I said. "I did on Friday. Don't you want me to make a good impression, since you got me this job as CEO?" Might be petty, but if he wants to see me more, he can just move me in to his 'Bachelor pad'.

He made puppy dog eyes at me but within twenty minutes, he was gone.

Joey really is a good man, and I'll be happy one day to call him my husband. For now, I'm focusing on running W.E.E.D.

First thing I see when I arrive Monday morning is a message blinking on Tiffany's phone. I ignore it and head to my desk. I message Tara and ask her to come to my office.

While I wait, I look out the window. I haven't had much time to since I'd taken over the office. There wasn't much to see. The Sacramento River, I guess. But with only a second floor office, you couldn't see much else beyond it. I was grateful that it was a more industrial part of the small city. A busier part of the river would result in obnoxious noises all day. A boring view gave me no reason to be distracted. Must be why Joe chose this hideous office building.

I reflected on my road map, making sure I was staying true to Joe's words. I'd only gotten through the first fifth of the book but it seemed to be the right amount to get me through my first couple of weeks.

According to Joe:

> *Your first week as the Chief Executive Officer requires a great deal of both reflection and introspection. Quiet contemplation will be afforded to you as all others clamber for the floor. There will be scant time to articulate your own observations, as the perfunctory song and dance of the other company executives will easily fill the time. Your role during this time is simple: assuage their worries while listening to their words. The milieu of W.E.E.D. can only be discerned in this careful and patient approach.*

He went on like that for literal pages. A long-winded way of saying: *do nothing.* Luckily, that means I'm already on track. Last week was my time to do nothing, this is my week of doing things.

Knock. Knock.

Tara opens the door and confidently closes the distance from my door to the desk. She says nothing to greet me and seems irritated.

"Close the door, please," I say, very politely. This does mean she has to turn away and walk back to the door. We are both silent as we wait for the door to click closed. I begin immediately, "Has Tiffany contacted you?"

Tara answers as she walks back towards me, "No, she hasn't."

I anticipated this. "I want her terminated as of today. I'll sign the documents when you have her final paycheck ready."

She had stopped midstride at the word *termination* as if she'd been given whiplash. "I would like you to reconsider that, perhaps with a cooler head."

Cooler heads prevail: Joe had written frequently. Seemed like something he could have told Tony. Good thing *my head* was cool. In addition to Joe's book, I had read the employee handbook. Also a skimmer.

"As the CHRO, I'm sure you know that *one* no call no show requires a writeup and that *three* no call no shows in a row is considered job abandonment, a voluntary termination. Certainly, you would advise me to accept a voluntary resignation over involuntary termination. Since involuntary termination is likely to result in back and forth with the unemployment division, even if unemployment is unlikely to be awarded. The CHRO would want to avoid that risk." I had also read legal advice on Google. And now I was reading Tara like a book.

Tara chose her words carefully. "With all due respect—" she meant none was due "—I think that's an overreaction. Tiffany has been with us four years and has *never* had an unexcused absence. If anything, I'm worried about her. I've called her and she hasn't responded. I had Jenny in accounting try her too since that was her closest co-worker. It is so unlike her. Her emergency contact was her ex-boyfriend, so there's no way to get ahold of her. I'm tempted to ask Tony to arrange a wellness check."

"Tony? Why?" I ask, making sure to pitch my voice up and feign curiosity.

"He knows the police chief. I'm not sure if it's the right jurisdiction. But I can ask."

Ha, so Ms. Know-It-All doesn't know about Tiffany and Tony. "Okay, you should." Tara looked relieved. I paused long enough to picture Tara approaching Tony and him panicking before realizing she just wants to use his connection with the police, not accuse him of misconduct. "Just have her final check ready today."

Tara blinked slowly at me, the only indication that she was furious. "I don't typically handle final checks, that's accounting."

I don't want to talk to Phil. "I'm confident that you can manage it."

"I will," she conceded, turning to leave.

"Before you go," Tara turned back to me, but only a quarter of the way. Her body language telling me she couldn't wait to get away and go gossip about me. "I want the position for Executive Assistant posted today. I'd like to see some solid applicants by Wednesday morning."

She nodded curtly before leaving me alone with my thoughts. Now is my chance to get organized for the day. Tara thought I needed her to tell me how to do my job. She told me I was being a poor leader. Most people would have been offended. Or they would grovel for her approval. Not me. I'm focused on results. Tiffany disappears because I had the nerve to tell her to do her job? A weaker person would beg her to come back and ask for all the passwords and Joe's secrets. Not me. I have IT working on the former, and for the latter I have Joe's book.

Last week was an anomaly. I have to remind everyone why I'm here. It's not because my fiancé got me the job. It's because Joe saw my leadership ability. He picked me over his own son. He saw my greatness and everyone else will too.

My heart raced at the thought of meeting Joe. Too many unknowns all at once. It was my first time going to Il Migliore. This was our first big client meeting, if you could call it that. After weeks of working with him, I was still learning what our business did. Joey explained we operated a series of holdings companies that would provide different consulting services depending on the needs of each company. A consulting company consulting on what? What were we the experts of?

But it didn't matter that I didn't understand it fully.

Joey was the expert of everything. I had learned to be comfortable with the butterflies in my stomach. I should have known then that it meant I had a schoolgirl crush on my new boss. I still get those butterflies when I see him.

I didn't have any *new* butterflies when meeting Joe. He was comfortable and kind, almost grandfatherly to me. I felt awkward around Joey and Collin, who were also present, but Joe helped me to feel at ease. I wanted him to like me.

I wanted Joey to see that Joe liked me.

Collin, whose primary purpose was the sommelier for the evening, had selected a wine for the table. While waiting for the server to bring it, Joe asked me about myself.

"Did you attend university, Ms. Sorella?"

"I did. UC Davis," I left out the part about dropping out after the first year, as Joey told me it would be unnecessary.

"I've known many UC Davis alumnus. What did you study specifically?" he asked.

Answer: Agricultural Science. But I didn't say that plainly since Joey said it would cause more direct questions. "I haven't found it to be germane to my career. Frankly, I should have pursued an MBA," I repeated what Joey had me memorize. Joey said Joe's favorite topic was himself and it worked to get him chatting. He went on for several minutes about his time finishing his MBA at UC Berkley while Collin tasted and approved of the wine. The server poured him a full glass and set the bottle down.

"Excuse me, young lady," Joe interrupted himself. The server looked at him raising her eyebrows. "There are four of us seated at this table. Logic would dictate we will need four glasses for our wine. I see one which you have filled—" the server visibly itched for Joe to be done speaking so she could reply "—and I see one other. A prudent server would note this and bring two glasses with the bottle." Grandfather Joe had stepped aside, leaving room for Joe the CEO.

"The table was preset for *two*," the server said, biting her tongue and ending it there. Indeed, Joe had insisted on *this* table and had two chairs moved. The booths we had been offered were unacceptable. Scootching in was undignified.

"We have uncovered two facts then. You can count *and* you are not a prudent server. Perhaps you can go on a fact-finding mission and determine the location of two additional glasses." Leave it to Joe to say seventy words when seven will do.

I stared at him while he studied the menu. I already knew to order whatever Joe was having so I didn't need to read. Instead, I studied Joe. I still wanted him to like me, even when I was beginning to not like him. His hair was white, his eyes a gray blue, his lips thin and held in a straight line. He was unmistakably Joey's father and Tony's future. But I hadn't yet met Tony to compare them at the time.

Joe was a raisin while Joey was the grape. Joey wasn't fat, but plump would be a fair word for it. He was big and strong and his hands didn't shake while gripping the menu as Joe's did. Both had medium olive skin.

Then, there was Collin. Collin was wine. He looked similar to Joey, but even if he was older I couldn't see him turning in to Joe. His eyes were brown. While his father and brother each had a nice head of hair, Collin's was much fuller. His eyebrows were bushy, and had been shaved where they should have touched. His chest hair poked out of his shirt barely able to be contained. Collin's skin was also more of a deep olive. What made him a wine was that he was a liquid going with the flow; sloshing about between different personalities as the situation called for it.

Joe and Joey were undeniably solid.

I was staring at Joe when he put his menu down and looked into me. What if he had read my mind and knew I'd called him a raisin? Collin poured him wine into the only other glass, and he brought it to his lips. He pulled his thin lips into a smile. "Tell me, Ms. Sorella, what brought you here today?"

Joey had coached me on what to say to this as well. "I met Mr. Caldarelli a few weeks ago while he was on a business trip. We started talking about his consulting business and I was immediately—" I stopped. Joe was shaking his head.

"No, no. I understand you have won over my sons, that much is plain. And I know of *the* Sorellas and their influence in the bay area." He said it, not me. "Tell me things I do not know. Tell me of your professional trajectory. Where were you before coming to work for Joe?" Joe senior leaned in towards me. He seemed genuinely intrigued, which felt weird. I didn't even know *why* we were meeting. It felt like an interview *and* a date, with someone my grandfather's age. Joey and I hadn't talked about the potential he would ask more about me. I had been assured Joe would do most of the talking.

"Well, for the last few years, I've been self-employed..." I paused. My eyes practically bulged out of my head as I begged Joey to save me.

"Vanessa, please!" Joey practically shouted. "You're too modest." Joey had most of his father's attention, but couldn't grab hold of his eyes which were focused on me. "She is the CEO of her own consulting firm. You can consider her joining the team as a merger. Before that, she was in Real Estate Development." My jaw dropped but Joe was staring at my hair. I collected myself and nodded; picking up my water glass for a sip. Demure.

"Hmm. Well, are you not a most interesting woman? So accomplished for a pretty young thing." I almost gagged. "I want to hear more. But first," Joe stood, grunting from the exertion. "I must excuse myself to the restroom. Never get old like me, boys. My prostate always interrupts my conversations with beautiful women."

I didn't appreciate the details about Joe's inner workings. But it gave me the opportunity to respectfully ask Joey what the fuck all that was about.

"Respectfully, what the fuck was all that about? Real Estate Development? I helped my mom close some sales."

"In Commercial Real Estate, which is going to involve developers and wealthy clientele. You'll learn that it's important to say as much as possible in few words when speaking to someone like Pops," Joey said.

"But it's not true. I just work for myself, I'm not a CEO." I rubbed at my temple, carefully avoiding my eye makeup. "I've consulted for small businesses. But I only helped them present business plans for loans." And they didn't always get them.

"Vanessa, it's semantics. It doesn't matter what you *have* done. It's important we convey what you're *capable* of doing." Joey looked at me when he spoke. I looked to my left for help. Collin was too physically and emotionally absorbed with the tannins at the bottom of his wine. Joey took my silence as complacence. And he kept it.

Now, I understand that he was right. There isn't much difference between being W.E.E.D.'s CEO and running my business except maybe half a billion dollars. Being a leader is completely scalable. Like flying a plane. What difference was there for a pilot of a private jet with eight passengers versus a commercial airline with eight hundred? None whatsoever.

The rest of that evening went smoothly. The server brought the wine glasses and took our orders. Joe's insistence of 'ladies first' destroyed my plan to copy his order. By sheer chance I ordered the gnocchi which happened to be the go-to of all the Caldarelli men. I found out that night that the red sauce at Il Migliore was disgustingly sweet.

Joe spoke for almost the entire evening. This was when I found out he fancied himself to be a writer. I soon found out (by reading his published book of poetry) that you can *fancy yourself* whatever you'd like as long as you have enough money.

By the end of the night, I had successfully charmed him. I went to shake his hand after dessert and, horrifyingly, he grabbed my right hand with both his skeletal hands and brought it to his lips for a quick kiss. "Ms. Vanessa, it has been my pleasure. I do look forward to any future endeavor which causes us to cross paths. You have my vote on whatever projects garner your allegiance. Have an enchanted evening. I already have."

Joe and Joey both believed in me. Whatever it was I did that night was all the boost I needed get me here. Now I am in exactly where I should be: the cockpit.

9

You will experience natural attrition during your inaugural ninety days. It is as certain as death and taxes when there is a change of the guards. Even if the individuals lost are of no particular consequence, this might ultimately reveal a crack in the dam. You must move hastily to fill the voids with loyal candidates.

Loyalty cannot be bought by traditional means. It can be obtained through trade. Whatever you trade must be disproportionately more valuable to them than their loyalty is to you. Impress upon them this fact. It is effortless to establish this when you hire someone new, more arduous to derive it from existing employees.

You will need to create it nonetheless. If you sense there is a mutiny in the works, curtail it by being shamelessly generous with your 'yeses'. Say yes to everything, particularly to your executive team. They didn't get to the top by neglecting their ego. A little bit of stroking will erect from them a desire to return the favor. Presently, they will become comfortable with you. Keep feeding them the carrot. Have your stick at the ready, you will need it next.

— Caldarelli, Joe* (2027). *Joe's First Ninety Days*

*Deceased prior to publication.

Five minutes before the meeting started, everyone else meandered in. Except for Vanessa, who would likely show up at the eleventh hour.

But Phil had arrived two minutes earlier than everyone else. Not because he had nothing better to do. There was always a high-level task of great importance that the Chief Financial Officer should be focused on, more urgent than this weekly meeting. But they depended on him to be the voice of reason, of logic, of numbers.

He had secured his preferred seat. The only seat that faced a glass wall and put distance between himself and the head of the table. There would be no distractions behind or next to him. Assuring him that when he spoke, they were looking at *him*. He detested trying to decipher what people's facial expressions meant. He didn't also want to guess whether they were looking at him or not.

Most of the managers became glassy eyed when he spoke, nodding their heads occasionally. They would bobble along to just about anything. Even Joe did this to express his agreement. If Phil said something finance related, Joe would trust it, even if the treasurer, Frank, disagreed.

It was Joe that had given him his first big break when he put Phil in charge of the finances of his new real estate developments. Over forty years ago. Phil had just gotten his bachelor's in accounting, having eked by with a 2.6 GPA. None of that mattered to Joe. Only that he was a *good man with a sense of duty*. Phil *did* have a sense of duty to his employer; *and* himself. The best position was one that allowed him to serve both. He worked hard for Joe and, in return, Joe stopped asking questions twenty five years ago. That was for the best.

Then Joe died. Merely two years before Phil was planning to soft retire. He wasn't going to work into his eighties like Joe. He knew to get while the getting was good, and then he was going to get out. No need to push his luck.

Tony came along as interim CEO and Phil contemplated retiring early. Tony questioned *everything*. While all the other managers looked at their laptops (Joe never would have allowed laptops at meetings), Tony laser focused on Phil.

His questions to the CFO were rapid-fire and prodding, poking in far deeper than Joe ever did. Phil would loudly announce there was a cash flow problem, to make sure everyone saw that *he saw* there were issues. This way, he couldn't be accused of negligence. But that was supposed to be the dance. He would tell everyone the doom and gloom. Then the marketing, revenue, and operations people would be tasked with improving numbers. They would just have to keep growing year over year. Acquiring new facilities and growing top line, or cutting prices if they had to. Making the shareholders happy.

By the time the price cuts hurt the bottom line too much to pay for the debt service, Phil would be retired and no one could blame him. But Tony's constant questions implied the onus was on Phil to correct the cash flow issue.

To shield himself from this, Phil had done un-Phil things. After decades of immunity he found himself forced to participate in the unthinkable: office politics.

To Tony's face, Phil agreed with every request and idea he had. He complimented him, calling Tony even more astute than Joe. He was even 'working on' a special deep dive project on the Giaimo loan: *Who signed off on it? How did we find that lender? What are their rates with other high-risk companies?*

Phil was buying time. He whispered many things about the company's direction under Tony to Frank. While most on the board were indifferent, Frank already hated Tony, insisting (if anyone) Collin should have been made the CEO. Phil couldn't even pretend to agree with that. He simply reminded Frank how very difficult Tony would be to control. Given Frank's great distaste for Phil, it was a miracle it had worked. He lucked out that he was the enemy of Frank's enemy.

It had helped, yet he wasn't out of the woods. The new CEO could be just as bad. He was still workshopping her nickname. He was very good at them. He wasn't a 'people person' but that didn't matter when it came to capturing people's essence in a nickname. Based on initial interactions, he had prepared several potentials.

There was Vanessa, the Vixen. Because she looked exactly like Joe's wife at that age; probably how she got the job. Vacant Vanessa was good, her stare during last week's meetings made it clear there was no one home. Like in a deer in the headlights when he spoke about EBITDA. Vacillating Vanessa would be good too; since she hardly seemed like a decision maker. But would she even understand the insult?

Alliteration was his favorite, but he also liked Loch Nessa Monster, in case she turned out to be a real bitch.

So far, she wasn't a bitch. She was just weak. Continuing to let Tiny Tony run the place. Tony was taller than Phil, who was just shy of six feet, but he was two inches shorter than Joey. And skinnier now. He would *hate* to be called Tiny... Another perfect nickname.

Seven minutes was a long time to let his brain wander. Phil was startled when Vanessa began speaking from right next to him.

"Good morning, everyone." She set her notebook down loudly next to him. She had chosen the opposite end of the table from Tony, effectively switching the head of the table.

"This," she gestured to the young man next to her, "Is Peter Liao. As my executive assistant, he will be joining us in these meetings. All schedule and meeting requests for me will go through him," she announced. Then quietly she asked, "Phil, can you switch seats so Peter can sit next to me?"

Switch seats! For some kid wearing his daddy's ill fitting suit? Phil had been here seven minutes, seven whole minutes in his carefully chosen seat. But *he* was the one that had to change seats? Maya was across from Phil, why couldn't she switch? She'd only been there for two minutes. Marketing's only job was to spend money and look pretty doing it.

He grabbed his stack of papers and, expertly betraying no emotion, moved to the other empty chair.

Vanessa continued to speak, but her words were only barely audible over the whoosh of blood around his ears while his head throbbed.

"You can think of Peter as an extension of me. He won't be making any decisions, but he represents me in my absence. He will attend some meetings for me," Vanessa continued. "Please help him wherever possible. I think you will find he won't take much time to ramp up. He may seem young, but in his twenty-seven years" −Tara cleared her throat loudly− "he has had many accomplishments. He has an MBA from UC Berkley and has worked for many top-level executives in the area." Phil thought Peter looked like he wanted to say something, but he sat down instead. Probably embarrassed by the attention. "Tony, can you take the meeting notes while Peter gets his footing?"

Phil secretly smirked at that. Tiny Tony won't be able to hide behind his little yellow highlighter. Forced to take notes while everyone else said their piece. He'd be unable to prod and poke Phil while scribbling down the minutes.

Peter handed out the packets and sat down. "Let's get started. Phil, you're up first," Vanessa said nonchalantly. As if she hadn't just disrupted the entire meeting curriculum.

Phil, first? He was never first. Phil was always last in the printed packets. It afforded him the time to talk for as long or short as he liked. It showed everyone that his was the most important section. His financial performance review and forecast was the aftertaste of the meeting. Reminding everyone that business couldn't function without the finance department, without the CFO, and most importantly, without Phil. As he was about to logically point out that disruption of the order would be confusing to follow along in the packets, he looked down to see his Profit and Loss Summary on the first page.

He acquiesced and began at the beginning.

____

Phil covered his section in record time with no commentary from the peanut gallery. That's how he preferred it. Let him get to the point. This is how all meetings would go if Phil was the CEO.

He didn't like the intense eye contact as Peter watched everyone with wide eyes, magnified through his thick lenses. His cheeks had a roundness that gave him a baby-face contrasting with his chunky black rectangular glasses. His hands clasped in front of him. His oversized tie. Peter looked like one of the local college students dressed for an interview. He would have blended in with any of the young service employees, funding cheap beer for their big house parties on tips whilst using their parents' hard-earned money to pay for college. Instead of picturing Peter in his underwear, he pictured him in a uniform. Serving burgers, selling weed, making coffee. It made him seethe. How was it that Phil found himself seated at the same table as this greenhorn?

For that matter, how had Vanessa found her way to the head of that same table? It wasn't due to her business prowess. During each of his colleagues' sections, Phil listened to Vanessa give the green light to request after request. It seemed she would say yes to anything, costs be damned.

During the human resources portion, Tara had asked for "an entry level addition to the team. We are buried in paperwork for agent card applications at the new Nevada locations." Vanessa approved it. Phil did the math in his head, multiplying the requested hourly wage by two thousand and eighty hours annually for the single FTE, added at least twenty-three percent for PT&EB... handed out like candy from a two-minute request.

Derrick angled for an upgrade to the firewall so that he could control what was blocked. The firewall blocking everything with the word *cannabis* was probably an issue. But for Vanessa to agree to a five-year contract without reviewing it herself was absurd.

Collin requested a one-week vacation, all expenses paid under the guise of "providing ground level support to our newest facilities during 420." She agreed immediately. Collin always did as he pleased and probably would have done it anyway but that was not the point.

They were trying to run a business, not perform Make-A-Wish for the executives. Vanessa stunk of a desperate desire for acceptance. And all the executives smelled blood in the water.

The biggest shark was Maya. Always trying to convince everyone with her marketing siren song of "you have to spend money to make money." She re-pitched an idea that Joe had rejected *three* times at Phil's urging.

"I think we need to launch something special this 420. I want to revamp our loyalty program," Maya sang. "Currently, it's so rigid. If people spend a certain amount, they get a set amount of points to redeem. But our customers aren't exactly the rigid type. What they're missing is a little sprinkle of surprise. It can't be one big thing every ten or twenty visits like it is now," she started speaking more quickly, excitedly. "With my loyalty program revamp, we would pick a different small reward each week, maybe a pre-roll or a battery or a gram of our newest strain. And they would unlock the reward every third visit with their loyalty pass." Maya slowed down deliberately for the grand reveal, using her hands to draw out the words in the air, "I call it: Puff Puff Pass."

The room was silent for three full seconds until two people spoke at once:

"I love it!" and "Absolutely not."

Two tense seconds of silence.

"Joe has rejected this multiple times," Phil chided Vanessa who had *love*d the idea. "Think of the starting cost, particularly to rush order this in a few weeks. And the tracking. How do you suggest we even begin to record the liability? I've already fought the auditors for the current loyalty program, do you think—"

"You'll figure it out, Phil. We need to be forward thinking and innovating," Maya urged.

"I agree," Vanessa said, definitively. "Maya, I want to see the ad copy, graphics for the passes, and your rollout plan by next week's meeting."

"You're agreeing to this with a portion of the information. Considering your ignorance on the industry—" Phil began reasonably.

"Ignorance?" Vanessa said, emotionally. "Phil, I do not care that the previous CEO didn't like it. I do not care that it's more work for you. I care about ideas that will make W.E.E.D. more efficient, more profitable, and overall better. You can decide if that's a good fit *for you* or not. Now, if there is nothing else..." she looked around the room for nods and agreement. "Good. Thank you all for your great ideas. I have some news that I didn't want to start the meeting with as it might be distressing to you..."

But Phil stopped listening, his ears buzzing. He was already *distressed* to see that the Loch Nessa Monster had been seduced by the treacherous songs of Maya the Mermaid. She had tempted the new CEO the same way as the last, only now she was more successful because the new one was an imbecile. She played with her thick charcoal hair and smiled with her dazzling white teeth.

Phil didn't know what her accent was, but he knew he didn't like it. Not that he was racist or anything, of course! But her deliberate and intense speech pattern enunciated each word so you had to listen. It was all part of her seduction. Phil was a happily married man, but even he found himself tracing his eyes up her toned bronze calves to the bottom of her knee length skirt that...

What had Vanessa just said? He tried to rewind it in his head, needing the recorded evidence to overcome his disbelief.

"Peter will be passing around a card for everyone to sign for his widow. He will be missed." She paused for a moment of silence. "We'll take a ten minute break between this and the next meeting so you can have some time for yourselves." Vanessa did not wait for any responses before stepping out of the meeting room, holding the door awkwardly for Peter who *had* followed her, but not closely enough.

Phil smiled to himself. Vanessa's list of allies on the board just got smaller, while Phil had one less person to question him. According to Vanessa, Frank Miller is dead.

10

The conversation started naked as all our best conversations do. It was one of those rare Thursday evenings that Joey and I were both completely free. He invited me over and spoiled me. He made dinner; clams in a garlic and white wine sauce, crostini on the side. I don't usually drink on weeknights, but we couldn't abandon the rest of the wine from the sauce. And the second bottle he opened…

I knew he was trying to seduce me when, after dinner, he grabbed a chilled tray of chocolate and berries for us to take to the room. As I lay in bed, head on his bare chest, left hand fingers interlaced with his, I stretch my arm across him to put a blueberry in his mouth. It was small enough he had to taste my fingers.

I broke myself a tiny piece of raspberry dark chocolate and said breathily, "I could really use a cigarette after that."

"That good huh?" he chuckled, trying to appear nonchalant. He was fishing for a compliment with greater detail.

"Mmm," I moaned. "It's like you've studied my body and written a dissertation."

"So I've got a doctorate in Nessa's pussy then?" he asked. I cringed but didn't let him see. I hate that word unless we are actively… engaged.

"Most definitely, Dr. Big D," I smiled up at him. He didn't have the implied big 'D'. Nor a doctorate in a woman's body. But he was almost two decades older than me, and I'd long ago granted him tenure to my body. The act of seduction was more important to me than the act of sex and he didn't need a giant dick for that. He always made sure I was satisfied.

At least eighty percent of the time.

His heavy sigh brought me out of cloudy headed bliss. "Nessa." I squeezed his hand but laid my head back down on his chest. This felt like bad news. "I have some great news. I called Stephen on Tuesday and he—"

"Stephen? Why?"

"After Frank died—"

"Oh Stephen *Fischer*, like the chairman of the board?" I was confused. Obviously, there was no reason he should be talking to his ex wife's new husband, also named Stephen.

"Yes," Joey answered, dragging it out to make me feel absurd. But I wasn't absurd, he shouldn't have been talking to Stephen Fischer either.

"Why were you talking to a member of *my* board?"

"Nessa, don't be silly. Frank was an old family friend, not just some member of W.E.E.D's board," he said as if that explained everything.

My body tensed. "You knew on Tuesday that Frank was dead? You didn't tell me until yesterday." It was hard to keep the accusation out of my voice. I sat up and pulled away.

"You're missing the point, I said I've got *good* news." I opened my mouth, but let him keep talking when I found I had nothing to add. "Frank left the treasurer role vacant. Stephen offered it to me. They'll have to vote on it, but the other board members hardly care. They just listen to whatever Stephen and Frank tell them. With Frank gone they'll *have* to—"

I couldn't let him continue, "They'll what?"

"If you would stop *interrupting* me, I would tell you. I'm going to be the treasurer."

I interrupted his dramatic pause with an important fact. "You can't be the treasurer while I'm the CEO."

"Hmph," he huffed, exaggeratedly. "I thought you would be happy for me."

No, he didn't. He thought I'd be upset. That's why we had sex *before* he shared his news. Always had to make sure Joey got his first. "This is going to look bad. What will the board think about us? And everyone else will see the convenient timing of my future husband getting on the board. It'll completely undermine me."

"They don't have to know about us."

I had to laugh. "So when I change my name to Vanessa *Caldarelli*, everyone will assume I'm Joe's long-lost daughter?" I was joking, but I was also stalling. Biding my time so I could process what I knew he was really saying. But this elephant could not be ignored. "You don't want to get married." Backing away to the edge of the bed, I stood up.

"Vanessa," he said sternly. "You are being short-sighted. I love you more than anyone. I want to marry you, in a few years. It's not the right—"

"*Years?*" I breathed through the pain.

"We're going to be together for the rest of our lives. What's a few more years? You'll learn how little time that is in the grand scheme."

I am too naked.

I pulled a blanket from the bed and held it against the front of me. I didn't want him looking at me, leering at my breasts while judging me for being younger than him. He mistook that to mean I was naïve. The man I'm about to marry shouldn't be telling me I'll learn one day like he's my *father*. I felt like throwing up. I wanted him to cover himself up and feel shame. I didn't want to see his sad cock, shriveled up now shorter than his sagging old man balls.

I gathered my clothes from a pile on the floor where I had teased Joey barely more than fifteen minutes ago and I backed into the nook that held the shower; out of sight from the bed.

He said, softly, "Don't be mad."

I dropped the blanket and pulled on my underwear, then my skirt and blouse, ignoring my bra. I hurried, loathing the idea that he might be able to see me in the mirror.

"Stay the night," he cooed. But all I could hear was a father telling his adult daughter what to do. I said what *she* would say.

"I don't live here, don't tell me what to do." I walked towards the bedroom door, bra in hand. Passing by the bed; Joey grabbed my hand. I was surprised, but it wasn't aggressive. He looked up at me and I couldn't ignore the resemblance between him and Collin. Pathetic.

He was so pitiful when he begged, "Please, I just want to be with you."

I knew then I had to stay.

It was getting late. I found some pajamas I had left there and changed in the closet. I washed my face and brushed my teeth and when Joey was certain I wasn't going anywhere for the night he changed his tune.

Turns out, he didn't just want to *be with* me. He wanted me there to witness his greatness. He talked *at me* until two in the morning. I heard all about his plan to request an annual retainer as treasurer. How he could best secure equity and what that would look like considering Joe's equity was in his estate, much of which would eventually make it to Joey. He offered a few reassurances to me that he would support me as CEO, making sure I stayed in the good graces of the board. He kept saying how lucky I was that this position opened up.

Joey kept making the point that he didn't need the money. I knew it wasn't true. He wasn't poor, but he wasn't as rich as his taste was.

He talked so much I wondered how he didn't run out of things to say. It seemed like he'd had a lot more than two days to think of it all, but that's just how Joey was. Always thinking of the grand *scheme*. He rambled too much and kept talking about Joe. Joey felt guilty, he blamed himself, couldn't understand how things had gotten so bad that his dad killed himself. I'm not sure if it's just a first-born son thing, but Joey was obsessed with making his dad proud.

By comparison, Tony never really seemed to like Joe. He emulated him, but that was as far as it went. He was a momma's boy. Creepily, it made me think *that* was why he wanted to be like Joe. To get the same husband-like affection Joe would have.

Joey never spoke about his mother, which was strange. She can't have been dead long when I met him. But I didn't bring it up because I didn't like talking about his past. It made me think of his ex-wife and his daughter, Laura. Laura was eighteen years younger than me, I was seventeen years younger than Joe. I didn't love being reminded of that.

I want to meet Laura, but she is down in LA. I might as well wait until she was an adult. Skip the whole wicked stepmother thing. After we are married... if we ever get married...

My mind continued to wander rather than sleep. My dreams were uneasy as I imagined Joey was still talking at me. Thursday night bled into Friday early morning. I desperately needed sleep, but I gave up at six in the morning and went home in a trance.

I came to while driving into work, Morning Boost coffee in my hand. All these thoughts of Joey's family made it impossible to push down memories of my own messy relationships.

Joey's family seemed better than mine. I had been looking forward to the day they'd become my family. I thought I'd have two brothers in law, plus Collin's wife, a father figure and even a stepdaughter. I romanticized those things. I thought a new family could replace my missing family pieces.

My dad wasn't bad, when he was there. He traveled a lot for work. Mom stayed home until I was eleven and I loved that I had her all to myself. I was an only child and they both treated me like a princess.

I answered the phone one day to woman asking for Mom, saying it was about Dad. My eleven-year-old brain assumed he was dead and stayed on the line when Mom picked up. That would have been a horrible way to find out. But sometimes I wish that's why she was calling.

She was *actually* calling to say that Dad, or Eugene as I call him now, was cheating on Mom. With that woman's sister. Mom didn't believe her but when Eugene came back from another exhausting work trip he saw her face and sat down and emotionlessly confessed the whole thing.

I listened as he admitted to being in love with this other woman, Maria. He blew my mind when he said they had three children together. The oldest was seven. Mom's solution: an ultimatum.

He chose Maria and her children. They had us outnumbered.

Mom was so stubborn (pronounced stupid) that she let him keep shared custody and pay no child support. She wanted to keep the Sorella name. Used in the right situation it can be advantageous. Her real estate agency got off the ground immediately thanks to high income customers believing she had excellent financial connections.

As for my attachment to the name, I saw my father and his family one week each year until I was sixteen. Then not again until I was twenty-five. I reached out to Eugene because I was about to get kicked off of Mom's insurance and I couldn't stand working for her one more day. I needed *money*, he gave me a job.

He put me in charge of small business loans for the Sorella family's private banks. It was a huge responsibility for a twenty-five-year-old, or anyone with as little experience as I had. I was approving loans anywhere from five thousand to a quarter million dollars with no oversight; I was doing important work. Or so I thought.

After years of learning the lingo, assessing the viability of these businesses on little more than an elevator pitch, I learned that it had all been pointless. Sorella Financial Services, SFS, didn't care if the businesses were viable. In fact, they targeted desperate small businesses who couldn't say no to the outrageous interest rates. I got tired of little old lady's coming to my office in tears, forced to close their family's restaurant after thirty years because they couldn't afford their debt.

SFS used the outrageous rates from these loans to fund lower interest loans for their ultra wealthy clientele. Disgusting. I know. I can hardly be blamed for my part in that. They would've done it without me. I was just a pretty face. But Eugene put me in that position. Two years in, I got the courage to confront him.

I had said plainly, "I want a raise, Eugene. And a promotion." He smiled at me warmly, his glasses and balding head glinting in the light. Did he look like Phil or did all men in finance look the same? Thank goodness I had Mom's genes.

"Vee, honey. Is that any way to address your father?" He paused, waiting for me to correct myself. I had nothing to correct. He said, "I thought you would be pleased with the opportunity I've given you."

I approached him while he was seated behind his desk. He's shorter than me. I stood over his desk. "I have been in the same position for the same wage for years."

"And if you had been doing it exceptionally you would have gotten a raise. Or my approval. Is that what you've come here for? You would like some of daddy's praise."

"No!" I was taken aback by his mocking. "I want what you give the others." I had meant love, but he had heard money. Words he found interchangeable.

"Your siblings? Vee, you must accept your life is different from theirs. I give them money, because they will always have it. They don't need to *earn* it or learn its worth. You do. And it's a father's job to give his children what they need, not what they want." He had not left it open for discussion.

I'd wondered how one man could possibly have two families, but I learned that day that he never did. Maria, Sophia, Marcus, Juan: they were the chicken, the fries, the toast and the dipping sauce. Mom and I were the fucking coleslaw. "You should be grateful that I brought you into the *family* business."

"Because I'm not really family?" It was the teenage girl inside me, speaking up for herself.

"Because you take after your mom. She's a real bitch," he said. The lack of inflection told me how little he cared. Like the coleslaw, he didn't even properly hate us, he was just going to ignore us or throw us away when he'd had what he wanted.

This is the part of the story where I tell everyone my great comeback quote. Or sometimes say I smashed something in his office. I once claimed to have punched him in the face breaking his nose and glasses.

In truth, I said, "Thank you for the opportunity," and went back to my office.

I worked there two more months before giving notice. That's when I went off and started my own business, coaching small businesses on the loan process. I had learned everything a loan officer would want to hear. I outsourced all the spreadsheets and data.

This is usually the part I start crying. Thinking about only seeing my dad's— Eugene's family every once in a while on holidays. Seeing the lives my half siblings were living compared to mine. With my tiny little consulting business. They were actually very kind to me, they must also have taken after *their* mom. I wondered what type of people they would be *without* money. It tends to change you.

And that's why I would cry. Being cynical and alone is painful.

I didn't cry today. My eyes twitched as if I might, but they were too dry. I blinked hard as I pulled into my parking spot, feeling the movement of my lid as if it was scraping the surface of my eye. I need to sleep. TGIF... unironically.

I dragged myself and my too heavy purse to the office, hearing a slight rattle. No wonder it's so heavy. After I got to the second-floor landing, I hung right and headed straight to Tony's corner office. I knocked on the door but didn't want to give him the chance to tell me 'no' so I entered on the second knock. "Tony, I..." I started before trailing off, processing that he wasn't there.

I'd never been in his office before. I counted the steps as I walked the distance to his desk; at least a full stride less than mine. His office was decidedly smaller. I set my purse down and dug around by feel. I scanned the office as I did so. Uncanny. Similar furniture, identical arrangement. Like a 4 : 5 ratio version of my office.

One, two, three, four. I lined the bottles up at the edge of his desk. The label was peeling off of one and two had a little lip gloss on them. A side-effect of rattling around my purse for over a week. Better leave a note so he knows that I *know*.

Thought you could use these, have fun!
-Vanessa (CEO)

I left his office hurriedly, feeling exposed, and made my way to my office. I was happy to see Peter, *not Tiffany*, at the desk before my door.

Peter was a symbol of the changes I was going to make. The first thing that was *mine*. Genuinely smiling I said, "Good morning, Peter. Nice to see you bright and early!"

Apparently, I startled him. He looked around his monitor and sputtered, "Y-yes. It's morning."

He has got to get through this awkward stage. He was so different at the Morning Boost... "Did you send Frank's wife my condolences?"

"Oh yeah. For sure," he nodded eagerly. "But there weren't any flower shops open that late. So I just sent him his regular order," Peter said.

"That's fine, doesn't have to be flowers. It could be...." I stopped, registering what he had said. "What's his *regular order*?"

He smiled and was very pleased with himself. "Yeah, so I found Tiffany's passwords to everything. She had a file on the executives and board members. She used to get them all free samples from the dispensary. Frank had a monthly order I got it myself and brought it over." He must have seen my look of confusion and frustration. "Don't worry though. The note says it's from you."

I was tempted to rub at my dry eyes, but fortunately remembered I had mascara on at the last moment and rubbed at my temple instead. "You brought weed to an eighty-year-old widow?"

"Y-yes." There was his stutter again. Maybe he had a good reason to lack confidence. "Yes." He repeated. "Tiffany's notes said Mrs. Miller also used it. Could help her relax right?" I couldn't let him think I approved, so I kept my face blank. He was the type that desperately had to fill the silence. "And I got access to her voicemails. Mostly just people looking for her, they didn't leave any details."

"Probably people in the office. They'll come see you or they can email if they need anything. You can delete those." I sipped my coffee as I turned to head to my office.

"There was one for you," he said, pausing dramatically.

I faced him. "And?"

"It was from that Frank guy, before he died."

'Before he died'. I am going to call him Lieutenant Obvious… Perhaps one day he will be Captain.

"It was from Friday the 26th," he said. That Friday evening replayed in my head. The one that concluded with Joey getting a call from Frank mere days before Frank's passing. Peter read mechanically from his notepad. Somehow it gave perfect justice to Frank's rambling. "This message is for Ms. Vanessa Sorella. We need to discuss the loan from Mr. Angelo Giaimo post haste. It has come to my attention that Mr. Giaimo and little Joey, that's *Joey Caldarelli*, were alumni of the same university. And further it seems they are affiliated. This is entirely abnormal. I was led to believe *you* found this financier. I wish to you speak with you right away. I'll be calling Joey for his—"

"Thank you. Can I see that?" I grabbed his notepad. I've heard enough.

"But that wasn't—" Peter protested as I ripped out the sheet with the voicemail and tore it up.

"Go ahead and delete them all," I said, tossing the page into his desk side trash can.

I walked straight to my office and locked the door behind me. Unfortunately, the door was only made of teak. It wasn't strong enough to keep out my fear that my fiancé, who had a lot to gain, had something to do with Frank's sudden death.

11

She slid into a familiar maroon booth. Her short skirt pulled up as she sat, allowing the cracking vinyl to cling to the underside of her thighs. The server handed her a menu and placed a second in front of the seat opposite her. She smiled and gave him a head bob adding, "Gracias."

He hesitated only briefly before a split-second judgement. "You're Welcome." He promised to return when her companion arrived.

She gripped the menu, made up of six oversized pages, each printed front and back, then shoved into a sheet protector. This was theoretically for easy menu changes; the only thing Maya had seen change at Las Tortillas Asombrosas was the price. They hadn't been discreet about the changes, handwriting in the new prices on top of tiny white labels rather than reprinting the menus.

She already knew she wanted the birria taco plate with rice and beans and that the price was irrelevant. She wasn't thinking about the menu. She *was* thinking about the way the server chose to reply in English. It reminded her of herself.

When she was a teenager, she would help check-in guests at her family's hotel. Her family wasn't wealthy but they did well enough. Their boutique hotel in Baja California attracted all kinds of people and, to Maya, they had all seemed rich. They would use her to practice their Spanish in preparation for their journey into less touristy areas. Sometimes their accents were terrible; their Spanish too formal. Or she would pretend not to understand and reply in English instead. They saw her as practice and not a person. Being a service worker meant she was their captive audience. But no one helped her when she was learning English. They mocked her practice and her accent.

Now, she was so far separated from her first language that a fellow native speaker wouldn't engage her. She didn't expect an authentic experience from a white-washed place called *Amazing Tortillas*. But she knew her server spoke Spanish, had heard him engaging with his co-workers. He had rejected her bid for connection with two simple words: *You're welcome.*

English speakers treated her the same way. Like they felt she was still practicing English. It *was* her third language. Her Mexican father had ensured she was fluent in Spanish. Her Indian mother had taught her enough Bengali to interact with the family. When she was twelve, they both pushed her to learn English. She learned it well enough to teach her three younger siblings, then her parents. With more than thirty years of living in the United States, her parents still *barely* grasped conversational English. Yet they teased her for her diminishing Spanish and Bengali accents when she went home.

Every English speaker picked up on her stilted speech. They never let her forget that English was not her first language. Maybe if her first language had been French or German they would have been kinder.

She would always be foreign here. But she hadn't been back to Mexico in five years, and even then, just for vacation. It seemed that no language, nor country, could be called home for her. The server reminded her she was a foreigner to Mexico now too. In his defense, she *was* trying to use him for practice.

Everywhere she went, they refused to accept her as she was. She changed to survive. She had not been called for interviews until she simplified her name from Maanya to Maya. Marketing companies wouldn't keep her, criticized for her rigid adherence to proper grammar in ad campaigns.

Until she adjusted her writing. She never used to get dates until she changed her body, her hair, *and* her idiolect.

She had fought herself every step of the way to earn her position as the Chief Marketing Officer of a public Cannabis company. She found that cannabis users were elitist about their knowledge of the product, ostracizing her for never having bought an eighth under the bleachers in high school.

They could make her feel as unwelcome as they wanted to. Maya Montoya would be whoever she needed to be to succeed.

She was distracted and didn't notice Tara come into the restaurant until she appeared at the table beside her. They smiled at each other and Tara scooted in.

"Thank you for waiting," Tara said. "Jenny grabbed me on the way out of the door, worried because Tiffany never came by for her final check. She's been calling and texting and couldn't get a hold of her. I finally convinced her to mail it out and be done with it."

"That is strange. Tiffany was always working overtime for the extra pay," Maya offered.

"True." Tara leaned in. "I wasn't going to say anything, but seeing as she is no longer in our employ... Tiffany's grandfather was exorbitantly wealthy. *And...* he just died. I highly doubt she is counting on her piddly little W.E.E.D. paycheck."

Maya asked skeptically, "How do you know he's dead?"

"Well, I don't want to gossip," Tara said.

"Okay."

"But if you twisted my arm, I'd tell you. Frank Miller, the treasurer, was her grandfather."

"No!" Maya was only moderately scandalized. But she knew Tara wanted some hammed up reactions.

"Oh yes! They weren't on good terms. But Frank pulled the strings to get her the promotion to Joe's assistant. Frank disowned Tiffany's mother when she became pregnant with Tiffany as a teenager, but he still had a soft spot for Tiffany. His other kids didn't have children. She was the only grand baby," Tara had to take a sip of her water. "Except for the new kid Tiffany's mom had. But Frank hated the father, so I doubt that matters. I'm sure he left Tiffany a hefty sum in his will."

"How do you always know these things?" Maya was genuinely curious.

"People come and tell me. Human Resources. Everyone thinks every problem they have is a Human Resources issue."

"They just come to complain?" Maya already knew this. But she also knew that Tara wanted to talk about it.

"Oh Lord, yes! Every company I've ever worked for. And their favorite topic in W.E.E.D. is favoritism. *So and so* did nice things for them and not for me. I don't know what they think I'm going to do about it, as if half the people working there aren't related to someone high up. You know about Vanessa of course?" Tara said it like a question, because it was very unlikely Maya knew.

"What about Vanessa?" Maya asked.

"Oh, I shouldn't say," Tara teased. "But you'll hear about it anyway. You know how we all thought Joey would be CEO when Joe quit? And that Vanessa was working for Joe?"

"Uh-huh," Maya encouraged.

"Well, turns out Vanessa is Joey's *fiancé*," Tara smiled widely at the reveal.

"Woah!" Maya was fully scandalized now. "*Before* she got the job, or after?"

"They've been engaged a while now. Joe had Tiffany send them a congrats gift, sometime last year. I don't know," Tara added. "I don't get *all* the details."

"Isn't Joey the *oldest* son?"

"Yes, he is. And I know exactly what you're thinking. It gets even weirder than that. Did you ever meet Joe's wife, Victoria?" Maya shook her head and Tara was already continuing. "Not only is Vanessa young enough to be Joey's daughter, but she's also the spitting image of his mom. Not now, but from old pictures... Mm-mm-mm!" she clicked her tongue. "That boy's got some mommy issues. And I'll bet..." Tara stopped herself. "What am I doing? It's Friday, it's our lunch break. Let's not talk about work."

Maya nodded and pushed her hair behind her ear.

"How's the dating scene going, Miss Thang?" Tara said playfully. She was only ten years older than Maya, but Tara referred to most people slightly younger than her in a maternal way when she wasn't at work. It took Maya years to realize she was being caring not condescending. She'd been the youngest woman around in most executive situations, fighting for scraps of respect. Now, with over two decades of experience behind her, she finally started to feel less defensive about it. Selectively.

"Dating is... good," Maya said unconvincingly. "I do have one man I've been seeing for a month. He's alright."

"Sounds promising," Tara joked. "The future Mr. Montoya. At your wedding, I can recount this story of how Mr. Right was just *alright*."

Maya played with her straw in her water glass. "Not like that, he's just, so old! I hit my mid-forties, and suddenly, every man who wants to date is ready to retire. I haven't found any man that really excites me. I don't have to marry them, but I would like a man that's fun. Or interested in something besides sports or having children or *grandchildren*."

"Oooh, that's your problem right there!"

"Children?" Maya was surprised since Tara loved kids.

"Ha!" Tara threw her head back and her short hair flipped into her eyes. She shook it out. "No: men. You may not find *a man* out there good enough for you."

Maya laughed. "Not all of us are lucky enough to find a wife as good as Sierra. Some of us have to settle for men."

"Don't I know it. She is too good for me. Only took me forty-six years to find her. You still have time," Tara smiled. Her warmth took away the slight chill Maya felt in the early spring air.

The server came over to refresh their waters and tried to take their order. Tara waved him away. She was still undecided. Maya's stomach grumbled; she hadn't added the chips and salsa on the table to her calorie tracker, having saved all of her calories for the birria. But if Tara kept talking, she wouldn't be able to resist.

"How about Sierra? How are she and the fur babies?" Maya asked, knowing it was a dead-end topic. Tara could talk all day about everyone else. She was private about her own life.

"Sierra is as good as ever, and the babies too." Tara reached for a chip and scooped some salsa. Maya nodded, and picked up her menu hoping Tara would follow suit. She did. After only a brief pause, Tara put her menu down. "You know what Sierra sent me today? An article for W.E.E.D. on *Touch Grass*."

Maya put down her menu too, *this* was something worth delaying tacos. "What did you think of it? It should be the top banner now through the 20th. Joe never let me spend the money on digital that we should have. I got Tony to approve it last month. I'm thinking of getting Vanessa to approve a video right before 420."

"Oh no, not the *ad*. I did see that too," she ate another chip and Maya wished Tara weren't so polite because she had to wait for her to finish chewing. "It did look good." That was not worth the wait. "Sierra sent me that article, *Women of W.E.E.D.*"

Article? Maya indexed her recent initiatives in her brain to make sure before she said, "I didn't know about an article."

"There's a whole photo spread of her. It's a little absurd."

"Who?" Maya was confused how she, the CMO, knew *nothing* about an article.

"Vanessa. I assumed you knew. Relieved to know you didn't because I have to say, it was in poor taste. Must have been from before she started," Tara said.

"What was it about?" Maya was interested and also starving. She broke a tiny piece off a chip and scooped some salsa. *One less bite of rice*, she calculated.

"Nonsense! Supposed to be about women in cannabis leadership, but what does she know? We've been with W.E.E.D. from the start and she strolls in talking about empowering women in the workplace. And a whole bunch of garbage about piloting a plane and having women in the cockpit. Meanwhile, they slap our name at the bottom like we're the stewardesses," Tara was getting heated and Maya worried she would never look at the menu. "Anyway, let's not let Vanessa ruin another minute. No more work talk."

The server returned and Maya feared the worst, knowing Tara hadn't so much as skimmed the menu.

"Are you ready to order?" He asked. Maya nodded but looked to Tara.

"I'll have the number two lunch special with chicken please," said Tara.

The same damn thing she always ordered.

The table was strewn with a nearly empty chip basket, two empty margarita glasses and two off-white oval plates which each had a smattering of beans and rice left. "You should have seen her poses. Mostly silly, using cannabis as props. Pretending to be a professional. Others were downright inappropriate. Something I might do for Sierra, Lord knows you wouldn't catch me making bedroom eyes for the whole darn internet to see." Tara shook her head and lifted her empty margarita glass to her lips, seeing if there was a drop she had missed.

Maya made a mental note to look up the article herself. Considering how conservatively Tara dressed and how much she disliked Vanessa; she took Tara's assessment with a rim of salt. She resisted the urge to lift her own glass and test for some reappearing margarita. This calorie deficit had her craving the sweetness. "She is very different from Joe," Maya conceded.

"Hmm," Tara vocalized without parting her lips. "You've got that right," she nodded agreeing with herself about some unspoken thing.

"I don't think that's a bad thing," Maya asserted. Tara looked taken aback. "You can't say Joe was perfect."

Tara shook her head. "No, I cannot. But he was consistent and eventually I got used to him."

"He was a dick."

"The man had experience. Which I can respect."

"He had experience. Old white men have all the experience because they keep giving the jobs to each other," Maya pointed out.

"You think the future daughter in law of the old white man is better?"

"She could be," Maya reasoned. "At least they're giving a woman the chance."

"She's just a puppet. Doing whatever the board says. Carrying on Joe's legacy, and pulling the ladder up behind her." Tara was as salty as her margarita.

"It's not like I want to be the CEO. If she listens to our input, I'm happy."

"You're just happy about the whole Puff and Pass."

"Maybe." Maya allowed. "It's the Puff, Puff Pass. It's very clever, if you say it correctly."

"I agree. You are very clever," Tara said. She meant it. "Time will tell if this Vanessa is clever too. Or just another person at the right place and the right time."

"It is fun the way she makes the men squirm," Maya smiled, imagining their faces. "She had Tony with his head down taking notes. He's never been so quiet. And Phil! Talk about upsetting the old white men. He looked like his head was going to explode during EC. I could see him adding all the numbers of everything she approved in his head. Joe used to let Phil control almost everything, and Tony controlled everything else. We were always under one of their thumbs. Maybe Vanessa will give other people a chance. And what about Peter? His background sounds impressive. Tiffany was manipulative and unshakeable. Never did figure her out."

"Uh-huh," Tara hesitated. "I'm not so sure about *him*. He came out of nowhere. One day, I post the job. Next day Vanessa shows up with his resume after lunch. He started the *next morning*. Didn't even have time to call his referrals. And she did not give me enough time to run his background check."

"I like him. It's kind of cute how skittish he is. I bet we could get him to work with us. Maybe influence Vanessa." Maya reached for the check the server had just dropped off. "My turn." She placed her credit card on the check.

Tara nodded. It was Maya's turn to pay since she had paid last Friday. They each picked up their phones and began scrolling through their missed emails.

Neither of them spoke about the disruption Vanessa had caused to the delicate ecosystem that had allowed their friendship to exist. The only real thing they had in common was being the only women in a male dominated environment. They had bonded over *where* they were, but they rarely talked about *who* they were. Because the truth for them was that they both broke through the glass ceiling, and like Vanessa, they never concerned themselves with those that may have been cut by the falling shards.

12

You are not creating leaders amongst your leadership team, you are the leader. You are looking for followers.

Promise them the world and dote on them. Do not do this to everyone. Choose specific flowers to water and this will give them reason to owe you. You might give them a title promotion, approve an idea of theirs, or build them up to their peers. The less deserving they are of the promotion, the more idiotic their idea, and the more inflated your flattery the more they will owe you. No person will reject these things, they will just ask how much they cost. Wait until they're at the check-out lane before you tell them.

Years ago, on a visit to New Orleans, I saw an older man approach a young man and begin shining the young man's shoes. Complimenting him on his shoes, telling him how a rich good-looking man like him needed quality polished shoes. The old man completed the job and the young man handed him twenty dollars with a smile on his face. It's a common scam and most other savvy tourists avoided the scammer easily. But this young man was different. Maybe no less savvy than his tourist compatriots except: he was with a young woman. In front of his audience, the young man was trapped. He either had to call out the scam artist for what he was, negating the compliments he had received, or add on to the facade that he was rich and not bothered with the loss of a measly twenty dollars.

After having distributed many accolades, you can now test if they have been effective on your subjects. Tell them no, tell them they are wrong, make sure there is an audience. They will be forced to accept you *are right about this or they will have to give back any perceived value that you previously awarded them.*

If they see you as the King, they will respect your authority to knight and behead accordingly. Either way, their heads should be bowed.

-Caldarelli, Joe* (2027). *Joe's First Ninety Days*

*Found deceased on his own private toilet prior to publication.

That was... a lot of mixed metaphors. Are my employees flowers or subjects? Am I the king or a scam artist? Am I giving them trophies or groceries? A lot to take in. Every page of this book is just as dense. Like eating a rich chocolate cake, I could only take so many bites. Unlike eating a rich chocolate cake, I didn't want to have any more.

Don't get me wrong. Joe's book has shared valuable information. It just takes effort to distill it into something useful. Today's section: *Knock them off their high horses. Tell them no.* Easy, simple, elegant.

Last week's executive committee meeting was surprisingly fantastic. I got to give everyone some little win. Except Phil who thinks he doesn't need to ask my permission. Nor Tony, since I had him with his head down taking notes. To his credit, he did it dutifully. His notes were excellent which I, begrudgingly, 'replied all' on the email chain to show support in front of everyone.

It was thrilling to show up with Peter, unannounced. Tara was visibly shaken. She needs to learn her place.

Not like that! Not all misogynistic and evil. Not a 'woman's place is in the kitchen' type of thing. I *am* a woman so I'm a feminist. I just mean, if Joe had wanted to hire Peter she wouldn't have been all "does his experience align?" and "I think one of his professional references is his mother." She would have just started the paperwork like I told her.

Regardless, it was a positive meeting. I hadn't wanted to talk about Frank but I didn't want them to gossip about it without me. I should have been gentler with the news for Tony and Collin. I forget he was like an uncle to them. Tony was as stone faced as ever, but Collin looked devastated.

Collin also called in *sick* for the rest of the week. I suppose being hungover *is* being sick, so I can't fault him there.

I didn't ride the high of that Wednesday for long.

When Joey asked me over on Thursday with his big romantic meal, there were so many things I thought it could be. Maybe he was ready to set a date for the wedding. Perhaps he had seen the article, *Women of W.E.E.D.*, and he was impressed... I had forgotten the release day myself until Mom called me up to tell me she was proud, and my hair needed trimmed and how smart I sounded and how bloated I looked.

Worst case scenario, I assumed he was just horny.

Any of those would have been better than reality. They existed in a world where Joey considered me in his life decisions. Like a future husband would. He was only ever thinking about *him*self, *his* career, *his* house. If *I* fit in it was by force. Wedging my way in there, like a chisel squeezing into marble.

Which is exactly why it wasn't working. If he was marble, I was just slowly chipping away at the areas I wanted to fit in. If he didn't soften or make room for me, I could turn him into David, but I'd still just be a chisel. I'm not so sure how much more I can force my way in. He is keeping me at a distance.

I still have no idea what Frank said to Joey a few days before he died. The message Frank left made Joey's friendship with Angelo seem more nefarious than I had imagined. But Frank did that. He was always doom and gloom. But if someone is doom and gloom and then they die... were they right?

That's silly though. He was just another octogenarian dying of *being old*. Although the only other one I knew *had* killed himself. I still don't know why someone of that age would kill themselves unless he was terminally ill. Joey's family must know more, it's not my business.

Because that's the point. I'm not Joey's family. I'm not my father's family. And not that I want to be, but I'm not part of this work 'family' either. Aside from Wednesdays, no one in the office talks to me unless I talk to them first. It makes sense in some ways, I am the CEO. But Joe didn't have to put his office on this isolated island that no one came to.

An image overtook my mind. Me, on my private toilet: dead. Peter finding me.

No! That won't be me. I'm not going to kill myself because no one invited me to tacos on Friday. It's human to want to connect. But these people are not my friends. They aren't even my co-workers. They are my subordinates. They should be spending their time hoping *I* like *them*. Not the other way around. Which is why I'm going to run this executive meeting and remind them all who is flying this plane.

Having learned that the most important people at meetings don't have to bring anything, I left my office empty-handed. I closed the door, but apparently not loud enough to get his attention.

"Peter," I said. He jumped a little, then turned to me. Eyes wide behind his glasses. He froze so I added, "Meeting."

"Oh right." He glanced at the time. He hurriedly finished stapling the meeting packets. I left him to it and headed to the meeting room. If he's late because he can't figure things out for himself, that will be on him. Three minutes until the scheduled start time.

I took larger than normal strides, the satisfying click of my heels on the hard floors announcing my approach. I saw Collin heading to the meeting room which was closer to him than me. He adjusted his pace so that we met at the glass door.

"Good morning," he said, looking an absolute wreck. He was wearing designer jeans and expensive bright yellow sneakers. He paired it with a graphic tee from one of our flower brands in Arizona. In a different scenario, I would have chuckled at the design. The front had a gray alien rolling a joint and it just said "The gray market." Not a great marketing design because I couldn't even tell which of our brands it was for. The alien's eyes were red, as if irritated from smoke. Collins eyes matched. His outfit was fine, or normal for Collin, and his hair wasn't disorderly. But I knew him and knew there was something deeply wrong.

"Morning, Collin." I watched his tired eyes give me their best *hopeful puppy about to get cheese* look. He leaned into me, like he was about to say something. Before he could, I whispered, "Get your shit together," maintaining perfect eye contact.

Luckily I was quiet because one moment later, Peter walked up behind me. For once, it wasn't Peter making things awkward. Shifting the meeting packets to one hand, he just said, "Uh…" and moved past me to open the door. He opened it wide, indicating we should go in, acting as though we had struggled with it.

Collin broke our eye contact and walked into the room. I followed him, noticing the back of his shirt which was a giant road sign that said : *Area 420.*

I rolled my eyes. Subtle.

I proceeded to my spot at the head of the table. Peter dutifully followed behind me. We both immediately noticed Phil. He was seated in the same damn spot as last week, the one I asked him to move out of. I sat. Peter remained standing and passed the meeting packets around. When he finished, he looked at me like a lost puppy. What's with all these grown men being puppies?

Discretely, I motioned my head toward the empty seat, letting my eyes follow. Inexplicably, Peter came to me. I look at him and ask quietly, "Did you need something?"

He said too loud, "I thought you were calling me over here."

I shook my head lightly. "No," I said, trying to keep from embarrassing him and me. He hadn't given me much choice. I pointed at the empty chair. "You can sit there." He moved around the table and sat down.

Phil smirked to himself. Like he's won something. The creature of habit seems to think he can force his will onto me. Working with him a couple of weeks has made it obvious he is not one of the followers I need. Best case scenario, he stays in his crate when I put him there.

"Phil," I said, loudly enough to make everyone think the meeting was starting.

"Hmm?" he mumbled, not even bothering to look at me as he flipped through the meeting packet trying to locate his section.

"I need you on notes this week."

Before he had time to process, he just said, "okay" while looking down. Then, his eyes snapped up to look at me and he squeezed his almost touching eyebrows together and exclaimed, "What!" That's one upset puppy. "I can't," he protested through gritted teeth. What he really meant was *'you can't...* tell me what to do.' He had enough common sense not to say it. "I need to cover my section. Isn't that what he—" he gestured to Peter "—is here for?"

I hate that my gut reaction to angry men is to apologize. *Never mind, I'll do it,* I'll say. But I wasn't asking my husband to 'help' with the dishes after a long day of caring for our kids. That husband could just say 'no' while I quietly seethe and spend twenty years plotting divorce or a poisoning. Phil was my employee. My fossil of a CFO who outsourced practically everything to his team and whose only contribution was to come to this meeting and read numbers off a page we could all clearly see. *He* had to do what I told him.

Realizing I had left Phil to stew for longer than intended, I sighed so he would know I was irritated, not intimidated.

"Peter is *my* assistant. He's still learning the ropes. This is a simple ask. You should be able to do both, since you're the only one who talks during the financials." Phil didn't argue. Nor did he agree. I added, reasonably, "You could record the meeting and summarize it after. Though that would take more of your time."

Phil remained silent. Tony slid the yellow legal pad and pen to him. Phil had his own notebook, but took it anyway. It was symbolic. Like a dunce cap passed from Tony to Phil. Maybe I'll never have Peter take notes.

Phil's snarky behavior contrasted with Tony's response last week. Now that I think about it, since that first meeting, Tony hasn't questioned me or condescended me once. He deserves a little watering.

"Tony, since you provided that excellent overview last week, I'd love to hear from you first today. Any updates?" I said so smoothly, it was like I planned it.

He looked surprised but he immediately played his part. Look at us, improvising together. "Why yes, Vanessa. I'm happy to update." Tony sounded so professional like we were a team of news broadcasters and I'd just kicked it to him for a weather update.

"With 420 coming up, we need to look at our inventory on hand. Last week, I met with the head of cultivation at our new Vegas facility, and it looks like we have a bottleneck in packaging due to the last-minute requests for the sales initiatives. Collin and Maya, I've asked you both to please be at least three weeks ahead on the promo schedule document, but the team is saying they aren't getting updates for 420 yet."

And he went on like that for five straight minutes, making me regret my decision.

———————

The meeting was business as usual. Almost everyone took their turns before I realized, I hardly spoke at all. It made me self-conscious. Is Tony still running the place and I'm just the face, the smiling flight attendant giving the seat belt instructions and passing out snacks while the pilot does the flying. Or worse yet, the gate attendant scanning tickets and letting everyone on the plane while I stay behind as it takes off.

I felt more engaged last week, but I hardly understood what I was agreeing to. They all seemed confident, why not let them do their thing? But I couldn't shake the feeling I should be contributing somehow.

WWJD? What would Joe do?

I made myself cringe. But Joe *would* know what to do. I recalled that I should be testing the team's loyalty. I need to focus. Hard to do when Tara is boring me to tears. "Please remember, before anyone can start work, I need at least three to five days for background checks and agent card processing for all new hires." Tara looked directly at me. "That includes the corporate office."

Because she was staring at me like she wanted something from me, I added, "Everyone, please remind your managers of the process."

"No exceptions," she said, still looking at me.

"Right, no exceptions," I echoed, building her loyalty. "Thank you for the reminder. Anything else?" Tara opened her mouth for a second. But then she shook her head. Not sure what that was about, but if I ask her, who knows how much longer she'll go on? I looked around the table, trying to remember who hadn't spoken. "Maya what do you have for us?"

"Just a quick update on the Puff Puff Pass. We're pushing for a 420 roll-out so everything should be final and ready to go by next week. I need to get the actual cards printed and they'll be sent here and then I'll overnight them to the locations. I'll have some ad copy for the banner out to you all by Monday. We can start socializing it to the dispensary teams by the fourteenth and by then—"

I was shaking my head but she did not stop talking.

Tony cut her off, "The fourteenth? Vanessa told you to have everything to us *today*. What's the delay?"

Tony was right. It was nice that he was defending me and helping me hold the line. But I really did not want to make an example out of *Maya*. She and I seemed to be so aligned. Please have a damn good reason Maya...

She began, "We have six different retail store names, in eleven states. They all have different registries. No the re-re-reg… the rules." She was instantly on the defensive. I had never heard her stutter or forget a word. In fact, I had gotten so used to her perfectly timed cadence, that her deviation from it was jarring.

I knew what I had to do. Just like Joe had said. *Tell them no. Tell them they are wrong. Make sure there is an audience.* Fuck, Maya. Why are you making me do this?

"Are you saying you have *nothing* finalized for the deadline?" I said, sternly. It wasn't really a question; I was dragging out the inevitable.

"I wouldn't say *nothing*. We just can't r-r-roll everything out right now. Most everything is nearly done, but there are many moving pieces. I just need—" Maya was talking so fast now, I put my hand up to stop her.

"I understand there is a lot to consider. But didn't you know we operate in eleven states before the meeting last week?" I didn't know until *just now*, but that's beside the point.

"Yes. You have no idea how much time that adds to every single campaign," Maya said. It looks like her own fumble caused a turnover, but now *she* was on the offense.

"You're right," I conceded. "I have no idea how to do *your* job." Dramatic pause. "But *you* do. Which is why you are seated at this table. And you knew when you agreed last week to have this done that it would not be possible. Tony, would this give us enough time to push out to the dispensary team?" I already knew he would say 'no', but why not share some of the guilt?

There was no hesitation in Tony's reply. "No, this would not be enough time."

"There's the answer then. No Puff Puff Pass for 420 this year," I said.

"But—" Maya pleaded.

I didn't feel bad interrupting her, because I was still talking. "Table it. We can circle back in a few months and decide if we want to launch it for summer."

Everyone was looking back and forth between me and Maya. Maya was staring at me. I looked at her for a second and had to look away. Her eyes were glistening.

"Thanks everyone, good meeting," I said. Was it a good meeting? I don't know… my tummy sure hurts. "Phil will circulate the notes and I'll see you each at your department meetings."

Maya was the first to leave, even though she had to brush past both me and Phil to exit. A *man* may have mistaken her welling tears for sadness or 'being emotional' like they insisted all women were. But the truth was, she was displaying the same emotion I had seen every man in this room whip out just as easily as they whip out their dick to pee on a wall.

She was pissed.

13

They don't prepare you for the fact that when you become the boss, there's no one to tell you what to do. I know it's like an implicit perk. I got a taste of it when I was consulting; I could choose my hours and which projects I took on, but I was still beholden to what the clients wanted. I do still have to please the shareholders. But the shareholders and the board just want more money. Year over year top line revenue growth that will flow down to dividends for infinity. Aside from that, I'm left to my own devices. There definitely *is* a right way of doing things, but no one is telling me what that is.

Every time I try to talk to the C-suite outside of Wednesday's meetings, I get brushed off. They're busy doing things. I've been engaging with the people who report to them instead. They'll gladly talk to me as long as I want, sometimes giving me valuable tidbits. I can tell right away if they like their manager, their coworkers, or their job. It's obvious whether they are competent or bullshitters. They always reveal when they have extensive formal education when they try to flex on me with their big words.

I also know when they want to be me, when they want to screw me, when they want to impress me, or manipulate me. They all want something to do with me because of my powerful role. The key is knowing that every single person around me has a motivation.

I've always been phenomenal at guessing the twists and plot points in movies. All you have to know is that every word a character says and everything a character does is pre-ordained by the writer and it always serves a purpose. If something they said or did is incongruous with their previous behavior that's something the writer *chose*. You do have to occasionally weed out some useless details, like when the character is eating in every scene because the actor is Brad Pitt. Useless in understanding the character, might be helpful in understanding Brad Pitt. And, like Shania Twain, that does not impress me very much.

Because I do not care what all these side characters in marketing and accounting are motivated by. It's Tony whose motivations I cannot figure out. He's been uncharacteristically supportive. It's partially manipulation. But surely, *he knows* that *I know* he's trying to influence me, which essentially voids the manipulation component. If I sift out all that unnecessary sediment, I'm left with a few possibilities.

First, Tony is lazy and agreeing is easy. How many days has he left early to go golf with his doctor pals who keep odd hours? How many long lunches has he had with old corporate lawyer friends? How many late starts after a night out drinking with his cop buddies? I don't know. *Maybe I should have Peter tracking it.* The point is, under the guise of *net*working, Tony loves *not*working. He always claims to have a good reason. Doctors can prescribe medical marijuana. Cops can push loiterers out of our parking lots. Lawyers can be allies against regulators. The excuse list goes on and on.

Second possibility, and this one's pretty unlikely, he *actually* agrees with me.

Third possibility, his rivalry with Joey trumps his rivalry with me. Tony hated that his dad chose me as predecessor over him. But long before that came the constant teeter totter for dad's approval between the two eldest sons. Tony's big head intimidated some, but Joey being two inches taller and more filled out meant he could plant his feet firmly on the ground while Tony was left dangling in the air. If Tony enlisted me, together we could catapult Joey off the opposite side. With Joe dead, there was no one left to pit them against each other. Until Joey got himself on the board as treasurer. This would put Joey back in a position of power and Tony would be outdone by him again.

Their form of brotherly love was contradictory. Family get-togethers were always pleasant. There was occasional tension, but generally there was mutual respect and love. I didn't have many interactions with my half siblings, but I couldn't imagine them getting together *by choice* to share a meal. It was part of what made me want to join the Caldarelli family. They were always able to put aside their differences to be brothers. They helped each other out. Tony always 'knew a guy.' Joey always had cash to loan. Collin was happy to exploit both resources. I once found Joey's little black book, a ledger, with Tony's substantial debt to him on top.

If Tony knew that Joey's move to become treasurer had put a wedge between *us*, he might think it's his chance to even the score. If I became one of the 'guys' Tony knew, he probably thought he could get me to pull strings for him. Cancel out his debt to Joey or something.

In the end, Tony's motivation, while interesting is irrelevant. He is effectively my 'yes man'. But since I can't trust that he is loyal to me, I still don't have anyone to talk to. Leaving me alone with Joe's book.

I always assumed Joe's officially published book was written by a ghostwriter. Not the poetry one, he clearly wrote that. The self-help book, something about business. I didn't read it, but I did buy it and casually leave it on my counter for Joey to see before we started dating.

Now Joe was advising me from beyond the grave. Turns out he *is* the ghostwriter. It would have been better to talk to him in person and ask questions. He had some good points, even if it was buried under a lot of other stuff; like a zombie just awoken from his grave. Having to bust its way up through its coffin then the cold, hard ground. Finally able to break free and go... kill people? Okay, bad example. But this is what I mean. No one to talk through ideas before just saying them makes them garbage. So much of Joe's writing is trash. I'll have lots of people proofread my memoir or preferably hire someone to write it. About life in the Corporate Cannabis fast lane also known as: The *High* Way.

There is some great stuff in here. I flipped through the pages, stopping on one with my sticky flag. This section. I've been thinking about this all week. Ever since last Wednesday's Executive Committee when I had to make an example out of Maya. I was following Joe's advice, but I have no reassurance that it was the right move. I've had nowhere else to look but deeper into the book.

Each week continues this cyclical hell. Mondays and Tuesdays, the week starts fresh and positive. Wednesdays, meetings day is a blur. Thursdays, meetings day hangover. Someone is always pissed at me. Fridays, everyone barely works, looking forward to the weekend. Weekends, I used to spend most of with Joey, now it's mostly alone.

I'm trying to keep my playbook going, follow the plan. Has admonishing Maya in front of everyone made her more loyal by forcing her to agree with my rejection to accept my prior praise? Will hiring Peter pay off? Is Collin even working? I can't tell if anything is going to plan.

All I can do is follow Joe's guidebook. This little section, marked with a sticky neon yellow flag could hold all the answers.

———————————

One of the foremost things you will do as the headman is find your most resolute followers. Your disciples, or as the young people say your 'homies' or your 'ride or dies'.

They can be comprised of two key types of people: People who know things; people who know people.

The people who know things will be the more intellectual among your followers. This is what makes them both valuable and dangerous. You need them, but keep them in their lane. Make it clear that they shouldn't be fraternizing among average people. Convince them they are exceptional, but their power can only be unlocked by you. Tell them you are giving them special opportunities rather than 'assigning them work' and they will thank you. Keep them away from other people who know things, or you may have a mutiny.

Your other lackeys, the people who know people, have a value that is more inestimable. It is paramount that you determine the quality of the type of people they know before becoming buried in the quantity. It is crucial you keep a variety of them around to serve various needs. You will want to eliminate any who predominately know people who have greater than your own level of influence. Those particular People who know People may be attempting to usurp your position. While they themselves are usually idiots, they can achieve high levels of success as puppets for other, smarter people. Look around and you will see many front facing, out in the open, morons in 'power'. These are people who know people, but they are already under someone else's control. You need to find your own and catch them early, so you can harness their horsepower for your career engine.

To be most effective as a leader, you must become both a person who knows people (your acolytes) and a person who knows things (how to control your acolytes).

-Caldarelli, Joe* (2027). *Joe's First Ninety Days*

*Found deceased by his top henchman prior to publication.

When I first read that, it sounded like utter nonsense.

But the more I thought about it, the more I realized he seriously was onto something. As evidenced by the fact that my natural leadership instincts already had me doing this.

Right now, my pool of followers is limited to the employees at W.E.E.D. Joe would have already vetted them for me but I was subconsciously sorting them.

Derrick, the Chief Technology officer was a Things Person (person who knows things). He set up my laptop.

Tara and Maya: also Things People. They each have their specialties and God knows I don't want anything to do with human resources.

Phil's not a Things Person. His team, especially Jenny, does the actual work while he reads numbers off a spreadsheet during meetings. He knows Joey, but I also already know him. The only other person of influence he knew was Joe and he's dead. That means he's not a People Person either. Phil may have outstayed his usefulness.

Then, there were the brothers. It's possible Joe only kept them around because they were his sons. But I think there's something to them.

Whatever Collin's usefulness is, I can harness it. Since his big screw up on my third day, he looks at me with pleading eyes. He wants to make me happy. Tony is a People Person. He knows half of Sacramento. The question is if he'll fall in line. After the loss of Joe, he should be free game for me to snatch up.

I'll circle back to them.

Finally, I had Peter. The only one on the team that *I* chose. I'm still not sure about him. Maybe I fired Tiffany too quickly. I never tapped into what she had to offer. But she's the one who disappeared, I needed *someone* in the role. I hired Peter on a whim. As long as my assistant is loyal to *me*, I have made the right choice. I just need to figure out which type he is. He was always talking about his MBA pursuit at the Morning Boost which suggests Things Person. But he's implied that he comes from wealthy connections, so not ruling out People Person.

I have a lot to figure out about my team. But my weeks are a concatenation revolving around Wednesday's meetings. Instead of being a leader, I'm forced to follow the morbid procession of meeting after meeting for all time. Everything is either preparing for the meetings, attending them, or 'circling back' on items from the meeting. Joe was the office poltergeist, haunting my every move. I was forced to follow the processes prophesied by the ancient texts. He was dead and buried, but maybe it was like the pet cemetery in that Stephen King book, because every decision he made came back to life, worse than before he died. Threatening to take a razor blade to my ankles.

Later sections of Joe's book were contradicting its earlier chapters, encouraging me to deviate from the meeting schedule. He wrote frequently of 'boots on the ground' and the need for the troops to see their leader. Can't do that *and* keep his rigid meeting schedule. After three weeks of business as usual, it is time for me to break this horrible routine.

Looking at my phone I see it's 9:02am. Shit. Despite my tardiness, I shuffled to the meeting room. Everyone is waiting there, except Collin. I decide to start without him. Even Tony, with all of his excuses, has *never* been late to these weekly meetings.

"Good morning, team," I say, breaking up all the micro-meetings with one singular sentence, reprimanding them as if *they* were late. "I know we are all busy, let's get started. First, I have an announcement. I will not be here for the meeting next week. Peter is booking me a flight—" I'm announcing to the group but also reminding Peter in a non-nagging way "—down to Las Vegas. I'll be spending a few days at our new facilities. I expect you will all keep—"

"Do you think that's a good idea?" Phil, who was sitting where Peter should have been, jumped in.

In the history of that question, no one has ever meant it as a question. It was just a statement that meant *that's a dumbass idea.* I chose to answer anyway. "Yes. As the *CEO*, it is my job to have face time with everyone on the team. Starting with the newest facilities will—"

"You should reconsider the timing," Phil interrupted again. What is wrong with this man?

I hardly had time to ponder before Tony stepped in on my behalf. "I think it's an excellent plan," he offered. "I can hold down the fort. If you would like, I'll head up the meetings."

"Yes. As I said, business as usual while I'm gone. As *COO*, Tony will be the go-to when I'm gone. He can handle anything urgent, Peter will arrange everything else to be addressed when I get back." Phil tapped his pen on his meeting packet in irritation. I chose to ignore it. I also chose to ignore Collin's absence and lack of meeting packet contribution. I can't draw attention to anything that could be perceived as a weakness of mine.

Before Joe's poltergeist starts hurling coffee mugs around the room, better get this meeting on track. I rejected the silent treatment Maya had been giving me. "Maya, why don't you start us off with marketing?"

I regretted my decision as I skimmed the top sheet of the meeting packet to see 'follow up on Puff Puff Pass' as the header of the first section. For a person who knows things, Maya sure *doesn't know* when to quit.

14

I reach for the armrest to my right to find it occupied by a pale hand with skin that clung to the bone. I don't have to look to know the hand belongs to a thin old man with heavy bags under his eyes and a bulky knit sweater. I try to grab the left arm rest instead, this time met with a large hairy hand with thick fingers ending in extra wide finger nails. My eyes follow down his legs. I notice his knee lightly touching mine. I look up to his face discreetly, but he sees me, clearly having noticed that I was looking between his legs. He gives me a perverted smile, enough that I can see the glint of his too-white teeth.

I recoil my knee and stretch my legs in front of me. There is not enough room to extend them. I clench my purse between my ankles and press the tops of my feet lightly against the underside of the seat in front of me, desperate to hold on to something as the weightless feeling takes over my whole body. Except for my stomach which is filled with lead and threatening to crawl out through my throat.

The seat pinches at my upper thigh at the two ends of the seatbelt. I was here on time and boarded early enough to get a window seat. No thanks to Peter. I don't want to be one of *those* people, but the CEO of the company shouldn't be in boarding group *C*. Next time I hope he remembers to check in twenty-four hours before my flight.

My predicament wasn't entirely Peter's fault, it was partially mine; letting these two grown ass men beg and bully their way into the window seat (because *he* gets 'claustrophobic') and the aisle seat (because *he* has prostate issues and needs easy access to the restroom). Silly of me to assume that *if* the gorilla and the crypt keeper were going to force me to be in the middle, they would at least give me the freaking armrests. Everyone knows, aisle and window each get *one* armrest, the middle gets *both*. Instead, I'm sitting bolt upright, unable to lean either direction. Trapped between smells of spearmint competing with bad breath and too much cologne.

It's been more than a decade since I've been on a plane. I don't remember them being so small. I am *aware* that my ass has grown and is part of this equation. But I'm still the same height and my knees are practically crammed against the seat in front of me. The two men next to me are encroaching; perfectly comfortable taking up more space than their fair share. The fragile looking white-haired man was supporting his head with a decidedly oversized travel pillow, covering some of my own headrest. The gray-haired man (technically his head hair was dark brown, but his gray knuckle hair gave away the game) thought I was ogling his junk. I was *actually* ogling the space between his legs. The empty space, where his legs should have been rather than touching mine.

My stomach settled as we reached our cruising altitude. Soon the seatbelt light would turn off and the flight attendants would come around. Maybe I could get some ginger ale or some vodka with a soda. Do they still do that? The pandemic changed many things, but they *have to* serve tiny booze on a flight to Vegas, right?

Woah! What was that? It takes me a moment to put together that it's just a little turbulence. I scanned around and no one was reacting. That's a good sign.

Using my feet I lifted my purse slightly, angling the handle towards me. Careful not to touch the men, I grabbed it. There wasn't enough room to put it fully on my lap and search, so I held it in one hand and felt around. I pulled out my earbud case and put one in each ear. I put the case and purse back before pulling out my phone. I had jammed it between my thighs for safe keeping. Navigating to the latest true crime podcast episode I had downloaded, I pressed play. Knowing it would probably last me the whole flight, I locked my cellphone and eased it back between my legs. That bad boy wasn't going anywhere.

I half-listened for a few minutes before I heard the comforting sound of the seatbelt light turning off. I listened harder, expecting some kind of announcement to follow, but the only communication is the light. I relaxed some; letting my shoulders disconnect slightly from the chair I hadn't realized I'd pinned them back against.

I grabbed my phone again, finding it easier to skip the ads there rather than on my ear buds. How many more times would I have to hear the first seven seconds of *this* mattress ad or the last five seconds of *that* ad for socks? I must be the target audience for these ads which makes me feel old. I did cave and buy an expensive mattress a couple of years ago, Joey's requirement if he was going to stay the night. Hard to believe that they're targeting *me* with the same ads as Old White Hair to my right would get. I could see his compression socks because his pants didn't reach the top of his loafers.

The plane bucked up. A woman standing in the aisle had been trying to get her bag from the overhead bin. The sudden movement of the plane caused her to grip the seat next to her as she almost fell into the lap of the woman sitting across the aisle from the old man. She scurried back to her seat without her bag, half-heartedly trying and failing to close the overhead bin. I lost sight of her as she sat down, disconnecting from the only person around who seemed to acknowledge something was off. The seatbelt light turned back on as if to say 'whoops, my bad.' Why would the pilot turn the light on if we were going to hit turbulence? A flight attendant started walking towards us. Not fast enough because another jolt of the plane had him falling against an aisle seat. Luckily, the cramped quarters didn't allow him to fall all the way down.

The jolt was just the start of several continuous bumps that resulted in a terrifying crash as the right engine exploded into a fireball!

I desperately tried to get a view out of the opposite side of the plane. I gripped the armrest to my left and grabbed my chest with my right hand, taking a sharp breath in. The armrest wasn't covered in cold hard metal as I had anticipated, but instead a warm shag rug.

Craning my neck, I surmised that the engine hadn't exploded, though a heavy burgundy briefcase falling out of the overhead bin next to me sounded *identical*.

The flight attendant rushed to grab the briefcase and secure it in the overhead bin. I smiled apologetically at the man on my left, withdrawing my grip from his arm, springing my hand into my lap. His smile in return had me wanting to crawl away from him. The only place to go would be in the lap of the old man who was, miraculously, asleep. I stared down at my feet. Why were men so good at making me feel embarrassed? Ashamed?

My mind wandered to Joey whom I once thought of as a life raft when I needed saving. But would he really do anything more than the man next to me was doing now if he were here? I doubt Joey would do anything other than smile at me and make me feel foolish like Sasquatch here had. He *might* let me use an armrest, though.

It would be on me to save myself as it always had been. Put on my own oxygen mask. Use my seat as a flotation device. Or the most likely outcome in a true catastrophe: die quickly like everyone else on the plane would.

I took a deep breath, regretting it immediately, remembering how many others were breathing in my same vicinity. The plane continued to shake intermittently, changing altitudes at unpredictable intervals.

What in the hell was this pilot doing? He spoke to the whole plane over the intercom once... once! Just to say the seatbelt light would be remaining on for the duration of the flight. I was trapped, held strapped to my seat with no further explanation. The pilot had to know more. There were patches of sky where it felt like things could be smooth. As soon as I was comfortable, my parched lips eager for drink service, it would get bumpy again.

My body rose and fell with the plane but my stomach stayed at the same altitude, jumping into my throat or pushing down into my seat when we climbed. I had convinced myself that a tiny plastic cup filled with ginger ale and ice cubes I could suck on would save me. It never came.

I have no control.

My eyes welled with tears. I dabbed them with my sleeve before they had a chance to streak my face. The only thing in the whole world I had any agency over was what *I* did. And here I sit, held captive by my fear. Because I'm just a passenger, riding along while everyone else did things around me and to me. I *can* control what I do, yet I've relinquished this power. Letting everyone else push me around like an inflatable sex doll forced to crowd surf at an outdoor concert.

Move to the middle seat. Show up to the meeting at this time and sit quietly while they talk. Wear this outfit to the photo shoot. Don't ask about Angelo. Never question Joey. Eat this gnocchi. Get on *this* damn flight on a Sunday. Maybe all I have to do is push back; do what I want and don't ask forgiveness. That's what I'm afraid of. Terrified that what I want is wrong, so I do nothing instead.

If I'm not ready to be my own compass, at least I can follow Joe. He won't gain anything by manipulating me. I'll fake it until I make it like all the greats probably did. And a year or two from now, when I'm writing my book on success and excellence in the cannabis industry, this moment will be a distant speck to me. As far away as the ground below.

———————

As the airline would probably say, we landed 'without incident'. The turbulence continued the whole way, worsening as we prepared to land. The hairy man assured me the Las Vegas airport was always windy in the spring. He said his wife never flew with him here because of it. He guaranteed me his frequent Vegas 'business trips' made him a pro at riding out the bumpy landing. He talked and talked and talked... until I pushed out of the plane while he struggled with his overhead luggage.

"Uh," I grunted, rolling my neck back and lightly stretching it for the first time in hours. Relief washed over me, followed by a tidal wave of dread. Leaving an airplane but still having to be in an airport. It makes it feel like I stepped on to a much larger airplane. Then into a shuttle to get my luggage. Into a bus to the car rental place. Just being squeezed through different sized metal tubes repeatedly, like how I envision sausage is made.

The car rental hub is like a smaller airport. I had to give myself repeated pep talks throughout while I waited in the giant line for a car. It was worth it because after hours of being shuffled around by others, when I left there I was finally the one in the driver's seat.

My hotel, as requested, was not on the strip. It was in an area called North Las Vegas. The front desk discouraged me from venturing around alone in this neighborhood. They instead suggested a few places for food delivery.

Spending an afternoon in a hotel room was better than the middle seat squeezed between two selfish men. I checked the bed for bedbugs (I got the feeling I needed to) then sprawled out on the bed, kicking my shoes off. I wanted to peel off my travel leggings and shirt, but I'd have to grab my food from the lobby soon enough.

Just as I was reaching to plug my phone into the charger, it rang. Without looking at the ID, I answered. Please be Joey.

"Hello," I croaked. God, it's so dry here. "This is Vanessa."

"Good afternoon, Ms. Sorella," a man's voice said. He had an indiscernible European accent… Scottish? "I was hoping to talk to you about the finance operations of the Wellness Enterprise of Exceptional Dispensaries."

I sat up. Financing? Was this about Angelo? "Yes…" was all I could manage without giving anything away.

"I know the many challenges an enterprise like yours is likely to face given the current state of the industry you are in." He was becoming more East coast American sounding as he went. "You probably have a tired and underperforming accounting and finance team, struggling to keep up with both the daily demands and long-term planning. Most AI software professes the ability—"

"No," I said flatly, before hanging up. I rolled my eyes. Who do these cold sales calls work on?

I immediately started a text to Peter.

> *Good afternoon Peter. Sorry to message you on a Sunday. I received a call from a sales person today and I believe they must have gotten my number from you. Please do not share my number with anyone until you have checked in with me first. Hope you're having a nice weekend! Sorry again for bothering you.*

I almost hit send. *No.* This won't do. I'm the fucking CEO. I don't have time for flowery messages and sales calls. I started over.

> *Peter, do not give my personal number to ANYONE.*

Send. Before I can start doubting myself.

I waited for the alert that my food had arrived, trying not to let my mind wander on paths that were unsafe and poorly lit.

I thought about the quality of the mattress. Subpar. You really can't put a number on a good night's rest, and I wouldn't be getting that here. I rubbed my calves. I did a lot of walking at the airport. Then, a lot of sitting on the plane. The combo had really made my lower legs sore and even a little swollen. I probably shouldn't be wearing heels to the office every day either, I always wind up standing and walking more than I think. ... Do I need a pair of compression socks?

Desperate to dodge that question, I thought about dinner last night with Joey. It was so cold. Not just because he arrived late, well after it was hot and ready. I had ordered pizza. It was from the fanciest wood-fire place that delivered. Joey loves wood-fire. He didn't even mention my thoughtfulness. He just showed up and we ate hovering over the box in the kitchen.

The only thing that got him talking was his new role as treasurer. The board is scheduled to vote this upcoming week, but he's pretty much got the job. With all of his demands fulfilled. He talked until he had finished half the pizza. I only ate one slice, nervous about my flight. Now, my stomach rumbled, that lousy slice was all I'd eaten since last night.

When I tried to steer the conversation to anything else, I hit a wall. I was talking about my travel plans and what I had hoped to accomplish as part of my first ninety days. Joey was saying nothing until—

"I'd better head out so you can rest before your flight, my love," he said.

"It's only seven thirty." I protested, "This is our date night."

"It was nice. I'm sure you want me out of your hair so you can pack." He sounded caring and reasonable. It made me want to apologize for fighting before we started.

"If I wanted that, I would have said so. Stop assuming you know what's best for me," I said.

"Vanessa, I just want to relax for my Saturday night. I don't want to talk about work or stand around and argue while you pack." He drained his wine before setting the empty glass back on the counter.

"I want to relax too. With you," I pleaded, trying not to be a nag. I had already packed. I put my hand on his arm meaning to squeeze it, but he pulled away so all I could do was brush it.

"We both know that's not going to happen," he accused.

I didn't know that. I didn't know what was going on between us at all. Only that he was stressed and so focused on this sudden 'dream' of becoming the treasurer.

I gave up. "I love you," I whispered.

"I love you too, Nessa," he said. I thought he was changing his mind about staying when he quickly closed the distance between us. He gave me a side hug and a peck on the forehead and left.

Now, I flipped from the food delivery app to my contacts and called one of my *favorites*. The phone rang twice and as the third ring started, I hung up. No use wasting one more second on hope that Joey would answer.

I picked up Joe's book and flipped to a section near where I'd last read it. One thing about skimming is you don't really use a bookmark. Though I did have an absurd amount of little sticky flags in that first third of the book.

It was hard not to think about the way Joe died when I read his book. He didn't seem unhappy or cynical, just realistic. I felt like a realist most days. Not at all optimistic about my relationship with Joey, trying to be more positive about my future with W.E.E.D. It was difficult to look on the bright side of things when there's no one to bounce the negative thoughts off of. They kind of just bounce around in your head and find a way to erase all the positive ones. Canceling them out until you're left with whatever feels like reality. Not good, not bad, just there.

Is following Joe's advice going to make me think like him? It hasn't made me dress like him or talk like him. It shouldn't make me want to kill myself like him. As long as I don't start wearing tweed jackets and talking like I sniffed the glue of a thesaurus's spine, I think it's safe to keep reading.

15

"You have to smell this one," Tyler said. He brought his fingers up to his nose and breathed deep.

I took my gloved hand and gently squeezed the bud, rubbing the scent into my gloves. I brought my fingers towards my nose and sniffed, not as deeply as Tyler. I learned from the first few that I did not enjoy the smell. "Oh yeah," I said convincingly. "I'm really getting a lot of limonene off of this one."

"Hmmm," he sniffed again. "I'm getting more pinene." I straightened my back, bracing for a lecture that didn't come. "Each plant can be a little different. Which is why cross breeding is such a challenging endeavor. I almost gave up on Grandpa's Titties." I stifled a laugh by quickly pretending to clear my throat. Thank goodness I'd prepared myself for this one by looking at the two strain names before we entered the grow room. Grandpa's Titties was accompanied by the much more tamely named Sour Diesel. But nothing will truly prepare you for a man in his early forties, with a lab coat over his scrubs and a hair net holding back a bushy beard looking you dead in the eyes while talking proudly of his Grandpa's Titties. "Did you need some more water?" Tyler asked, seeing my struggle.

"No, I'm okay, I've still got this one," I waited until we stepped out of the room to unscrew the cap and take a sip. They had found me a water bottle after I nearly coughed myself to death at the drying room. It wasn't an *unpleasant* smell, but the air coming out of the drying room was thick with it and incredibly humid. The combination of the dry Nevada desert and suddenly being immersed in a weed jungle irritated my throat and nose. I couldn't even step into the room.

My tour had started there. I was dumped off by security to meet with Tyler. He wanted to walk me through the facility in order, starting with the mother plants. He kindly suggested we skip the drying room and go straight to trimming then packaging from there.

The long tour would have me exhausted by the time of the team lunch I'd planned. I had to meet Tyler at the facility at six that morning. They were early risers as he was already deep in the facility by the time I was checking in.

The big and tall security guard made me wait to be buzzed in. I saw him through the glass; he put down his phone picked up his coffee mug for a long gulp, set *that* down, stood up, stretched his arms and finally pressed the button on top of his desk.

When he opened the door, I said, "Good morning. I'm Vanessa Sorella. Tyler is expecting me for—"

"Name, agent card number, time of entry, purpose of visit." He tapped the screen of a tablet in the entryway.

"Okay," I said to myself, filling it out. I pressed *submit* and he handed me a badge on a lanyard that said 'visitor'. "I don't really know if I qualify as a visitor," I joked. The security guard grunted as he pushed the door open, leaving me just enough room to squeeze through. He turned left down the sterile white hallway and walked away briskly. "Sorry, did you say where Tyler was?" I asked.

"No." He halfheartedly gestured for me to follow him. The air conditioning pushed down on me, creating a curtain. I scuttled after him, feeling like a little mouse chasing a house cat who didn't give a damn about catching me. Fitting, given the maze-like structure of the facility. I tried to figure out where he was taking me. It may have been to a murder dungeon given the lack of windows and his inhospitable behavior.

We made another turn before the hallway opened. There were separate sets of double doors on either side. We got to the end of that stretch and turned right. We saw Tyler standing outside a set of double doors talking to a petite woman swallowed by scrubs.

"Got someone from the state here to see you," the security guard said.

"Actually—" I started to correct him futilely. He had already turned to leave.

"Another audit?" Tyler questioned.

"No, I'm from the corporate office," I corrected. My shoulders drooped. I wouldn't demean myself by explaining that I was the CEO. I hadn't expected them to roll out the red carpet. But maybe to read the press releases or the team email or the article in *Touch Grass* or look me up on LinkedIn.

"Oh! Vanessa!" Tyler said, much warmer than the security guard. "Jasmine," he turned to the woman. "Can you help Vanessa get geared up? Meet me back at dry room two when you're ready."

When the tour started, Tyler, with his older hippie vibes, made me feel more comfortable. Every room was information overload; talking about mothers, veg, cloning, peat moss. I had to hear the phrase 'neem oil' three times before I realized, they were not saying 'Nemoy.' They had strains named Cheetah Piss and Purple Panty Dropper. Was it so wild to assumed one was named after the actor who played Spock in Star Trek? Context clues should have told me that neem oil, which was sprayed on, couldn't be a strain name. But my current surroundings were befuddling.

Tyler certainly seemed friendly. He gave off uncanny valley vibes like he had created a persona with which to greet me. He was probably a real human, but the person who was giving me a tour was a practiced, informative, helpful robot.

Everyone knew I didn't belong here. The click-click-click of my heels, muffled slightly by the blue boot covers they gave me, drew unnecessary attention. They were aliens and I was a human, aboard *their* alien spacecraft. It was filled with cold steel tables and LED lights of a different brightness and configuration in each room. They had plants stacked three levels high in some rooms, with sliding ladders to maneuver between them. The 'moms', as they called them, were bigger than me. The other plants were all different sizes. They filled entire rooms in seas of green and it wasn't clear where one plant started and another ended. In each room there would be one or two workers who would pop their heads up and stare at us over the mini forest. Even when the workers were alone, I got the distinct feeling we were interrupting a conversation.

One particular employee took my presence as a massive inconvenience. She kept coming up to us and asking Tyler questions that seemed non-urgent. She did not acknowledge me. I later learned her name was Jessie.

Tyler gave an engaging tour. He was the alien ambassador, equally capable of talking to visitors or to the plants. He was passionate about what he did. While walking me to the trimming area, he continued the explanation of Grandpa's Titties.

"What I found was that we were getting these excellent yields off Orangutan Titties. But the THC was low. Then we had Grandpa's Breath. Excellent THC, low yields," he said. "So I'm thinking, what about a new crossbreed, best of both worlds."

"Right," I encouraged. I didn't want to say too much as parroting back the words I had learned during the tour would only get me so far. Almost made a fool of myself with 'limonene'.

"But wouldn't you know it: first harvest, low THC, low yields. Doesn't mean it won't work so we give it another go and... Aspergillus. Could happen to any plant," he shook his head sadly. "Third time's a charm. By week three in the flower rooms, these plants were different." He pointed at me to fill in the blank.

"Big yields and high THC?" I answered in the form of a question.

"Ha! I wish I could tell that after three weeks," Tyler chuckled, under his beard like a moderately amused Santa Claus. "No, they turned hermaphroditic. It was over the Thanksgiving holiday, had some less experienced growers on. Room was a quarter seeded by Monday, when I got in." I nodded, knowingly. Or at least I hoped it seemed that way. "I thought of pulling them all, but we'd already plugged three other rooms a week apart. You know the big push to get variety out for 420. This is all the time we had to experiment with new strains. The rest of the year we already have our schedule. Need Wookie Cookie and Skywalker Og before May the 4th. Gotta build up our oil before 710. That kind of stuff. I put all my eggs in this new strain's basket and it might've been a dud. Then late January testing comes back and I have the strain I'd been working towards: high yield, high THC. Got out samples and everyone loved the smoke. Nice big frosty buds too, great for display." His talking had sped up as he went, his excitement infecting me. "Then we rushed to get more in time for 420. I think it's going to become a regular strain of ours. Who knew Grandpa's Titties would come from top tier genetics?"

I froze.

I wanted to laugh.

It's a professional setting with a man who takes his plants very seriously. But isn't there the slightest chance he was telling a crude joke? I'm sure literature professors make silly references to Balzac just to see who was listening.

I couldn't risk it. I kept a straight face as we continued the tour.

Tyler was noticeably less passionate about trimming and packaging. These rooms looked more industrial. They were filled with staff, all working rapidly to trim down then eventually weighing and packaging up the final product. The previous rooms had workers lovingly caring for these plants. These rooms seemed more factory-like and morbid. Used for dissecting the corpses of the plants the cultivators had gently grown. Tyler was less engaged here, saying the bare minimum. Like a baker who had spent days crafting a gorgeous multi-tiered wedding cake, watching it get cut into tiny pieces by joyless faces. He seemed relieved when we arrived at the production side of the facility.

"If there are no more questions," Tyler said, knowing damn well I hadn't asked a *single* provocative question. "I'll radio Connor over. He's the Production Manager."

"That would be great, thank you." I shed my nitrile gloves. I reached through the little slits of the lab coat into my pants pocket and pulled out my phone. Seven texts, countless app notifications and two missed calls. One call was from Joey; he can wait. Two of the texts were from him too and I didn't open them. A text and a call were from Peter and... four from mom. Enough to be concerning. "Where's the restroom?" I asked.

"Around that corner," Tyler pointed. "Then hang a left. Make sure to hang the lab coat outside of the door."

I nodded and started walking to the toilet, opening Mom's texts as I went. They said:

Are you okay?
Please call me Vanessa.
Where are you?

The final text was a link to an article. I clicked it: *Unidentified body found by hiker, Folsom Lake.*

"What the hell?" I whispered to myself. Another text came through as I was looking at the screen.

Call me???

I made it to the bathroom, hung the lab coat on the hook and stepped inside. I pressed the phone symbol by my mom's name. Better get this over with. She answered, interrupting the first ring.

"Vanessa?" She said frantically. "You're okay?"

"Good morning, Mother," I said because I'm at work and 'Mother' seems more professional. "What's this article?" I remained monotone, trying not to match her energy. I switched her to speaker so I could reference the article and started skimming it.

"Oh my goodness! My heart stopped when Kathy sent this to me on The Facebook!" she said.

"Because they found a dead woman at the lake?"

"I thought it was you!" she almost shouted, making me regret using speaker.

"Why?" I laughed.

"You and Joey have been to that lake. And it says it was a woman with long dark hair. Unidentified. And I haven't heard from you. Plus, my phone has been on the fritz. What if the police had been trying to reach me?" she asked, working herself up more.

"Okay Mom. I'm reading: it says she's a *petite* young biracial woman. Everyone from Sacramento has gone to Folsom Lake at some point. You can't let everything you see online panic you. This article was posted like three weeks ago. We spoke two days ago," I said.

"But, I thought—" she said, clearly distraught.

"Mom, please. I am at work. I know you thought I *died*." Could she hear me roll my eyes through the phone? "But you're talking to me now. It's fine. I'm fine. I am not every woman with dark hair that has been found dead."

"Yes.... But I worry about you. Living all alone," she was becoming more frantic. "Can't you move in with Joey? I can't handle this stress, I'm getting older."

I *didn't* say that I knew how old she was because she was only two years older than Joey. I *didn't* say that odds were, if someone killed me, it would be my domestic partner, so I'm safer living alone. I *did* say, "I'm not dead, but I am busy. I love you. Take a break from social media please?" I hung up before she could protest.

I looked in the mirror. My 'makeup free' illusion was being foiled by the humidity of the building. I took a paper towel and dabbed under my eyes where the mascara had bled.

I also had to pee. Sitting on the toilet I thought of my office restroom. A private restroom, for one person at a time. I had thought of it as minimalist, but *this bathroom* truly was. No frills, just a room designed for one purpose, painted white to remain clean and sterile. My private bathroom was no more minimalist than I was 'makeup free'.

I've been living in a world so different from the one I grew up in (since Eugene left my mother), but had I ever registered the change? Or was I simple-minded goldfish, slowly adapting to my new tank, upgraded from the water filled bag I came in and never knowing the difference? By comparison, Joe's bathroom was opulent, excessive, gaudy. This bathroom was functional, clean, and met the need.

I wonder if my own standards have become skewed; my expectations of what qualifies as 'good' increased.

I used a paper towel to open the door, then grabbed my lab coat. I rounded the corner and saw Tyler talking to a man I presumed to be Connor. Tyler was *at least* half a foot taller than me. Connor looked to be shorter than me. Yet I got the distinct feeling that he was looking down on Tyler. Connor was bald, with immaculately kept facial hair consisting of a dirty blonde mustache and a strawberry blonde goatee. Tyler looked like Big Foot pretending to be a doctor. Connor looked like a small mad scientist (both mad angry and mad crazy). I couldn't see his other features at this distance, especially given the protective goggles. One thing was certain as I approached them: these two men did not like each other.

"You're going to have to fit it in, Connor."

"I have a busy production schedule, Tyler."

"My team is busy as well," Tyler pressed.

"Yes, your *team* is busy. *My team* can't operate without me, they need me to monitor their progress. Your team is fine talking to plants without you," Connor, a boy in his late forties, said. "You can keep babysitting her all day for all I care."

"Eh-em," I cleared my throat loudly (competing with all the sounds of various machines). Tyler, who *hadn't* seen me approach, had the good grace to stop his petty arguing and introduce me.

"Vanessa Sorella, this is our Production Manager, Connor Addington," Tyler gestured to the short bald man. I guess full bald isn't sexier on every man.

"*Director of Production and Extraction.* Eight years," Connor, who *had seen* me approaching and decided to refer to me like a toddler anyway, said.

"All right, I'll leave you to it and go talk to my plants," Tyler said as sarcastically as he could. It didn't suit him at all. "I'll see you at lunch with the team, Vanessa."

"It's been a pleasure," I said, as Tyler walked away quickly. I also had thought of Tyler as a man who talks to plants, at least I had the decency not to say it. "Sorry about that introduction, Connor." *Why am I apologizing?* "I should explain a little more so we're on the same page. I'm replacing the CEO, Joe." Even through his PPE goggles, I could tell there was no recognition. "Caldarelli."

He thought for a moment, "Caldarelli? Tony?"

"No, Joe. They do have the same last name. Tony was the *interim* CEO until I was brought on board," I corrected.

"Oh! Good that self-important jerk strutted all around here—" he was one to talk "—demanding we change everything. He didn't know his head from his ass. Probably because they were fused. Glad he's gone!" Make mental note to laugh at this later, refuse Connor the satisfaction by laughing now.

"He's still around, he's the COO now," I said.

"Oh, good. Faith restored. Glad to know it's business as usual over in corporate headquarters," Connor said flippantly. The tone fit *him* like a glove.

"I'm not sure what you mean. But maybe we can clear up some of your misconceptions," I tried desperately to give him the benefit of the doubt. "As the new *C-E-O–*" I emphasized by saying each letter clearly "*–*I want you to know I'm a boots on the ground leader. I have a democratic leadership style. I like to get your input. I wouldn't ask any of you to do something that I wouldn't do myself. My approach–"

"I'm going to stop you right there. I know who you are. I know why you're here. And I've heard this speech." *Impossible! I just wrote it in the hotel last night.* "This is our third time being acquired. We get a ton of visits before the acquisition, and a boatload of promises. After we get acquired, we get few visits and no more promises. Just marching orders. I can assure you, *I am* the boots on the ground. I am in the trenches. And every day, I do things you cannot do because you do not know how. Once or twice a year your kind visits the facility for a tour or come down to Vegas for the *MJ Biz Con.* Then you go back to your corporate offices and let me run the facility." Connor barely took a breath. "I have made it through eight years and three acquisitions. I am good at my job. Great actually. If you question that, you should fire me. Or, you can expect me to give you a quick tour so you can go have lunch with the team and I will get back to the real work. Can we do that? Or are you going to ask me to put on a dog and pony show?"

He stopped. I waited for a punch line, but it seems like he was just punching. Did I really want to go three rounds with this tiny but intimidating man? What if he was the linchpin of this facility's production and extraction and I pulled that pin and the grenade explodes?

I paused to think. I wanted him to believe I was considering my options rather than being backed into a corner with only one move. "After you." I was unwilling to give him more.

He began walking at a breakneck pace, too fast for me in my heels. Thankfully most of the slick flooring was covered in rubber mats with holes in them. I looked silly while I played *the floor is lava* as we moved about the facility, but it was preferable to falling on my butt in front of this ass. "To your right is our newly completed CO2 extraction room," he said, passing it.

"Can I see—" I started.

"We will not be going inside. It is currently in use so that would be unsafe. You also do not have your OSHA certification." Under his breath he added, "It would just look like a room to you anyway."

I wanted to grab and squeeze his bald head, popping it like a pimple. Disgusting.

Lunch with the cultivation team was even more odd. It turned out to be a bar that served food rather than a restaurant. The team claimed it was the only place in the area that would seat the twelve of us. That may have been true. Perhaps a coincidence that it was the only place that would let them smoke their vapes incessantly while eating.

It started off pleasantly. After the frigid welcome I received from Connor, anything would feel warm. He was too busy to join; which was amazing news. Everyone else was superficially friendly. They were sharing war stories from the day we 'went rec' (the day recreational marijuana could be sold to non-medical customers) in Nevada. It was somehow also the good old days, despite the wartime type talk. They were all clearly bonded.

That's when things got a little off course. They grilled me about my job history and experience with cannabis. They asked my name three times. They told inside jokes and laughed across me, forcing me to get out of the way by receding into my chair. When I went to the restroom to gather myself, I returned to a round of shots.

It was a test. I knew when the *mean girl*, named Jessie, grabbed the first one and said, "To our new CEO," and held it up to *cheers* the air while everyone grabbed their shot. While everyone else threw theirs back, Jessie looked at me, I *clinked* the air with my shot and took it the same time she took hers.

Uck... cinnamon. At least it was pre-chilled, not something a bar like this would normally do. Another indication that lunch here was a frequent occurrence. They would all come to this bar and smoke their vape pens (either weed or nicotine) in the middle of their lunch shifts, drinking cinnamon whiskey and paying with the company card. Tipping more than thirty percent to get special treatment.

Jessie looked at me, defying me to be uncool and balk at their little game.

Knowing that we paid for Collin's occasional bender meant this little shindig and twenty more like it a year were darn near irrelevant in comparison. But the principal. They had the industry knowledge and therefore all the power. Sure, the company owned the intellectual property. But how much was written down as compared to kept in their heads? What was I going to do to stop them?

Truthfully, nothing. I don't care about these expenses. I don't care about the little Jessies of W.E.E.D. I am the *CEO*.

This put things in a whole new light. Everyone at the corporate office was trying to kiss my ass. But these mother fuckers were hazing me. The frustrating bit was that they wouldn't have done it to Joe.

Would they have gotten the chance? It didn't seem like he had bothered coming to this facility. No one knew his name, except for Tyler and he admitted they hadn't met. So much for Joe's advice to visit the team and learn operations. What else had he preached that he refused to practice?

I didn't go back to the cultivation facility after lunch. For how much they drank, I doubt the team did either. They were celebrating something. I went straight back to my hotel room. I didn't read Joe's book, instead spending the time watching that kind of TV that you only watch in hotel rooms because nothing else is on. I showered twice, thinking I could get the skunky smell out of my skin and hair. But it turned out to be my clothes and shoes and purse that reeked of W.E.E.D.

I lay in the bed, the extra pillows I requested surrounding me, trying to relax. I doubt the dispensary tours tomorrow will be nearly as exhausting. The manager, Willow. Is that the name of a mean girl?

16

He balanced the three pink boxes in his left hand, unwieldy due to their long flat shape. He pulled the door outward with his right hand. To enter, he had to squeeze between two people with their backs to him. They stared at him uncertainly.

"Excuse me." He held the boxes out in front of him by way of explanation. "Fuel for the crew." The two people smiled and parted for him. Once he passed, they instantly recovered their places and guarded them seriously.

Overcrowding made the two separate lines leading to the intake windows difficult to distinguish from each other. Every person was carefully watching the person in front of them. Moving up to fill in gaps, like one continuous stream. The mood of the room was light, the conversations bubbling along.

But make no mistake: there would be absolutely no cuts.

Collin was thankful that he was tall. He lifted the boxes above his head and above the crowd. His ticket to the front of the line. He got a few glares on his way through the lobby which held about fifty people (uncomfortably). Their mood softened when it was obvious he had no intention of swooping in to get the last deal. Every deal was advertised as having a limited quantity. It didn't, but 'scarcity created urgency', according to Maya. Judging by the packed room, she was right.

The lobby was filled with a hodgepodge of people. Cheap deals attracted Vegas tourists and locals alike. Collin pushed closer to the front and thought 'one of these things is not like the others,' as he spotted someone incongruous.

One line wasn't moving. A woman standing in front was holding it up. She spoke to the young man facing her by bending down slightly and speaking through a hole in the plexiglass that divided them. Her shiny beige stiletto heels and tight green pencil skirt with matching blazer made the bend difficult. Her dark hair trailed down her back, leading Collin's eye to trace her curvaceous figure. She was chubbier than he liked, but he could be persuaded.

But why was *she* here? Checking up on Colllin?

"No, no," she said louder. "I am here to *meet with* Willow." The young man's name tag just said 'Hi I'm New'.

"Yeah man," Hi-I'm-New said, his eyes only half open. "She's in the back. We're not doing requests for budtenders today. I can get you checked in, but like, you gotta wait in the line," he spoke slowly and loudly enough Collin could easily hear him. His eyes flashed to his co-worker, begging her to help him out.

Both were young, but she looked much more prepared. The young man withdrew into his hoodie with the sleeves rolled up. The young woman pulled his window intercom microphone towards her. Her face was covered in piercings, half her head shaved, the other half bright pink. Her name tag said 'Hi I'm Korey'.

She made it clear she was not in the mood for bull shit. "Hello, ma'am. You need to wait like everyone else. Just because he's new and soft, doesn't mean you can bully him." The young man looked ready to argue, but weighing his options, shrugged it off. "And if you speak up here—" Korey pointed at the intercom, "we can hear you better."

Vanessa stood up straight and spoke into the intercom. "I don't want to buy anything. I have a meeting scheduled with Willow. I am the CEO of W.E.E.D."

"The CEO of weed? Sure, you are. And I'm the High Priestess of CBD."

"W-E-E-D. The Wellness Enterprise of Exceptional Dispensaries. We *own* High and Mighty," Vanessa protested.

"I've never heard of you. And the 'owners' wouldn't be here on 420," Korey rolled her eyes.

"Unless they brought donuts!" Collin said from behind Vanessa. She jumped in shock, almost hitting the boxes of donuts Collin held at his waist.

"Hey Collin!" Korey was suddenly chipper. "You can go on back."

"Don't worry about this one," he gestured to Vanessa with his chin and winked at Korey. "She's with me."

Vanessa's irritation melted into an appreciative look when she realized Collin was rescuing her. Hi-I'm-New and Korey looked at each other. Korey moved back toward her own intercom, reaching under the desk for the button to buzz them in. Following Collin's lead, Vanessa went to the big wooden door with a metal door handle.

She waited for the buzz, turning the handle and pushing the door open. She had probably tried and failed to open the door, learning she needed permission.

Entering this room unleashed a more chaotic experience. Rather than a large group of people barely moving, as in the last room, this room was less populated and more active. About two dozen people in total were paired in groups of two or three all about the room. Some were at the sales counters which formed a broken *U* shape around the room, split down the middle for access to the back of house. There was twice as much space in this room but whatever wasn't counter was reserved for shelving and displays of all kinds of bright cannabis product packaging. Three long tables were in the center of the room lined with white lighting and topped with evenly spaced clear smell jars showing off a variety of flower buds. Tablets secured to each table to scroll through the products. Ten separate conversations created a cacophony bouncing off every hard surface.

Collin laughed to himself seeing Vanessa look around the store like a kid in a candy shop. She was looking at the walls filled with TVs showing footage of the cultivation facility or scrolling through the menus. The room itself was a sterile white with no windows. White counters, floors, walls, shelves. But every décor piece set on the shelves and in the glass case lining the counters was eye catching. The displayed products were different sizes and shapes, colorful or lit with neon lighting. It was kind of like a candy shop. Since none of the exhibits were infused, they mostly *were* candy. Albeit stale and covered in resin for display.

He scanned the room. When he saw she didn't actively have customers, he approached a tall woman in jeans and a black graphic T-shirt and said, "Hey Willow!"

She took a moment to recognize him but when she did, her smile seemed to be genuine. "Oh, hey Collin!" Willow moved around the counter to greet him.

"Great 420 today. Lobby's packed!"

"People were lining up before the doors opened."

"Nice! Dope shirt, new design?" Collin asked. She was wearing a store branded shirt that said 'High and Mighty'. A cartoonish character who looked like Popeye but wasn't (for trademark reasons) was smoking a pipe and crushing a can that said 'Hash' while flexing his giant arm muscle. Willow had pulled the shirt tight with a knot in the back and cut a *V* into the neck. It wouldn't look as good on him without some key missing assets that Willow possessed but he asked anyway, "Can I get one?"

"I got them in the back," Willow offered. She led them to the door and scanned her key fob to access the back room, holding the door for Collin. She went through and almost closed the door on Vanessa, who had been following but not closely enough to slip in. "Oh! You can't—" Willow started.

Before Vanessa could object, Collin threw in his, "She's with me," cool guy phrase. Willow propped the door open lightly with her hand, releasing it and following Collin once Vanessa had a hand on it.

Collin rounded the corner of the tight hallway, to the right. Had he gone left, he would have hit the product vault. To the right, he passed through the call center, which previously held the sales floor. It looked similar, just smaller. An *L* shaped counter rather than a *U*. They passed through a doorway to the break room. The lobby shared one wall with this break room, but it was reasonably soundproof. The back of house was more inviting with gray carpet flooring, green accent walls and yellow toned lighting. There were no windows so it still felt like a basement. The break room was basically a mini kitchen in said basement. It had a fridge, counters, toaster, coffee machine, and a four-seat table.

"Hey guys, donuts!" he said to three people in the break room standing around, setting them down on the small metal table.

"Sick!" one of them said.

Another said, "Cool," with much less enthusiasm.

While the third said, "I can't have gluten."

Willow looked irritated at the team then chimed in, "*Thanks*, Collin. We really appreciate it!" A choir teacher getting her students back in tune.

"Thanks," the three of them said with no uniformity.

Collin flipped one box open and said, "Got you some apple fritters."

"Oooh yes!" Willow grabbed a paper towel from the counter and put a fritter on it. Pushing her long braids back, she took a bite.

"I'm Vanessa," Vanessa said, as if someone had asked. She extended her hand when it was inopportune.

Willow wiped her right hand on the paper towel and hesitantly shook Vanessa's hand. "Hi?" Willow said, month partially full. Her eyes flicked to Collin who was distracted with grabbing his own donut.

Snatching the question from between the lines Vanessa answered, "I'm *the* Vanessa you have a meeting with today."

"Today? Girl, you got your wires crossed. I don't schedule meetings on 420."

"My office sent you a calendar invite."

"And did I accept it? No. You saw the zoo out there."

"You could've replied, rather than wasting my time," Vanessa pressed.

"I don't even remember your invite. I didn't ask you to come here. Who—"

"No, no," Collin put a lightly glazed hand up. "Willow, don't worry about it," he moved himself between Willow and Vanessa, turning his back to Vanessa. "You keep crushing it out there!" They fist bumped before the glaring Willow departed, another bite of fritter in her mouth.

The other three employees, none of whom were allergic to gluten anymore, cleared out of the break room with donuts in hand. "What the hell was that about?" Vanessa was incredulous.

"I was gonna ask you the same thing," Collin took a bite of a maple bar that was sprinkled with pieces of bacon. "What are you doing here? Checking up on me?"

"Excuse me, I'll go where I want. I'm the CEO."

"Yeah, you keep saying that. We've all heard." Collin took another bite.

"Except for Willow, apparently. And everyone at the cultivation facility."

"Ah, so it's *not* about me? You really did come down here to tell everyone you're the CEO?" Collin took a bite before continuing, only chewing once before saying, "on 420," with a mouthful.

"I didn't know it was 420."

"You got on the plane and didn't know that it's April 20th?"

"I didn't know what 420 was." Vanessa crossed her arms defensively. "I see now it's a big deal, but they could've told me."

"Told you what?" Collin asked, shoving more donut in his mouth. "About a holiday everyone in the industry—"

"Can you please stop with the donut? I haven't eaten today and it's making me sick to my stomach watching you talk with your mouth full."

Collin shoved the whole donut in his mouth. Around it, he said, "There. Happy now?" He started laughing. Vanessa laughed some with him. Collin started laughing even harder. Then he was choking. Vanessa's face got serious. He put his hands to his throat.

"Collin?" She was worried.

"Water?" He barely managed.

She swung open the fridge and pulled out a bottle, unscrewing the cap. Before handing it to him, she saw he was laughing again. He reached for the water but she withdrew it and took a big gulp. "You're a jerk, you know?"

"Guess that's why they made *you* the CEO," Collin teased. "Next time I'll send the town crier to announce your arrival on the busiest day of the year. Does that work your *high*ness?" he emphasized 'high' and picked up a few small pieces of green confetti cannabis leaves that were strewn about the break room, placing it in her hair.

"Hilarious." Vanessa immediately plucked them out of her hair. "So I'm an idiot. I came down here for a half assed cultivation tour and then what? I just fly home and hope no one asks about it during Executive Committee?" She deflated. "I was making headway with them, I thought. Now they're going to think I wasn't paying attention when we talked about 420."

"Were you?" She glared at him so he back-pedaled. "Join me! Spread the holiday cheer!" He clicked his heels together, drawing attention to his bright green shoes. "Tell them that was your plan. Or don't tell them at all. You don't have to answer to Executive Committee. Just stop telling everyone we meet that you're the CEO and they'll like you a lot better. We'll get you a branded shirt and you can ditch the suit jacket."

"You want me to wear that?" Vanessa pointed to Collin's shirt. It was a white graphic tee depicting giant *God* hands emerging from the pearly gates offering a tall golden bong. *High and Mighty* appeared over the top of the gate in shiny gold lettering.

"Obviously not," Collin said. "This one's mine. You get your own." He grabbed a shirt from a stack of boxes that was piled up on the floor. "Next stop is to pick up pizzas for the strip location. Coming or not?"

He offered his hand. She accepted. She trusted him. And why shouldn't she?

"I don't know about this," Collin said. "Seems kinda fucked." He stared into his glass before taking a sip of the *Weekly Special*, a coconut margarita with a rim of tajin. Joey mocked him for the order and got himself Glenlivet neat, which seemed to get the bartender's nod of approval. Collin didn't care about the bartender's approval; he deserved a tasty drink. Now, if the bartender had been a beautiful blonde....

They found a spot in the corner. *Old* Saorise's Pub had modern soft seating. An ornate wooden coffee table was placed in front of their loveseat. It was nice they didn't have to look at each other; less ideal that their knees were touching.

"You don't think it went well?" Joey asked, taking a sip of his scotch and sucking air through his mouth as a chaser.

"No.... it was fine." Collin sucked his drink through a tiny cocktail straw. "Why are we involving *Vanessa*? Some woman you met a couple weeks ago at a club and took back to your hotel to start talking business? Seems weird."

"*You* were at that club and it was *your* hotel room too, idiot. Being black out drunk doesn't mean you weren't there," Joey teased in a brotherly and *not* friendly way. "And so what? Not like I'm a *married* man bringing girls back to my hotel room."

"This isn't about me. I'm talking about her."

"What about her? Pops loved her, you saw him at dinner tonight. It was like Ma from thirty years ago walked in the room." Joey leaned back, no longer setting his glass down between sips. "He was smitten. He didn't even hear what she said. Good thing too because she doesn't know what she's talking about."

"So, she looks like Ma," Collin cringed when saying it. "But why bring her in?"

"Look, I'm playing chess, you're playing checkers. You keep clacking your pieces around the board, maybe someone will king you. Me? I'm already King."

Collin furrowed his brow. "You think I'm stupid."

"You did walk into an Irish Pub and order a *margarita* from a man named Sean."

"It was the special!"

Joey laughed. "And how is it?"

Collin had made a face at the very first sip, so Joey already knew the answer. "That's not the point, Joey," he said. "But if you want me to be your partner, you gotta treat me like one. Let me in on the plan."

Joey did not respond at first. But when it became clear Collin wasn't going to give up, he broke the silence. "Fine. Yes, I met her at the club. I wanted her to get her friends to go back to the hotel, so you would crash, like always, and they would leave."

"I don't always crash!" Collin protested. "You were the one who started the shots!"

"Do you want me to tell you or not?" Collin opened his mouth, but decided against speaking and put the straw in his mouth instead. He nodded and Joey continued. "When we got back to the room and you and the other two girls passed out—" *Two girls? I'm going to need more details later,* Collin thought "—Vanessa and I stayed up talking. She sounds eager and desperate to be someone great. I ask about her background and I flirt a little." Joey turned to Collin as he was speaking, partially putting one leg on the couch to turn his body. "She starts telling me everything. How she didn't finish college but she got this incredible gig working for Sorella Financial Services because, get this, her father is *Eugene Sorella*. But, here's the best part, she doesn't talk to him anymore."

Collin set his drink down and turned to face Joey, also putting one leg on the couch. When the silence went on uncomfortably long, Collin said, "So?"

"So?" Joey was incredulous that Collin hadn't put the pieces together yet. He loosened his tie and took a sip of his drink before setting it down, freeing his hands to talk. "See, this is where the chess comes in. You gotta stop thinking about all the pieces like they're the same. You have to know what every piece can do for you. It's not about *Vanessa*, this college drop-out with daddy issues. Nothing special, a million of those at the strip clubs. No, it's about this woman who has a name and connections that she can't use. She's attractive too, but to *one man*, our Pops, she's the most gorgeous creature on the face of the planet. And all we need is for her to be there to persuade him. Lucky for us: I can be her daddy. All I have to do is keep her thinking I'm interested. I can keep her at arm's length by insisting it's just business."

"What do you want with Pops? We're already set making plenty on the side."

"I don't want *side* money, Coll. I want entree money, a big juicy steak of money. All our lives, Pops gives us jobs. You want to work until you die like he's gonna?" Collin shook his head. "Didn't think so. Yeah, we got a sweet thing going with Angelo. But we need something big, something we can milk for a long time. I'm tired of these small loans. We get one big one with W.E.E.D. we can skim millions," Joey lowered his voice and looked around. But Old Saoirse's Pub wasn't popular and the music was loud, that's why he chose it. "No one's gonna trust it if it comes from us. We want to keep our names far away. So Vanessa hangs around for a while, closing other small deals. Everyone gets used to her and trusts her, Pops already loves her. Then, we have our puppet introduce Angelo to him, like it's her idea. No one questions that a Sorella has money lending contacts. Meanwhile, no way Vanessa goes out on her own. She has no real connections, what's she going to do without us?"

"You know Tony would never stand for this. And he's got his hands all over W.E.E.D," Collin stated.

"So what? Pops doesn't listen to him," Joey waved him off.

"Ma does."

"No, *Tony* listens to her," Joey corrected. "What's your problem? Knowing you, you're gonna be working on another alimony payment soon. You need the cash."

Collin didn't deny and instead ignored Joey's dig. "We barely know Vanessa."

"You afraid she's a bad person? Gonna screw us over? Nothing I can't handle."

Collin sat forward looking away from Joey. "No. What if she's a *good* person?"

Joey looked offended. "You saying we aren't good people?"

"I think we should consider—" Collin started.

"You think too much." Joey downed his scotch and stood. "Want a real drink this time?"

17

Dropping off pizzas and fist bumping people is surprisingly exhausting. I was ready to crash by noon. Instead of crashing, we had a two-hour lunch with some sales reps of a new edible company. It was a 'work' meeting, that they paid for, but had we talked business at all? I can't even recall the name of their company...

We ended the day driving to two different sandwich shops to get enough sandwiches for the third High and Mighty dispensary. Collin dropped me off at the first location where my rental car was. The whole time, he avoided talking to me about anything real by putting the top down on the flashy red convertible that only a man in his forties would like. Or a man in his fifties. Joey and he had remarkably similar taste in everything except for clothing and women.

It felt like a long day, but I made it back to the hotel before five. Enough time to be bored in the tiny room. My flight isn't until tomorrow morning. I had thought about going to the hot tub, but every time I peeked out of the window, a family or two were splashing around noisily at the pool. I ordered a smoothie to my room, knowing I needed to get *something* despite the heavy lunch.

By eight, the families had gotten cold because even in Vegas, nights were still cold in April. The hot tub was empty. I changed and headed down.

I swiped my room key and as soon as I opened the door, I could see that I had been beaten. It was just one man which was worse than if it were a group. He had his back to me, and I debated turning around and leaving before he saw me. His back was exceptionally hairy. And recognizable.

"What the hell?" I said out loud.

Collin turned his upper body slightly, taking his right arm off the hot tub wall to do so. "Vanessa?" He seemed even more surprised than was, like he'd been caught. He took a moment to appreciate my red one-piece suit.

I approached the hot tub and put my towel and key down on a nearby pool chair. "Hey, Collin. Long time no see." Then, the smell hit me. The skunky, earthy scent I'd been ambushed with all day, now accompanied by fire and ash. While Tyler had eventually helped me detect the differences in prominent terpenes, those subtle variations all went up in smoke. I walked to the hot tub and descended the three stairs, the hot water slowing me as I adjusted to the temperature with each step. I looked at Collin, and he was staring at me, a blunt in his right hand. The tobacco leaf wrapping added to the unpleasant smell.

"*Not* here to check in on me?" he said suspiciously.

I lowered myself fully and exhaled, trying to let go of frustration. "No, Collin. I asked for a hotel off the strip and *this* is what Peter booked me."

Collin took a hit. "That checks out," he said. "Peter booked my room too. I asked to be far from the casinos. Didn't know he was going to put me in *North Vegas*. Your little assistant needs to do some research."

I rolled my eyes. "Shame on us for not being specific." I submerged as much of my body as I could without getting my hair wet. I felt a group of strands loosen from my bun and fall behind my back into the water anyway. I looked at Collin directly, "I thought you'd want to be near the casinos and all the 'activities'."

"I told you, I'm trying to be sober." I eyed his blunt. "I know, I know. It's helping though. If it keeps me off everything else, it's a net positive." He took another deep draw and offered it to me. I pushed through the hot tub and joined him on the opposite side, accepting the joint. "I've basically been sober since the last time we partied." I was attempting to inhale when he spoke. I choked and laughed instead.

"S-s-sure," I sputtered.

"I have!" His relaxed posture stiffened and our height difference became apparent.

"Collin." I looked him in the eye. "I caught you passed out on your desk weeks *after* that."

"That was dumb, I know. It was Joe's whiskey. It smelled like him, brought up memories. I wasn't trying to get drunk..... just connect to a feeling." Collin looked up. "I know I shouldn't have had any."

"It was my first big meeting, I needed you there." I took a quick drag, letting it cool in my mouth before sucking it into my lungs. I've been all alone. He should feel guilty.

"It was just a little. Bottle was mostly empty when I got it."

"Don't lie to me."

His eyes snapped to me. "I would never... I am not lying to you. I got there early, I had less than two shots in my coffee, didn't even finish it. What happened was weird, I'm no lightweight, but I was two weeks sober. Maybe that had something to do with it. I was hazy all day, that's never happened," he seemed desperate as he held my gaze. "I have been on my best behavior. I've been doing every report Tony asked for. Even this trip, no partying. I had a whole curriculum. Meetings every day, even the weekend, until today. I want to do what's right by you..." He reached for my face and changed his mind, grabbing my shoulder instead. "You as CEO."

Though I had been upset by his behavior, ultimately I knew not to expect much of Collin. And he had genuine remorse. I decided to let him off the hook. "It's fine, just don't let it happen again," I teased. "I don't really want to talk about work." I turned away from him, passing the blunt back.

"Oh sure, give me back the roach." He grabbed a nearby empty can of carbonated water and dropped the remnants in. He pulled out a joint. He worked at lighting it. "So, boss lady. If not work, what did you have in mind when you got into a tub with me, half-naked?" He elbowed me playfully. I knew he was joke flirting, something we did often.

There was also some truth behind it. He definitely checked out my ass before I got in the hot tub. I wasn't his thin-blonde-with-giant-breasts type. But all the Caldarelli men appreciate a nice ass.

"Stop..." I say unconvincingly as I give him a little splash. "I'm serious though. Let's not talk shop. We're friends right?"

"Almost family." I looked down at the water. "What?" he asked. Collin was no genius, but he was the most emotionally intelligent of the brothers.

The tiny bit of weed I've had is enough to get me to drop my guard. "Joey doesn't want to get married anymore!"

"What! What makes you say that?"

"He told me. Because of the whole treasurer thing. He wants to wait years for the right timing to announce our relationship."

"That's not so bad."

I shouted at him, "*Years!* If he doesn't want to get married, he should say so."

"Don't read into it," he took a hit of the joint and blew out. "He's an ambitious guy, he's always doing what's best for the hustle."

"Exactly! When I met him, I thought the whole consulting business was a ruse to get to me. After two years, I finally caved. But now I'm feeling like the relationship was some plan for the business." How much of what I'm saying do I believe? It's pouring out of me from nowhere. I put my head in my hands and turned away from Collin, leaning back on the hot tub wall. He put his arm around me and I put my head on his shoulder.

"Hey!" He said loudly, then more gently, "Hey now. Don't think like that. Who knows what Joey thought way back when you met? Who cares? Joey never wanted to get married again after Melissa—"

"Great, thanks," I moaned.

"Let me finish, would ya? He never wanted to get married again but... then he found you. And marriage didn't seem so bad. It's a testament to how beautiful and amazing you are."

"Joey has met lots of beautiful women." I was fishing and I didn't care.

"You're special, Nessa. You know it," Collin pressed into me as he reassured me. "And Joey is a man of his word. Give him time. When he's ready to get married, hopefully you're still there for him." Collin sat up again, suddenly thinking of something. "You're not planning on leaving him, are you?"

"I..." wasn't. But it would be okay to let him think I was. Maybe *he* could give Joey a sense of urgency. "I don't want to talk about it."

He took a long drag from the joint, and blew a cloud of smoke up. "Okay, we won't talk about that either."

I turned to him and held out my right hand. "I'll take a hit."

"This?" he looked down at the joint. "It's pretty strong, it's infused."

"You were just going to smoke the whole thing by *yourself*? After a blunt?"

"Long day. CEO's been busting my balls lately."

"Shut up! And hand it over. It is puff, puff, pass after all." I reached for the joint, which he passed awkwardly.

"Woah! Look at you. Who's been teaching you the cool kid's lingo... from a decade ago?"

"Quiet old man. I'm hipper than you." Hipper? God I *am* out of touch, spending all my time with these old men. I took a drag, blowing the smoke up above us.

"Take it easy there, Ms. Chimney." His shift from flirty too parental reminded me of Joey. I took another deeper drag, sucking it straight into my lungs. I started to blow it into his face, then a coughing fit hit me. "You all right?" Collin asked, opening can of bubble water and handing it to me. I drank it.

"Never better," I said with a husky voice, smoke still tickling my throat. And then I dropped low into the hot tub again, this time the bottom of *all* my hair got wet. My head started swirling.

We finished the joint in near silence. Collin got out once to turn the jets back on in the hot tub. I was glued to the cement, looking up at what would be stars if not for the neon lights, abrasive on my eyes. At some point, the heat got to be too much. Collin braved the freezing air to dunk his towel in the cold pool water and bring it back. We rolled it up and put it under our necks laying our heads back, arms out against the cement. My head felt heavy, but now that my throat was no longer scorched, I needed to talk more.

"What was Joe like as a dad?" I said, surprising myself.

"Joe?"

"Yes. Why are you always questioning me?"

"Well, you say some weird shit."

I closed my eyes. "I'm special remember? I have a unique mind."

"That you do." Collin said. A long pause followed.

"Okay the longer you don't answer me the more I'm imagining some crazy shit about your childhood," I said calmly.

Collin sighed. "Joe − Pops, he was fine. *You* know, *you* worked for him."

"That's not the same."

"Yeah it was. Everyone *worked* for him. He'd meet someone and decide how they could work for him. He prided himself on finding their hidden talents. He'd praise them for it and make sure he tapped into the talent. That's why he had so many people loyal to him. He had them convinced he was the answer to their dreams. But he was just giving them jobs."

"What was your job?" I asked, rethinking my own place with Joe... both Joes.

"I was the Olympian. I got interested in swimming as a kid watching Bay Watch. Thought I'd be swimming with babes. He installed a pool in the back yard and then my first job was to find a way to pay him back. By making it to the Olympics, which I did. Technically. By qualifying for '04 in Athens. I tell people the US won that year, but it was all Phelps. Never really made any money off it. Pops was determined to squeeze something out of me, so he's been dragging me to job after job, wherever he works. Like he's going to unlock my hidden talent for profit." Collin was melancholy.

"Can you still swim?" I asked stupidly.

"I *can* swim," he laughed. "But I had our pool built for my boys, not just me. Thought they'd get into it. Becky doesn't want them following in my footsteps. As if they're guaranteed to be an alcoholic Olympian. I wanted something I could do with them that I could be proud of. Kind of depressing to do it without them."

"Maybe if you weren't such a player, she wouldn't be so worried about the boys turning into you." I was only half joking.

"If it makes you feel any better, she left me."

"Oh, Jesus, Coll. I'm sorry. I didn't mean to...." I paused and struggled to redirect the conversation. "What about your mom?"

"Ma didn't exactly leave me," he started.

Damn... I kept putting my foot in my mouth. Bringing up his estranged wife, implying his dead mother *left* him. I felt clouds forming over my mind so I sat up, hoping for a 'weather' change. "No, I'm changing the subject." Wow... smooth transition. "How was she as a mom growing up?"

"Not very different from now."

Harsh. "She wasn't there for you? Joey thinks she babied you," I said.

"In a sense," Collin allowed. "I was the *baby*, by being the youngest. The baby who always had to be watched. I was an accident, that came too many years after the second son, and ruined their perfect nuclear family. Ma had to restart that eighteen-year countdown until I was out of the house. I made it easy on her by leaving when I was sixteen."

"I'm sure that's not true! Joey always said you were their special boy," I teased.

"Yeah, I got special treatment. No curfew, no rules. Pops gave me *goals* and *jobs*. But he'd hand those out to the paperboy if he lingered too long. He was in his fifties by then, and he barely even considered me his son." I looked over to Collin, his eyes were glistening with tears teetering on the edge without going over. Like an infinity pool. Put one toe in and all the water would gush over the sides.

"*Everyone* thinks that when they're a teenager. Joe had a strange way of showing people he loved them. Doesn't mean he didn't," I reassured him.

"He loved me, just not like a son," Collin paused. It went on and on. The silence made my arms itch, relieved only when he continued. "Ma and Pops fought constantly. Not even a fight, because Pops would never say anything back. Ma would just demand more and more and he'd give it to her, whatever she wanted. He knew about her and Frank, but he never said a thing."

Her and Frank? *What the hell?*

"Still treated Frank like family. Tony and Joey called him Uncle Frank. I refused. I'd either call him Frank or Dad. No games for me. So, Ma and Joe let me call him Frank, but I always knew…" Collin trailed off.

My head was swimming, the world spinning all around me. Frank and Collin? They *were* the two hairiest men I knew. It was no coincidence. I reached out blindly and grabbed his arm. It grounded me enough to speak.

"Are you saying that Frank is—" I started slowly enough that I deserved to be interrupted.

"I don't know what I'm saying. Must be the drugs talking," he laughed. "Ma hated Frank, just a little less than she hated Joe."

I don't need him to acknowledge what I've inferred. It explains why he was so distraught after Frank died. His bio dad dying months after the dad who raised him? That would be hard to take.

"I'm starting to think I hardly even know the family I'm marrying into." I was hoping to lighten the mood... and maybe, selfishly, get reassured. "Any other details I should know before becoming a Caldarelli? Or should I run away?"

"Um." Collin gave it some serious thought. "Run." He laughed heartily, which made me laugh. Hard not to when Collin started. The Caldarelli brothers speaking voices were similar, but their laughs were unique. Collin's was boyish and always at the ready. Sometimes making me take him less seriously, wondering if he ever took himself seriously.

"Run?" I pushed my laughter down. "Should I run on the wedding day or wait until the alimony kicks in?"

"I mean it, Nessa... It's like I said, Joey knows you're special, he doesn't want to let you go. He really wants to marry you someday. If I were just Joey's brother, I'd be saying, 'yeah wait. He's a good guy, he'll come around.' But maybe that's not what's best for *you*." We were both sitting upright then, looking at each other, legs touching. Maybe it was the hot tub talking (which we had stayed in well beyond the twenty-minute safety recommendation), but I got the distinct feeling that Collin was incredibly uncomfortable. Like you would be around someone you wanted to kiss but shouldn't. He stared forward, away from me.

"But you're not *just* Joey's brother, are you Coll?" I touched his right arm, lightly brushing it with my left hand, in a way that I hoped was kind, not flirty. "You're my friend."

"Vanessa," Collin used his arms to hoist himself out of the hot tub. He sat on what must have been very cold cement for another beat before continuing. "I am not your friend." He put no emphasis on any one word, making his joke fall flat. I laughed at the absurdity of the dull statement.

Collin was silent. He stood up, dripping wet, slipped his feet into his nearby sandals. The squish... squish... squish of his shoes would have been comical except nothing was funny about Collin anymore. He grabbed a fresh towel by the pool's exit and left.

Perfectly timed, the jets in the hot tub shut off. I sat in what was now just a warm outdoor bath, feeling naked as soon as the coverage provided by the bubbling water disappeared.

My sexy as fuck one piece bathing suit that I had turned to for confidence when I bought it is doing little to comfort me now. I shiver in the hot tub. Alone and exposed.

18

"This is technically *your* job," Derrick, the Chief Technology Officer said, handing over a sticky note of coffee orders. Peter didn't appreciate the smirk Derrick made from under his perfect dark blonde goatee. Peter had never been able to grow a beard since it was especially patching around the chin. At least he could look down at the much shorter and skinnier man. "Since you're new, I helped you out. Make sure to get yourself a coffee."

"Thank you," Peter said, because he was supposed to. But he was not thankful. He did not want to carry five hot coffees through the building up the stairs. He especially did not want to go back to Morning Boost. He didn't think he could say no. Anyone with a *C* in their title thought his time was free game. In fairness, he wasn't busy. Aside from reviewing everything Tiffany had done, Vanessa hadn't assigned him any work.

Monday, Tony had him hunting through files for some man with the compliance board. They wanted to call Vanessa too, but she said to never give out her number. She didn't answer when he called. They asked Peter questions instead. He was worried he might be in trouble when they asked about the weed he'd dropped off for that old man's wife, but he assured them Vanessa told him to and they backed off. It was interesting, until they sent him away to make copies of the files. Tuesday, he had to clean up the aftermath. Tony said they got what they needed and made

Peter shred a bunch of them. Pointless. He could have just given them the files instead of making them copies.

And now he was on another pointless task. Stuck in line, on what felt like the wrong side of the counter. They were taking forever.

Peter peered around the giant espresso machine and saw they had Trent on bar. Poor choice for a rush, Trent was notoriously slow. His chill hipster persona was possessed by an even chiller surfer bro who worked on his own imaginary timeline when they had him making drinks. Though it might be worse when he helped customers, since he took time to chat up each and every one.

They had Elyse on the register, a much better choice. Grumpier customers would have griped about her curt communication, but she didn't allow them time to complain. With her sweet narrow face, doe eyes, and blonde face-framing highlights she looked both too perfect and too innocently new to critique. She was the shift supervisor and she had no issues holding her own. She should have been made manager years ago, rather than the steady stream of corporate idiots. It would happen for her one day. Elyse always got her way, eventually.

When the person in front of Peter took too long to order, Elyse chimed in with, "If you like sweet, you'll love the chocolate covered cherry latte. My absolute favorite." It was a lie, but Elyse always got the bonus for pushing seasonal drink orders. This was one of the Valentine's specials they had ordered too much syrup for. They'd be pushing it until May.

"I don't really like too sweet," the timid young woman ordering responded.

"Oh, perfect. I'll make it for you half sweet then, what size?" Elyse pushed. Nine times out of ten, this worked. Not only did she get her drink specials bonus, she got her line moving. As the young woman agreed to a medium and paid, Elyse gave a tight smile to Peter, a tiny acknowledgement of recognition.

As he stepped up to the counter, Peter hesitated, "Um."

"Can I suggest the chocolate covered cherry latte? It's my absolute favorite." Elyse hardly skipped a beat. It was a cold greeting for someone she had known for five years. But that was Elyse, she never sugar coated anything, aside from lattes. Peter had learned this years ago when he asked her on a date. She'd simply said, "No," and then asked him to cover her Saturday shift because she had a Friday night date.

"No." Peter had a misplaced glee at getting to tell her 'no'. "I have a list," he said loudly. She stared at him silently as he checked his pockets.

"Yo, is that Pete?" Trent popped his head out from behind the espresso machine and stepped towards the register. Peter didn't bother reminding him that he prefers to be called 'Peter' for the hundredth time. It was good enough that he stopped saying P-Man. Peter hardly had to concern himself with what the *baristas* called him. Trent's energy was equal and opposite that of Elyse as he went on. "Where ya been, man? They got me on bar.... alone. Been cranking 'em out and missing you big time."

Peter decided neutral was the correct tone to cancel the out Elyse-Trent duo. "I don't work here anymore."

"You don't.... Nah man, you're pulling my leg."

"Oh you didn't hear?" Elyse said to Trent while looking right at Peter. "Peter walked out of here mid-shift. Quit to go take some fancy job. Working for that Corporate Suit lady he was always hitting on. Veronica something."

"What?! No way!" Trent extended his fist for a bump and Peter obliged. His hand exploded back, but Peter did not reciprocate, recalling a time where he got stuck in a seemingly endless secret handshake with Trent. He had a meeting to get to. "How do I get myself one of those sugar mommas?"

"It's not like that. I'm an Executive Assistant," Peter objected, regretting the fist bump. He didn't need a sugar momma. He had gotten into Colmubia's Business School. "I have an MBA. Almost."

"That's funny. Thought you almost had an MBA when I started working here," Elyse said. She didn't know he'd been booted from CBS because of cannabis or she would have rubbed it in by now.

Trent turned to Elyse. "It's not like it matters, babe." *Babe.* They were *dating* and Peter's sudden disappearance hadn't even been discussed after hours. Proof they were a good match since they were both self-centered. "He's an executive now."

"Right," Elyse let the single word fry so long it was burnt. "The big executive man on the coffee run." The three of them stood in silence until Elyse took the wheel. "Hey, back on bar, Trent."

"Oh right," he said apologetically. He stepped back to the bar. "Rooting for you, Pete."

"Hey." Elyse made Peter flinch. "Order?" She was the only thing about Morning Boost he really missed, and she would've crushed him under the heel of her shoe if she weren't so tiny. She was barely even going to know what she was missing. Peter would move up through the ranks at W.E.E.D. and never come back here for a coffee run again. She didn't matter, he liked older women anyway.

He checked his pockets, this time remembering he was wearing a suit jacket, which held the note. Pulling it out, he begrudgingly ordered the first drink on the list.

"One large hot Chocolate Covered Cherry Latte, extra sweet."

It was two minutes past the scheduled meeting start when Peter awkwardly pushed the glass door open with his butt while balancing a drink carrier plus one extra drink. Notably, none of the executives (who the coffee was for) helped him. They were pre-occupied reviewing the printed pages *he* had dropped off in the meeting room earlier.

Putting the loose coffee in front of Derrick, Peter said, "One chocolate covered cherry latte."

With no hesitation, Derrick asked, "Extra sweet?"

"Yes," Peter affirmed. "Okay, nonfat, sugar free vanilla latte." Maya raised her pen in the air and Peter walked around the table to set the drink down in front of her. "Americano with a splash of oat milk and hazelnut syrup?"

Tara said, "That one is mine." Peter reached across the table and set it down in front of her. She picked it up, warming her hands on it. "Oooh, thank you, Mr. Peter. Exactly what I needed."

He smiled at her kindness. It had been long, thankless morning until now.

"And a plain black coffee," Peter said. Tony reached out and Peter let him grab it from the drink carrier. Looking at the final drink, which was his, he realized he was one short. "I'm sorry, Phil. I didn't get your order."

"He didn't have one," Derrick said. "You can give him the receipt for reimbursement though."

Phil, who had been looking down at the papers and ignoring the room, snapped his head up at the word. "Reimbursement?" He asked; saying it as if he simultaneously hated the word *and* didn't understand it. "We don't reimburse coffee runs. We have a perfectly good coffee machine in the break room." He returned to his papers.

"No, you got Joe to agree that Tiffany shouldn't do coffee runs because she was too busy. Peter wasn't doing anything while Vanessa is gone," Derrick said. Peter wanted to defend himself and point out that he was making copies when Derrick interrupted him to go on the coffee run. But he didn't want to say anything to risk not being reimbursed.

"It is a waste of time and money. Joe and I decided." Phil looked at Derrick over the top of his glasses. "The CTO is in no position to override that."

"The CEO doesn't care what we do. The CFO should have more important things to do than wasting time nickel and diming me," Derrick shot back.

"Gentlemen, as the *COO*, I can break this tie," Tony slid his two cents on the table. Peter had never heard anyone say their title as frequently as the people on this team. "We can all agree that Peter shouldn't pay for *us* to have coffee." Peter was encouraged when he looked around the room to see each person nodding their head lightly. "Phil, you can reimburse him after the meeting."

"Fine." Phil crossed his arms defiantly. "But it's a one-time thing. I won't be doing this every—"

"Enough!" Tony slapped his hand down on the conference table. "We have the most powerful people in the company in this room. Unless a coffee run costs six figures, I don't want to hear about it again."

Peter silently and uncomfortably slid the receipt in front of Phil before taking an empty seat next to Tony.

Tony began the meeting, taking full charge and commanding attention in a way Peter had not seen Vanessa do. There were no further interruptions and, aside from Phil staring daggers at Derrick, everyone faced Tony when they spoke. The judge to which they appealed, sentencing to be decided.

They finished the meeting, which had started late, five minutes early. Tony canceled the remainder of the day's meetings. Peter thought frantically of what was next for him since he was supposed to attend the meetings and take notes all day.

When everyone else cleared out of the room, he approached Tony apprehensively. "Hi, uh, Mr. Caldarelli, sir. Vanessa told me to take notes for the meetings and I don't know what I'm going to tell her when she gets back today. Do you have anything you want me to work on for the day?"

"Of course I do!" Tony was far more jovial than he had been all morning. "I was hoping you would accompany me.

We have some essential networking and facetime with various shareholders scheduled for today. I'm sure that Vanessa won't mind. In fact, I'm positive she would want you to observe as her eyes and ears." He clapped Peter on the back. "I've got an extra polo for you. You're going to want something a little less stiff in the arms than this jacket."

———————

The rest of the day flew by for Peter. He'd had no idea what to expect. It turned out to be a day full of golf, lunch, and early afternoon cocktails. Peter quietly observed. He was introduced as an 'executive in training' which was a generous interpretation of 'executive assistant'. Though the day consisted of eating and drinking and jokes while hitting balls, it felt like his most important day with W.E.E.D. He tried to memorize names, faces, and titles. He searched for them on LinkedIn throughout the day but most of them didn't have profiles. He used to think having a strong profile indicated power and would get you the best positions. Online, Vanessa had connections and endorsements and an article featuring her, pinned to the top. These men had none of that, barely any footprint online at all.

But in person their presence was… palpable.

It wasn't the attractive and charismatic Chief Executive Officer who held the power. It was this calculating man who knew the most important people.

Peter would be like Tony.

19

My plane touched down in Sacramento before noon, but by the time I had gotten my luggage and ordered a car home, I was too tired to consider making it to the office for the tail end of meetings. I desperately need to shower Vegas off of me. Though I had rinsed after the hot tub, I hadn't washed my hair, despite the regrettable unintentional contact with the public hot tub water. I need an everything shower. And an entire bottle of wine to wash my brain after the bizarre conversation with Collin.

Last night, I came down from my high instantly following our interaction. Collin's words were a slap in the face, unpleasantly sobering only after I heard them. If only I hadn't been high in the moment, I could have made more sense of it. As I replayed the conversation all last night, fiction and reality blurred. It felt like Collin was telling me to leave Joey. Which was absurd. He had always rooted for us. He and Joey were so close that Collin and I had become friends... I thought.

I wish Joey were here to hold me. I texted him the details of my flight. Maybe he'll surprise me when I get home. He'll propose again, this time with a date for the wedding. It was an exciting daydream. As we approached my little townhouse, butterflies filled my stomach at the sight of a vehicle parked in my driveway. I let myself dream for two more milliseconds.

It wasn't Joey's sporty red car.

It was an imposing black SUV.

I had been eager to get home and peel off my bra; still sweaty from sitting on the tarmac, where the air wasn't circulating and the heat from the Vegas sun pushed in through the windows with no means of escape. Now I wanted to turn around. I didn't want to know what this man in the unmarked car had just stepped out to tell me.

I'd already paid for my ride. I could grab my luggage and run inside as soon as we stopped. I had my flats on in case any airport creeps needed a quick dodge. I'd have to test my juking skills with a carry-on and wheeling luggage if I was going to make it past the cop in my driveway.

I haven't done anything wrong. Why is he here and why am I nervous?

By the time I opened the door to get out, the cop had already made it to my curbside drop off location.

"Thanks," I said to the driver, not bothering to flash him a smile. If he hadn't made me wait fifteen minutes for pickup, calling me and claiming I wasn't where my pinned location was, I might not be in this situation. I walked around to grab my luggage from the trunk.

"Can I give you a hand?" the cop pretended to ask, while grabbing the luggage prematurely.

"Thanks," I said begrudgingly. He hadn't introduced himself. He didn't have to. He was the coppiest looking cop I had ever seen. He had the coppiest haircut and the most cop shiny black shoes with black casual cop cargo pants and tan polo shirt. This was not an outfit that would look good on anyone else, or him. Even though he was relatively fit, the tucking in of the polo shirt drew the eye to his midsection in an unflattering way.

He was only a couple of inches taller than me, but without my heels on, I felt even smaller. He started to wheel the luggage up the driveway. "Are you, uh, Ms. Vanessa Sorella?" he asked. Another non-question since he must know.

"What?" I stalled. It was believable that I wouldn't have heard him, the bag being wheeled *was* noisy. I immediately felt irritated with him. He came to *my house* and asked who I was before introducing himself, pretending to help me as a guise to approach me... It's on wheels for goodness' sake. Not like someone helped me *in*to the car with my luggage. "Sorry, who were you saying you are?"

He stopped and turned to face me. "I'm Detective Hernandez. Do you have a moment to speak Ms. Sorella?" So he did know who I was.

"I'm on my way in to change and then off to a meeting. Is this urgent?" I spoke with confidence. But I was hyper-aware of the fact that my bag and hair both reeked of W.E.E.D.

"I won't take long," he reached into his pocket as he spoke. If I had been the cop and *he* had done that without warning, I probably would have shot him. This must be a baby detective, new to interacting with the public without a uniform to hide behind. He showed me a clear plastic bag labeled 'evidence'. "Does this seem familiar to you?" It contained a shiny white bag with a zip top. A scent proof bag for cannabis.

"Yes, it looks like an exit bag that dispensaries give you product in." I didn't realize I had been clenching my fists which I relaxed, relieved when my nails stopped digging into my palms. It occurred to me that I had been worried this was about Joey. Though no one should know he and I were together, I hadn't heard from him since before I left for Vegas. I was stupidly paranoid because this man was just here to talk about my job.

"From one of *your* dispensaries?"

"From most dispensaries. We all order the same ones. Cheap. In bulk. From China," I couldn't quite put my finger on what he was accusing me of. But he had shown up without warning.

He looked at the bag and pointed to a smaller piece of paper inside. "Says it's from you." I squinted closer at it and could see my name written on it. "Why would this be at the house of a murder victim?"

Holy fucking shit!

I ran through a list of names of who might be dead. It started with Joey, the love of my life. It ended with Joey. There's no one else that makes sense. "I have no idea what or *who* you're talking about. It would be best for us both if you just got to the point." My voice shook. Please don't let Joey be dead.

He looked unblinkingly into my eyes. He formed the name with his mouth slowly, letting his teeth pull on his lip as he said, "Frank Miller."

Stupidly, I laughed out of surprise. That was the last name I expected. "Frank wasn't killed! He died of being old. He's been dying for years. Surprised it wasn't sooner." Everyone expects old men to die. Who would bother *killing* him?

"Hmm. Not quite soon enough for you?" Detective Hernandez asked.

I gathered myself. I need to take this seriously. "I am as shocked as anyone would be to hear that Frank died of anything other than natural causes, but I have no idea why that package—" I cut myself off as I realized. *Peter* delivered it. "That package was part of a care package sent to Frank's wife. His widow. *After* he died."

"True," said the little snake apparently trying to catch me in a lie. "Mrs. Miller said you had a regular habit of sending these care packages. Through your assistant, Tiffany."

Peter *had* said he got the order from Tiffany's notes, but I never sent her. Detective Hernandez already made up his mind about that. I need to show him how silly he's being. "Are you here to arrest me for drug trafficking? If this is about providing cannabis to legal adults, you're going to have a lot of *CEOs* to question." Doesn't hurt to remind him the power of my title.

"The state may have a couple of questions about that. I'm only concerned about the tincture under Tiffany's name. Seems it had more than THC in it."

It took everything in me to keep from looking mortified. Whatever Tiffany did, I need to distance myself from her. "Tiffany doesn't work for us anymore. Maybe you should go harass her." I spoke placidly, but I was exhausted and irritated. I haven't done *anything*. "Come to think of it, it's wild you would just show up here unannounced. Without so much as showing me your badge."

He pulled his badge out, showing it to me while responding. "You see, I spoke to your assistant first. He told us you took a spontaneous trip to Vegas and you were supposed to be back in the office this afternoon. My partner went there to meet you, but I had a hunch. We asked about Tiffany Miller. Your human resources department seems to recall you and she had a nasty few days working together. Right before she stopped showing up."

"She *quit*. She was... disgruntled. Right before her grandfather - that's right *her grandfather,* whom she also hated, was murdered!" I almost shouted.

"We know Tiffany was related to Frank. Which is why we were already looking into her. But she disappeared. Didn't pay April's rent with her apartment and left behind all her belongings," he paused. He was trying to bait me into confessing or something. I let him sit. Until he said, "We located her. Found her body the same day Frank died. Only just identified her on Monday. She was already dead almost a week before he died. Disappeared the same day she and you got into it. *Everyone* thought she quit because of you."

"This is.... preposterous." Preposterous enough he had me using a word I hadn't uttered allowed possibly ever. I steeled my nerves. I wasn't ready to fully comprehend. Tiffany's body? Frank's murder? Nonsense words. "It is very sad. But I don't see what this has to do with me."

"Maybe this will help you understand." Hernandez had his phone out and took a step towards me, showing me the screen. His foot had been holding the wheely luggage in place. It rolled down the driveway, hitting the bottom and tipping over. The comedic timing was lost on me as I stared at the screen with a security camera quality picture. It was zoomed in on a grainy little red car. "This is outside of Tiffany's apartment. The driver pulls up, Tiffany gets in, they drive away. Maybe if *the driver*" —he said these two words like they were our secret— "could tell us when they came back, we could clear this all up."

Joey... you piece of shit. I'm gonna kill you. "When you find them, let me know what *the driver* says. I'm sorry I couldn't be of more assistance." I walked towards my fallen luggage. I picked up the hefty bag by the side handle and carried it: let him see how strong I am. I deliberately went around the other side of his vehicle to my front door, opposite of where he was standing. "If there's nothing else then I'll be settling in for the day," I called.

He came around the front of his truck to intercept me, "I thought you had a meeting to get to."

"I've just heard some shocking news. They'll understand if I need the afternoon off."

"Of course," he said, almost like a normal human. He stepped closer to me and handed me a ragged looking business card. Guess the Sacramento police department doesn't have much of a print budget these days. I shoved it unceremoniously into my pocket. "Call me if you remember anything. And maybe no more spur of the moment flights, hmm?"

He made me feel guilty, like I should apologize. But I haven't done *anything* wrong. He's not arresting me. He's expecting me to do as I'm told and to turn my boyfriend in. I walked my bulky bag to the door and called to him, "I have a business to run."

I'm the mother fucking CEO.

20

Every single one of the Caldarelli men is a liar, a cheat, and a coward. I called Joey all afternoon and the next day, he never answered.

Collin had the nerve to text me on Thursday:

You all right? You coming in?

No, I'm not coming in, you asshole. This company refuses to treat me like the CEO. They either kiss my butt only to mock me when I turn my back or they skip the first step and mock me to my face. The only thing real about my title is the paycheck.

I get paid whether I show up or not. So, on Thursday, I did not.

I deserved a day off. I needed a month off after what that Detective told me, but at least I can have a day. I wanted to connect with Joey, have him clear everything up. He doesn't have to explain what his car was doing at Tiffany's house to the police. But I deserve to know.

I can't imagine Joey as a cheater. I *had* imagined him as something worse. Before I even knew Frank was murdered, I wondered how Joey had been so prepared to fill his role. And about the voicemail; was Frank's call that night worth killing over?

I've witnessed Joey lying. So smooth, so believable. I always knew when he was lying and tried to understand how others couldn't see through it. But he never lied to me.... said every woman. I know it sounds foolish, but he's probably avoiding my call because he doesn't want to lie to me. Like I said, he's a coward.

This is how my thoughts ping-ponged through my head all day on Thursday. No, not ping-pong. It was a more treacherous pattern than that. It Frogger-ed through my head. Occasionally being smooshed by a truck or eaten by an alligator. Sometimes successfully evading both by riding on a log solemnly off screen into oblivion before I could encourage it to progress. No one thought prevailed and my head was an exhausting mess.

I took an infused gummy midway through the day to calm my mind. It glued my body to the couch while my thoughts proceeded anyway flashing before my eyes like a pre-programmed brainwashing campaign. It convinced me that my fiancé was a liar, a cheater, a murderer. Then it would erase those thoughts by reminding me that Joey was sweet, an amazing lover, an ambitious businessman. But those facts did not truly override the others. Joey could be a wonderful fiancé and also a bad man. I just need him to talk to me.

I had to go to work today. To show my face at the office and report back on my amazing plan to rally the troops at our new facilities on 420. There, I hoped to escape the thoughts of Joey.

Unfortunately, the Caldarellis surround me. I work with two of his brothers and carry around a piece of his dad in my purse. They are a part of my life. There was no avoiding Joey, but I have a weekend ahead of me after today. That's a reassuring thought.

Passing by Peter's desk, I see his monitor is on and he has his work bag on the ground. He's nowhere nearby. Gives me time to catch up on my emails. None were coming through my phone while I was traveling. I unlocked my office door.

Straight away, I realized things were missing. The office didn't have much, but now it was even more bare. Since nothing was mine, I couldn't piece together exactly what was gone. For sure some pictures, a lamp, a small side table. Good. Tony must have taken what he wanted. Next, I can get rid of this stupid desk and chair and make it *my* office.

I successfully loaded my email. I had only received two; one being Wednesday's meeting minutes. The second was a 'memo' from Phil about a moratorium on individual reimbursements until the policy could be re-evaluated.

My phone wasn't having issues loading emails: there were none. Four business days away and no one needed anything. My previous jobs I would have a full inbox if I had so much as left early for the day. Now that I'm the CEO, shouldn't they need me more? To make decisions, resolve disputes, lead them.

My office door, which I had left partially ajar, suddenly clicked closed. I heard the scratch of a key being inserted, locking the handle from the outside. My breathing intensified. My heart raced, pumping blood everywhere except for my half-functional brain. I panicked, feeling trapped. Who had trapped me? Was the detective here to lock me away?

No. Of course not. That is not how doors work. The after-effects of yesterday's edible still had me paranoid. I strode to the door, unlocking it and pulling it open. Poking my head out cautiously, I saw Peter looking at his monitor. I stepped all the way out, the clack of my heel on the floor enough to have Peter jerk his head to me.

His eyes widened and he grabbed at his heart. "You scared me!" he narrated needlessly, looking like he'd just seen a ghost.

"Did you... lock my office door while I was in there?"

He looked behind me at the door, only now realizing where I had come from. "I didn't know you were here! Thought it had been left open again."

Again? I wondered. "Thank you," I said reflexively. "Where did you get a key?"

He reached into his bag, which was under his standing desk. "Found them on the desk. I think they were Tiffany's.

There's a little *T* here." He showed me the ivory chess piece engraved with *TC* at the bottom. A pawn. "Did you need them?"

I thought for a moment. "No, that's fine. You can lock my office if it's open when I'm not here." I turned back to my door until a thought struck me. "Did someone try to go in there while I was gone?"

"Uh yeah. Someone from the state came by. He asked about it but Tony said not to let him in since there's no paperwork in there," Peter answered too hastily to be as innocent as he pretended.

"What did the state want?"

"He mostly spoke to Tony. But he asked for all of Tiffany's files and stuff. It was an audit I guess. He asked for your cell number too, but I told him you would absolutely not let me give that out." He puffed his chest out, proud of himself.

Irked, I said, "I meant not to give my number to random salespeople. You can give it to an auditor." I must have been silent long enough to concern him. I was tempted to reassure him. Nervous men stress me out. But I need to know what I'm working with. "Show me the files the man looked at."

"I can't. He copied some or took the original. But Tony had me shred some and he took the others."

I looked into his eyes. He avoided contact. "You didn't think that was weird? That you were asked to shred things?"

"No," he shook his head and shrugged his shoulders. "Once the state had the copies, Tony said we don't have to keep them anymore. *He* was cool with it."

"Right," I looked in his eyes with determination. This time: contact. He didn't look nervous. Just oblivious. Without another word I twirled on my heel and returned to my office, closing and locking the door behind me.

I heard a small regretful groan. Peter had more to say. He can keep it to himself. The state auditors are the least of my worries. But I made a mental note anyway. Next chance I get, I'm going through Tiffany's computer.

I somehow have no tasks again today. I pull open my banking app. I must have an important job here. For the second time now, I've received my biweekly paycheck direct deposited. It's huge. Ten times the size of my paycheck plus bonuses when I worked for my... Eugene. Practically everything from my first check still sat there. I'd once had credit card and student loan debt, but I paid that all off working with Joey. I thought about buying a new car, a bigger house maybe. But in my heart, I'm still hopeful Joey and I will buy one together.

Since he hasn't been working and getting paid, I thought he might need me. But now, as he makes God-knows-what as treasurer plus whatever job he and Angelo are working on, it feels like he doesn't need me. Ignoring me for almost a week now, maybe he doesn't want me either.

I have to get a reply from him. Just in case Detective Hernandez is watching his phone, I've been cryptic in my messaging. Calling and leaving no voicemail. Texting a simple:

Call me back, please.

Since that's not working, I need to say something that couldn't be used against him, but would also invoke a response. 'We need to talk' wouldn't do much. 'We need to talk about Tiffany' wouldn't be easy to explain to a judge. I settled on:

We need to talk about your brother.

And hit send.

As I waited on his reply, I decided to kill time with *Joe's Big Book of Hypocritical Advice.* The further I got in the book, the less wordy he became. Maybe that was a sign he knew he needed to get everything out before he offed himself.

Once you have properly vetted the loyalty of those around you, it is time to determine if culling is necessary. If you run a tight ship, it may not be. Simple nudges in the proper direction will keep you from the need to cut off any heads. If the team is properly trained and confident, they should be able to fully function without your direct oversight.

Unfortunately, if a lean team looking to trim fat finds none amongst themselves, they may instead aim to cut off the head. They cannot survive without the head, without you, but they do not possess the wisdom to know that. You will need to be one step ahead of them. Find the person who challenges you most. Are they truly competent? Or is this just bravado?

The one thing they need to be reminded of is that every single one of them is replaceable. The one challenging you the most will likely not be a gall bladder or spare kidney. They may be an arm or a leg. You must be willing to deal with any attempted usurpers immediately regardless of the rank they hold.

Though I would like to believe I've left you a solid team, you will be challenged. Luckily, I won't be going far. We can discuss these issues as they come up. But make no mistake, as my son you will be pushed and challenged. You must be ready to ride out and meet them, ending any rebellion before it can begin.

-Caldarelli, Joe* (2027). *Joe's First Ninety Days*

*Found deceased by his assistant who herself was later found dead, possibly at the hands of one of Joe's sons.

His son? *Joe's first 90 days* as in **Joey's** *first 90 days*? That can't be it. It's written to the CEO.

Me.

Joey said it was always supposed to be me. Joe's confidence in me is everything. That's how I know I'm supposed to be a great CEO. Because he said so. He never told me. He told *Joey*.

Or not.

But.... it makes no difference. Everything Joe wrote here wasn't some pep talk for himself. It was instructions for his son. To do everything he was too big of a coward to do. I've done all those things though. I told people 'no'. I went out in the field and showed everyone what it means to be a leader. And if I have to, I'll do something Joe never did despite all his big talk. I'll get rid of any appendages that don't work properly. Even if it turns out to be one of Joe's sons.

I know in my gut how to run this company. I don't need some dead old man to tell me that. My instinct tells me that after a big holiday week, it's time to rally the troops. A team lunch to discuss successes and failures. It's ten o'clock now, just enough time to pull this together. Anything to distract me from Joey.

I stood up abruptly, feeling invigorated. Look at me pep-talking *myself*. This lesson can go in my self-help book since it's all about doing things *my way*.

I realized after trying to open my door that it was locked again. My heart thudded, trapped like a little bunny. *I locked it, so I can just unlock it.* I did, swinging it open with enough umph that papers on Peter's desk fluttered. He turned to me.

"Peter!" I said too loudly. Then, in a normal volume, "I want you to order lunch for the executive team at noon. You're invited too, for notes. I think Nick's Deli delivers."

The blood drained from his face. Was he gluten intolerant? Afraid of phone calls? Was Nick his long-lost father?

"I can't. Tee time is in an hour," he said.

Was he... British? "Tea Time?" I asked.

"Yes. It's work-related. Tony said—" Peter mumbled but I heard nothing after *Tony said*. Tony the spleen.

Of course. Peter was wearing a polo shirt and business casual pants. He had worn a suit *every* day since he started. Until now.

Gone for a few days and Tony had already wormed his way in to take over my assistant. Peter was lucky I hired him. I can't let him be my weak link.

"Oh that's right." I was silently fuming. "Tony *asked me* about taking you golfing. Great opportunity for networking and discussing business. Have the notes for me by Monday morning," I lied easily, taking back the narrative.

"Yes!" He was too eager to please. I walked past him. "Have a nice weekend."

"You too," I said without looking back. I'll deal with him on Monday. I kept walking past the conference room, turning right, then right again. "Good morning, Tara." I almost bumped into her. She and Maya were standing in front of their offices, next to the cubicles. I caught a glimpse of the back of Phil, hovering by the cubicles for the finance team but chose not to acknowledge him. "Just the person I was looking for." Not lying, improvising. I'm 'Yes-And'-ing the hell out of this mess.

"Good morning to you." Tara eyed me with equal parts concern and suspicion.

"I was hoping you could help me arrange an executive team lunch for today."

"Today?" She repeated. "Maya and I were discussing our typical Friday lunch plans. We grab lunch together and connect on our department's needs."

"Perfect!" I said enthusiastically. "Where were you going? We can all tag along to your work lunch."

Maya's eyes bulged and she lightly nudged Tara from behind. As if I wouldn't see, used to disguising subtle clues from a nearsighted octogenarian without the social skills of a woman. "I'm not sure they can seat so many of us on such short notice."

"Peter and Tony can't make it, so it'll just be six. I don't know many places that can't handle six people midday, even on short notice."

"They are very tiny," Maya chimed in. "A small local place."

"Go ahead and call them and let me know." I called her bluff. "Or I have a few suggestions." Both women were visibly uncomfortable, and it reminded me of my intention. It was supposed to be positive. "I think it'll run long; so we can call it a day after lunch." Maya's face lit up, but I still hadn't hooked Tara. "Besides, if we go out as a team, we can have Phil reimburse us." This had Tara on my side, which was surprising considering her salary. But who didn't love a free meal?

From behind me, Phil cleared his throat. He was practically on top of me. "What exactly am I reimbursing?" Phil asked.

Nice to see you too, Phil. "Executive lunch. Clear your schedule. Noonish work for everyone?" I said, looking between them.

"No," Phil said plainly.

"I'm flexible. Eleven... one?" I offered, trying to goad a positive response out of him.

"No, we won't be reimbursing any more pointless expenses."

"Excuse me?" I said, loudly enough to get attention. I couldn't help but notice the cubicle workers turning their heads or poking them out above their little boxes.

Phil, speech at the ready, was looking only at me. "I have made it very clear in several memorandums, the most recent sent earlier this very week. There will be no more unnecessary spending. Reimbursement of these petty expenses may seem small but they add up. I haven't even factored in you and Collin galivanting around Las Vegas. I hardly think an executive 'fun' lunch is an appropriate use of funds." He put actual air quotes around *fun*.

I held back my scoff. "I am not asking your permission for—"

Tara cut me off. "My office is right here, maybe we should step inside." Notably, she had interrupted me and not Phil.

"I'm fine here," I insisted, now hyper aware of the crowd we had drawn. I saw Collin round the corner and freeze just behind Phil. Better make this count. "This is not a *fun* lunch; it's for team building. I expect you there."

"I don't have time for your silly lunch. I don't need team building. I've been doing this job longer than you've been alive." Phil's voice grew louder, "And whether they'll say it to your face or not, we all know *we're*" −he gestured to the other executives− "all going to outlast you."

We'll see about that.

"I don't doubt your capability," I said, calmly. "But as the CEO, I am capable of deciding how we spend our money."

"No you aren't!" Phil erupted. "I am the CFO and I control the purse strings. I have told you time and again that we have a cash flow issue, which you have been too stupid to comprehend."

"Phil, you should−" Tara began.

He ignored her and continued, "Let me make it clear to you. This company will do what I say when it comes to all things finance. You will stay out of my way. I am here because I am competent, I know what I'm doing. You..." Phil was red in the face and his eyes were wild. "You are here because you got down on your knees," he leaned in closer and said quietly, "and laid on your back." His smirk made it clear that he thought he was clever.

Tara gasped. Collin's mouth hung open. Phil glanced around, trying to make eye contact with his male employees. They quickly looked away. Phil's smile faded and he looked back at me. Everyone will recall how even my voice is, how reasonable I am. Get the fucking tourniquet ready... no time for an anesthetic before this amputation. "You can go home Phil. You're suspended without pay, pending an investigation."

Phil stared at me. He opened his mouth, then closed it. He did that several times. He looked like one of those singing fish where the batteries were low and no sound was coming out. He finally settled on, "You can't terminate me. Not without the board."

"I haven't. We'll be doing an investigation during your suspension. We'll let them decide whether or not to terminate you," I assured him, and every onlooker. I smiled as I said, "But we'll see what *Joey* thinks." I wish I knew how to wink without looking like an idiot. I settled on shooing him away with my hand. He stomped off around the corner towards his office.

The lack of professionalism was apparent in all the cubicle workers. Either it was the cannabis industry or the fact that they were young, but they did not possess the self-awareness to pretend like they weren't eavesdropping. Works for me.

"Tara." I stepped closer to her. "I'm sorry, but it looks like you'll have a lot of reports to take for the remainder of the day to help with the investigation. Please feel free to order yourself some lunch in, we'll reimburse it. Maya, let's grab lunch in about an hour, we can discuss the new plan for the Puff Puff Pass."

I turned away not waiting for their reply. My message was clear and I was confident they would each do as they were told. I started walking back towards my office, passing by Collin. He reached out his hand as if to grab me by the arm. Something on my face must have told him not to and he withdrew.

"I don't think this is a good idea," Collin whispered.

I pulled out my phone looking down at it when I replied, "If I want advice, I'll ask a friend."

Leaving him behind, I read Joey's text.

Date night tonight? My place.

I looked up just in time to see Phil, heading towards the stairs behind me. He glared at me and we played a game of chicken. He walked straight towards me veering off at the last second as he realized I wasn't budging.

I text back:

Get wine.

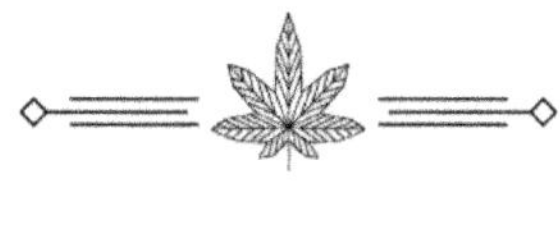

21

He did not get wine. He did, however, make us some Whiskey Old Fashioneds, because it's my favorite. Except it isn't my favorite. But one too many times I went along with it, even though I had never once said it was and I had never once asked for it. But I *had* asked for wine, which he did not get.

Aside from straight whiskey, an Old Fashioned is *his* favorite. I could correct him. But it was more convenient to drink the one he made as soon as I walked in the door. I finished it so fast that the second one was made before the ice from the first had time to melt.

It had been an abnormal Friday. Lunch with Maya was cordial. Partway through I got a surprise text from Tony congratulating me on the 'courage to dismiss Phil', lauding it as the right move; as if I needed his approval. It *was* nice to get. The day's events pushed me to drink even more of this not-my-favorite-drink.

As I stood in the kitchen barefoot, sipping the third drink and swaying lightly; Joey was starting on a late dinner. He was wearing a white undershirt that he had had on under a button up when I arrived, and some olive green slacks he hadn't even bothered to take all the way off before he pulled out his dick and asked me to suck it. He stood there drinking his whiskey, his attitude as business casual as his clothes, while I got on my knees on the kitchen tiles, doing exactly as he wanted because it was easier that way. He had whispered to me that he wanted to finish on my tits, but I swallowed instead. That way I didn't have to clean up *his* mess.

Now, cock away and presumably soft, he was humming as he cooked. Some old man song by Sinatra, even though that was too old even for Joey. My mother was his age and all her musical taste came from the '80s. He always hummed or sang a few lines when he thought we'd had mind blowing sex. He fancied himself a sexy suave ladies' man. Except he'd just shoved his dick in my mouth and hadn't even bothered to touch me.

It didn't matter. Even if he had tried − at all −I probably couldn't get there. I am running through my head all the things I need to ask him. The alcohol will give me courage; but too much and I'll forget what to say. Or what to do with the information if I get any answers. Joey always knew what to say. Hopefully, that means he's honest. It is easy to remember something if it's true.

I know I can't ask outright if he killed Tiffany, or was sleeping with her. Let's see what he'll volunteer.

"Detective Hernandez came to my house the other day," I said, like I was continuing an earlier conversation. He might not know the difference thanks to his cooking distraction.

"Oh?" Joey said; his back to me as he peeled some garlic. Not *who's Detective Hernandez?*

"He showed me a picture of what looked like your *car*." I spoke with a rising inflection, even though I had not asked a question. He smashed a garlic clove with the flat side of his knife. "I couldn't figure out why he was showing it to me. But I think it *was* your car." I may be tipsy, but my lack of detail is intentional.

He stopped, and looked up, like the answer was written on the cabinets above him. "You mean outside of that dead girl's place?" He knew exactly what I meant. He turned only a little, his face now in profile. "I didn't know either. We checked the dates. Turns out I wasn't even in town then. My car was with Tony's mechanic when I went down to LA. Remember?"

Right back to mincing.

I leaned forward slightly onto the island which was between us. I didn't remember, I wasn't given the date of the picture, but it made so much sense. Relief washed over me. "Yes! That's right. Is this something you can prove?"

"I did. Cleared it right up. They took my car in for a search."

I sighed. "Thank god! I'm so glad they didn't find anything."

"I didn't say that." He still wasn't facing me, but he had set the knife down. He put both of his hands on the counter. "They still have my car. Since Monday. All I told them was that *I* wasn't here."

"Monday? But they asked me about it on Wednesday. You said it wasn't your car?"

He turned around then. "My car *was* there. They must've asked you because—" he took a big breath in "—you're the only other person with a key."

"I've never even driven your car! You gave me that key for emergencies," I said. "How would they know about it? Did you send them to talk to me?"

"Not exactly. But they asked about significant others, other people who might have a key." I must have looked furious because he folded his arms in a defensive stance. "Hey, what did you want me to do, Nessa? They were questioning me for murder of some girl I don't even know."

"I don't know, maybe fucking call me?" I slammed my empty glass on the counter, too close to the edge. It fell, landing hard on the floor. The thin upper part of the glass shattered, the heavy bottom bouncing onto my right foot. "Shit!" I said, startled. I stepped forward losing my balance; landing on a piece of the glass with my full weight. I reflexively jerked back and grabbed my foot, which made me even more unbalanced. Joey ran around the counter grabbing me. I uttered a chorus of 'I'm sorry' and 'Thank you' on repeat until he helped me to his living room chair. I added in some additional 'sorry's' as I noticed the trail of blood, dark red drops appearing on the off-white carpet.

I sat propped up with my back against the arm of the couch, legs up and a paper towel under my foot while Joey got bandages and other first aid. He cleaned my foot and put a large bandage under my front left toe where the cut had only just stopped bleeding.

He was actually taking care of me. It was a sobering moment. Until he handed me a freshly made Old Fashioned. I didn't know how to continue, so Joey, sipping on his own glass, started.

He sat on the couch, lifting my feet into his lap, "I've been avoiding you, sorry if that was confusing. When that detective came around asking about Frank and then Tiffany... it was so messed up. Why would someone think *I* did that? The only other person with the keys was you... I guess I panicked."

My mind went to the kitchen tiles where my knees had been earlier, now covered in blood and glass. He let me suck his cock while thinking I was a murderer. "You thought I killed her?"

"No... Maybe," he looked down, then right at me. "You thought *I* killed her?" Oh God, I sucked his cock while thinking he was a murderer.

He held my gaze. Inexplicably, I laughed. He laughed. I laughed harder, the ice in my drink bumping against the edge of my glass, to remind me it was there. I composed myself and took a sip. It tasted better than the last one. I shouldn't drink this. A couple of glasses of wine over a few hours and I would've been able to drive home. This one drink mandates that I'll be staying the night.

"Who else could have driven your car?" I asked, relieved that we were both trying to solve this puzzle.

"*I* was in LA," he shrugged. "*It* was with the mechanic."

I rolled that around with the ice in my glass. How would the mechanic know Tiffany? Her boyfriend? Unlikely. The detective didn't say *when* she disappeared, but the last time I saw her, it seemed like she and *Tony* were flirting in the copy room and then leaving work together. "*Tony's* Mechanic," I said.

"I always use Tony's guy."

I swallowed. "Last time I saw Tiffany, it seemed like she and Tony were dating."

"Ha!" he guffawed. "Tony doesn't stand a chance with an attractive girl like that. She was a real—" he stopped himself, at risk of choking on his own foot. It made me question how easily I had ruled out Joey's presence at Tiffany's house. How certain was I that Tony was the brother sleeping with her? "Tony's not like that. He's a real asshole but he never gets involved in anything shady. He would never... He's just a little mama's boy. I didn't even tell him half the shit I have going on. He'd go run and tell."

"What do you mean? Tell who?" I asked.

"Look, the point is, Tony's too good for his own good. Other than, and I can't emphasize this enough, how big of an asshole he is," Joey said. He patted my legs, so I lifted them up. "I'm gonna grab another drink, you want one?"

His glass was already empty. "No, thanks though."

Joey stood and walked to the kitchen. I heard him cleaning up the glass and mess. I wanted to help but sitting feels nice. And I have to keep things on track. My brain is getting fuzzy. I have so many things I was supposed to talk to him about. I collected my thoughts.

I called out to him, "Tony's not as good as you remember."

"What?" he called back.

"Tony's not a little goodie two shoes anymore." I was louder and confident.

"What makes you say that?" Joey said from behind the kitchen wall. It was one of those *open* houses. But it was massive. Even just a room away, you had to shout.

I hesitated trying to think of how to broach the sensitive topic, but my tact had gone down with the second Old

Fashioned. "Pills. He had lots of pills. Just rolling all around."

Joey stepped back in the room. "Rolling.... like ecstasy?"

"No!" I laughed. "The bottle kind, like from doctors." English was starting to feel like my second language as I struggled for words.

"You mean prescription?" he pulled.

"Yes!" I pointed at him with my glass holding hand, extending it towards him. He took that to mean I wanted more and poured whiskey straight into my glass before I could pull it away.

"So, he has prescription pills. From a doctor. Kind of proves my point that he only does as he's told," Joey added, coming around the couch. I sat up. Letting my feet dangle made my left foot ache.

"No, not *a* doctor. *Lots of doctors.* Same pills different doctors. That's-not-right." Everything started blending into one word.

Joey was staring intensely at me. "What were the pills?"

My head lolled not wanting to stay upright on my neck. I let it rest on the back of the couch. "Not ones I've had. They had little warnings like : *caution may make you sleepy, or addicted.* There were four bottles, all the same."

"I need to see them." Joey was suddenly very intense. "Now!"

"I gave them back. I don't want *those* drugs," I was being playful. "I only deal pot."

Joey reached over and turned my head to him. "This is important, Vanessa. Think, were they opioids?"

"Well duh! Hydro…Something like that. He was hiding them. But it was a lot of them. I don't think they're all for him, He's not gonna OD or anything." Joey is focusing on the wrong part. I need him to understand. "He's probably taking some. Maybe selling them too. The point is: he's no law-abiding citizen, okay?"

"I'm calling him." He stood up again, heading to the kitchen and his phone. All the up and down was making me nauseated. I decided to stand and follow him. My foot throbbed when I put weight on it.

By the time I made it to the kitchen, Joey's obnoxiously loud phone volume allowed me to hear the tail end of Tony's outgoing voicemail. "Call me back. I know you know what happened with Pops." Joey hissed into his phone.

"Joey, what's going on?" I blinked at the bright kitchen lights trying to process what he was saying.

"You think my brother is a murderer?" He gestured at me with his phone. "Then, let's find out."

"No! No, I wasn't saying that." Well, *I was saying that*, but I didn't believe it. Anything to believe Joey wasn't involved. He was looking down at his phone, I verbally pawed at him for attention. "We shouldn't jump to conclusions. But it wouldn't hurt for Detective Jiminez – Hermanez? To have all the information." I got closer to Joey, and stroked the arm that held his phone. "My love—"

His eyes flashed up at me. "Why is Phil texting me?" Joey said dangerously.

Phil. That little punk ass bitch couldn't even wait until Monday to cry to daddy Joey. Fine. Two can play at that game and only one of us gives amazing blow jobs.

"Baby," I said, breathily. "Come on. Let's go back to the couch. Finish these drinks," I lightly clinked my glass on his and took a long drink, making eye contact as I did. "It's our date night and I haven't gotten to be with you all week." I winked at him.

"You're drunk," he said with disgust. *You've been making me drinks instead of dinner.* He turned from me reading his texts. I *am* drunk, but I finished the whiskey anyway. It wasn't as good as the Old Fashioned so I downed it quickly. Joey slammed his down as well, not tasting it. He clicked his tongue. "What did you do?"

"What did *I* do? Phil, he-he was disrespecting me! In front of everyone" I defended.

Joey set his phone down hard enough I worried he may have broken the screen. "You got your feelings hurt and decided: 'hey fuck Joey and everything he's worked for.' So you blow it all up?"

"This wasn't about *you*. Phil was challenging *me*. I had to do something. He was making everybody think that I didn't earn my title. That it just got handed to me. Like my hard work doesn't even matter."

"Oh, enlighten me. How did you *earn* that CEO title?"

I paused. I know there is an answer but my mouth struggled to form it. "By my knowledge. My experience. And Joe said so too. He knew I was the best for the job. He said I was intriguing and fascinating."

"Pops thought you were a silly little girl. He was *intrigued* by you because you look like a younger version of his wife. Before she got crazy. He didn't want to make you CEO. He wanted to rail you," Joey spat.

"Yeah? Then why didn't he make you CEO?"

Joey shook his head. "Because I told him no. I'm not going to captain a sinking ship. He thought I could save it. Screw that."

Flabbergasted, I choked out, "You sent me to go down with it instead?"

"No, Nessa, not like that." He rolled his eyes but seemed apologetic. "I was going to take you with me. I needed someone in the role who would do what I needed without question." He was saying it sweetly. It went down bitter. "And I *need* Phil back in there. I want you to fix this Monday morning. Better yet, call him tomorrow. Give him the week off, *with pay* and let everyone think he was suspended. No one will question you again."

I was already shaking my head. "No, *you* talk to the board on Monday. I want him out of there."

"We can't do that," he reached out and grabbed my hands. I let them hang there loosely. "Nessa, I really want to marry you. In a few years, we'll have everything we need. We can let W.E.E.D. slip under in the rear view, and we can be far away. Then, we can have each other forever."

It was like his proposal speech. It still made me want to cry. Except now it also made me want to scream.

"No. I know what I'm doing. I have to do this or no one will ever listen to me. And I don't want him there, he sucks."

Joey dropped my arms. I didn't stop them and they swung back hanging by my sides, like dead weight. "Don't be stupid," he said. "You are going to mess up the deal with Angelo."

"Angelo's loan?" I scoffed. "You think I care about some loan? I'm running a business. Whether you or Joe ever believed in me. I don't care. I'm good at this." Out loud but to myself I assured, "I'm gonna be."

"You wouldn't be here if it weren't for me." He moved towards me as if to pass me, but I stood still. He could go around the island if he wanted. I'm not his doormat.

"I'm done talking about this until you sober up and stop being such-a-stupid-*cunt*." His words slurred together.

He knows I hate that word. "Oh, I'm a cunt? Maybe. But if that's what I have to be so people take me seriously, then I will be," I said.

"What is wrong with you? I set you up in the perfect position. You just have to lie low and listen to me. We can both be set for life." Joey had been saying this all along, only now it was mangled and cruel. He was flexing and releasing his hands like he needed somewhere for his energy to go.

I stared down at his hands. "I didn't ask you to do any of that."

He started to pace then, in the small space between the counter and the island. He pointed at me, his finger in my face. "You're an ungrateful little bitch."

"Stop! Just stop!" I shouted. "You're the one who's ruining everything. I just stood up for myself. I don't have to be a little coward and bend to whatever Phil wants. You're the one who does as he's told! Whatever Phil says. Whatever Angelo wants. Whatever Papa Joe says. Your only job is to jump when they say so." I couldn't bring myself to call him a name, so I looked in his eyes and said something else that may have hurt him more. "You're the weak brother. At least Tony has the balls to stick up to Phil and support—"

My reflexes were slow. I stopped talking before he made contact, but I didn't flinch. I was frozen, staring at him with my watery puppy dog eyes. Eyes that asked him: *you wouldn't do this to me would you?* But his eyes were black, and they sucked my plea into their void.

The back of his hand connected so hard with the right side of my face, I almost fell into the fridge. I grasped the handle of it instead using it to prop myself up, shaking my head, try to erase the dizzy static filling my ear. My eyelid vibrated, desperate to close, something hard had caught it. His nail or ring scratched it. Joey's face was unrecognizable, distorted in anger. But from this moment on, this is how he will look in my memory.

I should reach my hands up and scratch his ugly face.

I should pound my fists on his wide chest.

I should kick and bite and fight him.

I *wanted* to want to do those things. But my instincts told me to say 'sorry' for being such an incorrigible bitch that he *had* to slap me; to lean in for a gentle and reassuring hug; to find anything but Joey to blame. Whiskey. Phil. Broken glass. Detectives. Empty stomachs. *Me.*

His face softened, his pupils shrunk. His chest heaved. His eyes watered. He reached out his hands to hit me again and I jerked away, only to realize he had wanted to pull me in for an embrace. He had the nerve to look hurt.

"Nessa," he said so softly I almost missed it. "I would never hurt you." He *can* lie to me. I knew the next thing I said would be begging for his forgiveness. So, I shut the fuck up.

I spun away, grabbed my purse and walked through the living room, straight to the front door, fishing for my keys as I did so.

"Vanessa, wait!" Joey called, following.

I bent down to put on my shoes and struggled with the sling back of my stiletto heels, realizing that my left foot was in unbearable pain. I grabbed the shoes, deciding to carry them instead. Joey caught my arm and snatched the shoes from me.

"You... you can't drive like this..." he begged.

He was right. I let my keys drop back into my purse and, struggling only briefly with the locks, I flung the door open. He tried to force it closed but I was already more than halfway through so he let me step out, grabbing my right arm so I couldn't go any further. "Stop! You can't go. Please. It was an accident," he pleaded. "I couldn't control myself." He was right about that part. "Just, talking about Tony gets me upset. And then Phil's message." He put his head in his hands and pushed his hair back with a heavy sigh. "We don't have to talk about that, or anything else. Come back and I'll make us dinner. Please I just," he paused to make a show of looking up and down the street. "I don't want you out here alone like this. It isn't safe."

I jerked my arm away from him. As soon as I was free, I started running. My bare feet ached as they slammed the pavement, the cut on my foot hurting a little less with each contact. Numbing.

I ran with everything I had stopping only when I was sure he couldn't see me and wasn't following. Joey was right, it isn't safe. There's a murderer living on this street.

22

It was eleven thirty by the time Lindsey finally found street parking and walked up to the cute little condo. Or was it a townhouse? Lindsey didn't know the difference. She *did* know that it wasn't as big as her house. Mostly because it was obvious, and also since Vanessa had obsessed over every house she looked at, making them look over the specs for hours while she decided. Rubbing in the fact that she was years ahead of her friends in buying her first house.

Lindsey had been happy for her, so she didn't care. That much. When *Vanessa* got her keys, Lindsey showed up with champagne. When Lindsey got *her* keys, only her husband, Preston, was there with her to celebrate.

She walked up the steps to the brownish red door, part of the natural color scheme that matched the bricks on the bottom third of this house (and every other cookie cutter house on the street). She knocked with her left hand, her right holding a bottle of cheap sparkling wine. She had learned who *did* and *did not* appreciate it when she brought real champagne.

When no one came to the door, she let herself in.

"Hi-hi, Ms. Vanessa. I hope you have the OJ, I brought—" Lindsey paused as she entered the kitchen where she saw the backs of two women, sitting at the marble kitchen counter on bar stools. "Oh, how did you beat me here, Court?"

"I had to help Nessa go get her car," Courtney sad, patting Vanessa's knee and giving Lindsey a *Can you believe her?* look.

Lindsey turned away from them to hide her irritation. She busied herself by grabbing orange juice and glasses. "Is that why neither of you made it to Pilates?"

"I... wasn't really up for it," Vanessa said.

Apparently she was up for brunch and sitting around sipping mimosas. No wonder those expensive leggings she gave her didn't fit Vanessa anymore. Lindsey only gave them to her because they were too big on her now. She should ask for them back and give them to someone who was going to at least *try* to fit into them.

Lindsey continued crafting the mimosas. Vanessa only had two long stem glasses, so the third had to go in a fat little glass tumbler. Vanessa and Courtney kept talking, facing each other, going on as if Lindsey hadn't arrived mid conversation.

"So, what's going to happen with you and Joey?" Courtney asked.

Vanessa sighed. "I'm not thinking about that right now. Last night was... a lot."

"Why, what happened?" Lindsey set the long stem glasses in front of the other two. Vanessa picked hers up and took a sip, not even *offering* to drink out of the stubby glass. Typical. She wasn't a good hostess. Usually, she at least opened her door and served the drinks. But this time, she didn't even get up. And the way they were seated, with the spare chair between them, there was no room for Lindsey to take the last bar stool without making it awkward. There was also no way for them to comfortably move to the dining room table, cluttered with random papers and pantry goods that hadn't been put away.

Despite a very intense workout, Lindsey had to remain standing at the kitchen counter, across from her two best friends. She sipped her mimosa in its whiskey glass and observed how easily the other two fit together and pondered *Can there really be three best friends?*

Vanessa was halfway through her story before she tuned back in. "Then, while he was cooking dinner I broke a glass and cut myself. He helped me take care of it and was really sweet. But when I tried talking, he got all evasive. After ignoring me for *a week*, he should really have been more...." Vanessa struggled for the word.

"Grovel-y?" Courtney offered.

"Uh, no," Vanessa scoffed. "I thought we would get together and we would just click again. Reconnect. And that he would have the magic answers."

"Well, Nessa. Guys don't really like when you're all needy like that," Courtney said, her glass already half empty. "Collin goes weeks without talking to me."

"Collin is *married*!" Vanessa snapped.

"They're separated!" Courtney argued. "And *I'm* the only one he's seeing. You know we don't hook up unless they aren't together. They had a big blow up. This time, I think they're done for good. I would appreciate you not acting like I'm some *other woman* homewrecker type."

"I'm sorry," Vanessa grabbed Courtney's hand and gave it a squeeze, "I'm just drained."

Lindsey noted that Vanessa, indeed, looked awful. Like she hadn't gotten any sleep. Her right eye was red and not opening fully, like she had been rubbing it. Maybe she would feel better if she had started her day with Pilates instead of carbs. Lindsey noted the wrapper of one giant muffin *and* a partially eaten croissant in front of Vanessa. If anyone had earned that, it was Lindsey. She popped a grape in her mouth and sucked on it before she chewed. She'd heard that activating her saliva from sucking would help her feel more satiated and have better digestion.

"Okay, he's been shitty and ignoring you," Lindsey said around a second grape, sucking inconspicuously. "But if there's any advice I can give as a *married woman*, all men act that way until they're sure it's serious. They just see it as a game."

Vanessa laughed lightly. "You and Preston have barely been together a year."

"Fourteen months," Lindsey corrected. "But he was serious about me immediately. We bought a house. You and Joey have been *engaged* longer than we've even been together. But he hasn't sold that Bachelor pad I don't see a ring on that finger."

"That's fair." Vanessa rubbed her ring finger. Joey hadn't given her a ring when he proposed, claiming he was *waiting* for his grandmother's. "It doesn't matter because I'm thinking about ending things. Last night was a mess. He... he... he's just really mean when he drinks."

"He's mean?" Courtney raised her eyebrows. "No one's nice when they've had too much to drink. You're going to judge someone based off that?"

"I feel like he's particularly bad." Vanessa looked away. "It gets really intense with him sometimes."

Lindsey and Courtney looked at each other. Lindsey raised her eyebrow to say *Are you gonna tell her or should I?*, and Courtney shook her head. Vanessa, being right next to them, 'heard' everything they said.

"What?" She asked suspiciously.

Courtney set her glass down and Lindsey followed suit, resting her hands delicately on the counter. "You know we love you, right babe?" Courtney asked. Vanessa nodded hesitantly. "Good. Then you know I say this with love when I say: you really bum us out." Vanessa took a quick shocked breath in. "Everything is *always* so much harder for you than for everyone else. But you seriously have *the* best life. You're the CEO of this huge company, making so much money, with full on articles written about you. That purse right there cost you as much as I make in *a month*, and you didn't even bat an eye when you bought it. And you have Joey, who, yes, is kind of old. But he makes you dinner and he's pretty hot; like dad bod suburban hot. But still, he's rich. And now you're telling us 'he's mean' when he drinks? Maybe he's just being blunt. Or maybe he's tired of hearing you gripe about your amazing life."

Vanessa huffed, "You both think I'm just a big downer?" she looked between Courtney and Lindsey.

Lindsey spoke up before Courtney had the chance. "Not all the time."

"Fair," Courtney eagerly agreed. "But I swear girl. You are set! What is there to complain about?"

"Co-workers, for one," Vanessa tried standing, wincing as soon as she put weight on her foot. She quickly sat down. "I had this guy call me out in front of the whole office. He's been questioning me for weeks. I had to fire him yesterday."

"Was it Tony? Er no... Phil?" Lindsey guessed.

"Tony has been way better. It *was* Phil," Vanessa confirmed reluctantly.

"See!" Courtney shouted. "That right there! We've never met Phil, why do we know all about that loser from your texts?"

Vanessa faced Courtney and Lindsey equally, a defensive pose. "*I* know about Lindsey's horrible co-worker, Steph the bitch from sales." She looked defiantly at Courtney. "And I know all about *your* asshole landlord who keeps sending the creepy repair guy, Ralph, to fix your fridge instead of just buying a new one."

"Exactly!" Courtney nodded emphatically. "Those are people in our lives that we don't control. We don't get to say what happens with the shitty people affecting our lives. You own your house, no landlord. And you are the boss. You can fire your Stephs and your Ralphs. Like you've said a dozen times. You're the fucking *C - E - O*." She emphasized each letter.

Vanessa bit her upper lip while the bottom one quivered slightly. She looked down at her feet. "You're right. I've been selfish... I thought this job would make everything finally come together, but it's been hell and then Joey started to pull away, I feel like everything in my life is falling apart.

I'm so emotional sometimes. I'll work on it." She dabbed at her eye with a napkin and picked up her champagne flute. Looking up she smiled. "What's going on with you both? I feel like we hardly ever hang out anymore."

Maybe if you bothered to come to Pilates... thought Lindsey.

Lindsey opened her mouth to speak but Courtney beat her to the punch. "I've been slammed with work! And Collin too." She took a sip of her mimosa and a sly smile formed. "My lease is almost up, and Collin has this big empty house now that the wife and kids are out. I'm thinking about asking to move in with him! What do you think?"

Lindsey quickly tore a piece off a croissant and shoved it in her mouth. A caloric sacrifice to save herself. Vanessa had nowhere to hide, so she said, "I don't know, Court. He really seemed like he was hoping they could get back together still."

Lindsey swallowed roughly when she realized the other two were looking at her. "Yeah. No. I don't think... Maybe the timing is... you did say Collin has been all moody lately." Courtney cleared her throat. "Like maybe if he comes to *you*, it might show he's ready to move on. Has he mentioned co-habitation?"

"No, not directly." Courtney crossed her arms. "But he's not forward thinking like that. If I asked him first—"

Lindsey interrupted, "Then he might just say *yes* because it's easier."

"That is Collin," Vanessa stated. "He goes with the flow."

"So what? As long as that flow is us living together."

"It's might be fine at first. But what's going to keep him from *going with the flow* when Becky comes back with the boys and wants to try again?" Vanessa said it, but Lindsey was thinking it.

Courtney pushed her hair behind her right ear, then her left ear. She looked at them each in turn. "I was hoping that my best friends would be more supportive."

"We are!" Lindsey rushed to add.

"Yes, we are. I think you should—" Vanessa struggled "—just ask and see what happens."

"Whatever makes you happy."

"Aw, thanks guys," Courtney said. "I texted him about it earlier. I'm just waiting for him to text back. I'll let you know what he says."

"O-kay," Vanessa sounded the word out, then tipped her chin up to Lindsey. "How about you? What's new in your life?"

Lindsey's eyes lit up with the opportunity to speak about herself. "Nothing really," she shrugged. If they want to know, they'll work for it.

Courtney prodded her, "There must be *something*. We haven't gotten together in like a month."

"Well, there is one thing," Lindsey milked each word. "But I'm sure you guys don't want me to bore you with my old lady married life."

"What? Of course we want to hear!" Vanessa reached across the counter and patted Lindsey's hand as if to say *aw, you poor old boring married lady.*

"Preston and I have been talking lately and..." Lindsey hesitated as Vanessa pulled out her vibrating phone. She looked down at it and pressed a button, ending the vibration. When she was sure she had Vanessa's attention again, she continued, "Preston and I have been talking and we think it's time for us to start the discussion on what having a baby might look like."

Courtney had her gasp locked and loaded. "Congratulations!" she said, clasping her hands together.

Vanessa was looking down at her vibrating phone again. She stood with an exaggerated grimace. "I'm so sorry, I have to take this. Excuse me." As she hobbled away, she hissed into the phone, "What do *you* want?"

As Vanessa disappeared into the hallway that led to the two bedrooms, Lindsey said, "Guess my news isn't that big."

"Oh shush, she's just busy," Courtney waved off Vanessa in the direction she had disappeared. "You know our boss bitch friend. But I'm sure she's excited for you, *I'm* excited for you!"

"Thank you! I knew you would be," Lindsey smiled, nodding to herself. "Preston thought none of our friends would want to hear about it because most of them are childless; like you and Vanessa. He thinks timing may not be right. But I'm thirty-six! If not now, when?"

"No!" They both turned their heads to the hallway, hearing Vanessa clearly. They had each been straining their ears at the potential to overhear something. But now they dropped the pretense and shifted gears to full on gossip research mode.

Lindsey, who was already close to the hallway, took two steps towards it. Despite their silence, neither heard another word from Vanessa. As Vanessa came back into the kitchen, Lindsey pretended to be reaching for more orange juice. Based on the blank look on Vanessa's face, Lindsey knew she could drop the act.

Vanessa's eyes were unblinking, her stare was focused on something a thousand yards away. Through Lindsey and through windows and walls. Courtney and Lindsey couldn't see whatever it was Vanessa was fixated on.

"That was Collin," Vanessa said.

"But he hasn't even texted me..." Courtney said reflexivity and regretted it. Lindsey glared at her.

"What did he want?" Lindsey covered.

Vanessa froze. She collected herself and took a deep breath. "Joey's gone. Dead."

Then, she collapsed.

Lindsey and Courtney ran to her. Not lifting her up. That was not what she needed. Instead, they crumbled beside her, becoming a pillow, a blanket, and soothing sounds. Knowing innately this is the comfort she needed.

There was no longer a question of whether or not they were best friends. No question of who skipped Pilates, who didn't bring champagne, who complained too much. It no longer mattered.

The moment was only about these three women being there for each other in whatever way they were able. Maybe they weren't best friends. Hadn't even been *good* friends for a long time. But their friendship had never been about sleepovers and pillow fights. It had been about the ability to drop all the petty bullshit and be there for each other when they needed it the most.

And Vanessa needed it the most.

23

She couldn't begin to imagine how she would react if it was her child up there in the open casket. But something about Victoria's countenance gave her the chills from across the room because it didn't seem right.

The service wasn't large, tucked away in the smallest room of the funeral home. There were about thirty chairs in four rows and not all of them were occupied. It wasn't much of a funeral. No one spoke about the deceased. They took turns going up to view his body. A large picture of Joey was set on a stand near the casket. Whoever picked the photo was going for the shock factor. It was Joey from at least twenty years and forty pounds ago. Couple that with the fact that he was dead and he didn't look his best by comparison.

He didn't look dead either. In that gray suit with the baby blue shirt and dark blue tie, Joey looked like he did after any work meeting, a little worse for wear, not as fresh as when he left for the start of the day, but professional. She knew if his eyes were open, the blue in them would really pop in this suit. They were, thankfully, covered. It had been a long time since she'd looked lovingly into them. But her heart couldn't bear the thought of looking into his lifeless eyes and knowing they would never sparkle again. She still had love for him, frozen in time with his passing. There would be no making up or forgiveness, neither would there be more fights over custody for Laura. It was safe to say their relationship just is what it is. Or *was* what it *was*.

She was only here now because of Laura. Laura, who so desperately did not want to believe her dad was dead. Mom was always the bad guy. And she had to be the bearer of bad news too. The worst news Laura had ever received in her whole short life. If telling her daughter that her favorite parent was dead hadn't broken her, nothing could. But she came damn near close watching her sob and say, "Daddy, wake up... please daddy," until her Uncle Collin pulled her away. He was still comforting her now while Melissa slid to the back of the room with the other non-family. Not her family anymore.

But that wasn't the only thing pushing her to the back of the room. It was this terrible feeling that Joey would wake up. It didn't help that they had put sunglasses on him. She was told the mortician had done everything they could. Only so many things work when you've taken a bullet to the eye. And with the sunglasses on, it was eerie how alive he looked.

Melissa had never heard of a dead man needing to stylishly protect his eyes from sunlight. Though some *un*dead ones might. Namely Blade. But this was no late nineties action-packed vampire movie and Joey Caldarelli was nothing like Wesley Snipes. Except for the tax evasion part. Joey was just a man. A man Melissa had once loved, and still loved in memories.

If she tried to conjure happy memories of him now, this is the image of Joey she would see. On their wedding day, or at Laura's birth, or their five year anniversary in Italy, or on the couch watching The Little Mermaid on repeat with their little girl. All she could picture was Joey, not laughing and smiling and crying as he had been, but stiff as a board. Arms positioned oddly so that his hands clasped over his pudgy stomach which looked deflated. Eyes blocked by sunglasses like some morbid bodyguard of their best moments together. Even the good memories were ruined now. By whomever had decided it needed to be an open casket.

Knowing the family, she was sure it had to be Victoria. She ruined every family gathering with her craziness.

Her positive memories had been despite, not because of, that woman. Luckily, Joey had felt similar, and they had cut her out more than a decade ago. It was no surprise that the matriarch shed no tears. She'd held a grudge against Joe, too, right up until his death and she hadn't regretted it, considering how she sat there stone-faced. Even after the violent and sudden death of her eldest son.

Collin was sweating more than she had seen him, barely holding back tears as he comforted her daughter. Tony kept clearing his throat and swallowing hard when they spoke. When it was *his* turn to view the body he looked mortified as if he had seen a ghost. The color drained from his face and he immediately returned to the seat by his mother, resting his head on her shoulder. Even this, watching her other sons be reduced to tears, did nothing to soften her visage. She sat there, back straight, occasionally patting Tony's head like a dog she had never wanted to adopt in the first place.

The room was quiet. Unlike most Caldarelli family gatherings. Melissa felt the unspoken tension. She couldn't know that *she* was the one about to snap from it.

Scrutinizing the non-family guests, she realized she didn't recognize them. She started to wonder if some were employees of the funeral home, waiting as politely as possible for the earliest opportunity to take down Joey's picture and flowers and wheel in the next body. One amongst them was grieving and distraught. This woman had scooted to the edge of her chair and leaned in towards the aisle to get up but was unmoving. Presumably working up the courage to see Joey one last time.

She should be nervous. *Why the fuck would she show her face here?*

She had a pretty face with long dark hair. She was more gussied up than was appropriate for the occasion. Joey always did expect his arm candy to come in a shiny wrapper.

Joey's latest squeeze was a decade younger than Melissa. Her demeanor made her seem younger still. Big doe eyes looking around the room, unsure of what she should do with herself.

She caught Melissa looking at her and perked up.

Shit.

Now was a good time for a cigarette. One of the benefits of being in the room furthest back in the funeral home was that it had its own exit. She stood and made her way to it, slowly pushing the bar open. It clearly read *no reentrance*. With her foot jammed in the door she looked around for a rock to prop it open. Back to the door, she felt the weight of the door on her foot disappear. Looking back, she realized the woman was holding it open.

"Can I join you?" she asked softly.

Melissa shrugged. "Free country. Don't let that door close though, I gotta get back in there."

She simply said, "oh," and stuck her foot in the door to keep it open. Melissa took several steps away and pulled out her cigarettes, opening the pack and selecting one. "My name is Vanessa."

Melissa put the cigarette in her mouth and spoke around it. "I know who you are." She moved farther away.

"Can we talk?"

Melissa turned around and lit her cigarette, sucking in to get it started. After the first draw she said, "You have 'til I'm done with this cigarette."

Vanessa looked around for a rock giving Melissa just enough time to look her up and down. She wasn't jealous of Joey's choice, just confused. Vanessa and Melissa were polar opposites in appearance. Melissa was blonde and thin with an angular face complemented by a blunt bob. Though both wore black for the occasion, Melissa had chosen a black button up and black pants with black sensible flats. Nothing about Vanessa's outfit seemed practical, especially not the four-inch heels, uneven on the gravel as she awkwardly hunted for a rock.

It's not that all men had to have a type. It's that Joey *did* and that type was Melissa. All of the women Joey had been serious with (or played around with while married) looked like Melissa. Aside from the clothing as Joey did like his ladies more dolled up, she was all wrong. The fancy clothes suited her better than any of Joey's other partners. Like she had always led a soft life. Joey preferred a woman he could introduce to the good life. One who hadn't experienced it on her own. A fixer-upper who needed him. Melissa certainly had. It made the divorce difficult, knowing she was walking away from an easier life. Easier financially. Life with Joey was no walk in the park.

It was hard to give up the financial stability and become a single mother. After their separation it became clear that, like his *nice guy* act, Joey's *rich guy* act was a sham. It was obvious, now that she had hindsight. The final nail in the coffin was the fact that this was not the funeral of a rich man. And *that woman* was not the trophy wife of one either.

As Vanessa bent over to grab a large rock, Melissa did note one very large *ass*et Joey did not compromise on in his new girlfriend selection. Vanessa used her foot to prop the door open, balancing on one heel better than Melissa could have imagined, shoving the rock in place.

"I'm glad we're getting a chance to talk," Vanessa said.

After a moment, Melissa said, "So talk."

"I just wanted to say how sorry I am for you and La- your daughter." Vanessa swallowed, not managing to get Laura's name out. She probably knew so little about Laura that she wasn't confident that was her name. "I was hoping to get your blessing to talk to her today. Let her know how much she meant to Joey. And to me. I wish this wasn't how—"

Melissa laughed, a forceful laugh that blew smoke straight into Vanessa's face. "You think you can—" she started, laughing again, too hard to continue. She stopped herself, catching her breath enough to take another long drag of her cigarette. "You aren't shit to me. And you aren't shit to Laura." Vanessa gave a little gasp and straightened her shoulders, pulling her head back some. "For all I know you weren't shit to Joey neither. Might be why you decided to blow his head off."

Vanessa's eyes swiveled around, refusing to settle on Melissa. "I didn't do anything to Joey," she said firmly.

Melissa stared in her eyes, refusing to back down. "You don't seem surprised to be accused of something terrible. You seem perfectly calm. And you sure got some nerve showing your face while the family is giving their last respects."

"Oh please, Melissa. Like you have any more right to be here than I do. Why are *you* here? Joey showed me your texts. You hated him."

"Yeah... well I had every right to. But those texts were for a dead-beat dad. Not for a dead one," she inhaled the grief and carcinogens. "And unlike you, I got some actual class. Laura needs me here. You're lucky I'm not going to cause a scene at her daddy's funeral. Otherwise, I'd beat your ass," Melissa took a step closer toward Vanessa, who remained in place. It was an empty threat. She had never been in a fight, but Vanessa didn't have to know that.

Vanessa shook her head. "I don't want to fight you. I don't have the energy to defend myself. All I wanted was to come here and talk to the people who knew and loved him like I do." She hung her head. Her slow movements and her cadence were awkward. *Is she high at Joey's funeral?*

"Don't come here trying to act all pathetic. Just cause I didn't like him.... Don't mean you can kill him then rub it in our faces." Melissa took a long drag, ash falling onto her shoe without her noticing. The sight of this woman made her furious. Joey was a shitty husband, and an even worse ex-husband. But he didn't deserve to be killed. At least not by *her*. For what? Money?

Vanessa shrank, deflating into herself. "Joey's death was a shock to me. I don't really care if you believe me. The police believe me. I have an alibi. Why do you think I'm not in jail?"

That can't be true. The questions the police were asking Melissa made it clear: Vanessa was the first and only suspect. Melissa pulled her cigarette up to her lips. The ashy taste told her there was nothing left to smoke. She dropped it on the ground and stamped it out. "Okay, so you didn't pull the trigger. Doesn't mean you aren't working with someone. Let me tell you, you keep working with all these dangerous people, you'll wind up like Joey. He said he swore off working with Angelo for Laura's sake. Then you come around and just like that" −Melissa snapped her fingers− "Angelo's back. Cops are one thing. You piss Angelo and them off and it don't matter how good your ass looks in that dress."

"Angelo?" Vanessa was oblivious and her reaction time was slow. "Joey's college friend?"

Melissa looked her up and down. The pathetic act might not be an act. Could be she *was* just a helpless little doe. "I don't know if you're fucking with me or not. If you aren't, you should get the hell away from the Caldarelli's. If you are... you should get the hell away from me." She moved past Vanessa and went for the door.

"Wait," a pleading little voice caught her sympathy. "Please. I'm just here to say goodbye. I don't believe any of the things Joey told me about you. Or anything else for that matter. I know you aren't my friend, but Joey kept us both in the dark on things. At least we can relate."

"Do you have a point?" Melissa crossed her arms.

"One question." Vanessa nodded, hair falling out from behind her ear and into her face. She didn't move it, instead allowing it to be a shield from Melissa's glare. "I'm afraid... to see his body. Every time I get close, that woman makes me feel out of place. Who is she?"

Melissa knew exactly who she meant. She smirked. Joey claimed he was going to *marry* this woman. And she didn't even know who his mother was? She slid the rock out from the door. "That's Victoria. The Mother." She pushed through the door, knowing Vanessa would have to scramble to grab it or be locked out. She returned to her seat in the back row.

Vanessa came back in with a new determination. She grabbed her expensive looking purse from her chair and marched to the front of the room, straight to Joey.

Melissa felt a tinge of regret. She hadn't warned Vanessa that Joey looked… surprising in his sunglasses. She could see his girlfriend stiffen at first. She bent slightly. She touched his hand or his cheek. She, like Melissa, confirmed he was dead. And feelings rushed her. She straightened up quickly, but it was clear she was uneasy on her feet rocking back and forth. Whatever she was on was wearing off. *Tony* stood and put his arm around her. She cringed reflexively away from him. Then she leaned into him, eventually melting into a hug. Her body shook enough that, even across the room, Melissa could see it.

Victoria suddenly stood and brushed past the two of them. It was a dramatic maneuver that every person in the room could see. Perhaps Victoria was finally moved to tears, God knows she'd never let anyone see her cry. Or she just had to pee.

Melissa was glad that it wasn't her up there. Had she stayed with Joey, thinking they were building a life together, she would be a true widow today. She still felt the heartbreak.

But for her, she'd been spreading the loss of Joey across almost a decade. You spread something out over a long enough time and it hurts just a little bit. Every day. It would probably hurt just a little bit every day until she died.

Today, she felt grief for Laura's loss. Aside from that, her only other feeling was anger. Towards Vanessa.

Misplaced? Perhaps.

If Vanessa really didn't know about Joey's shady life. If she didn't know the financial strings the Caldarelli matriarch pulled. If she really had an alibi....

Then it seemed unlikely that she had killed Joey. *For what?* She asked herself again. A fancy watch? A used Porsche, still on payments? A house with an outrageous mortgage?

Joey's money was all in *things*, that he mostly didn't own. From the child support payments, it was apparent that even less money had come in the last few years. No chance Joe left anything to his sons with Victoria still around. Unless Vanessa was an idiot, she wouldn't have killed him for money.

Tony helped Vanessa pull herself together. Melissa saw her walk out quickly after that. Tony didn't return to his front row seat. He walked down the tiny aisle between the chairs, all the way to the back row. Tony sat down by Melissa, leaving one empty chair between them. She gave a shrug intended to mean: *Not sure what you want from me.*

He seemed to understand her well enough. "Hey Lissa. Long time, no talk?"

She wanted to correct him. Only Joey called her Lissa. But since he wasn't around, what difference did it make? It made her heart sing a little melody of memories. The good ones. Maybe she'd keep the nickname. "Hey, Tony. Good to see you." He nodded, but continued looking at her silently. She needed to fill the silence. "Sorry about Pops. And now Joey. It just sucks."

Tony sucked in air as if preparing for a long-winded speech. "Yep." He exhaled, blowing out through his lips as if they would form the words for him. They did not, so he had to do the work himself. "Bunch of us are gonna meet up at Old Saorise's Pub at seven. Have a few drinks, tell stories about Joey. I'd really like it if you came."

That was shocking. Her invite to the funeral had been obligatory. This was something else, she was tempted to go but she had to ask, "Will *she* be there?"

"Ma? No, she hates bars," he chuckled.

"Good to know," Melissa laughed. "But, I meant *her*," she gestured to the exit. "Vanessa."

Tony nodded. "She was invited. But she was a mess just now. So I'm not sure. She's," he swallowed, "really not that bad though."

"Sounds like you're trying to convince yourself that."

"I get it. You're the ex-wife, she's the new wife—"

"New wife?" Melissa jumped in on cue.

"Fiancé." Tony corrected putting his hand up. "You don't have to be best friends. You don't even have to talk to her. We all lost Joey. Might be good to be together." She looked around the room, then looked at him. "I mean, might be good to be together *not* in this sterile room with a dead body in it. Who knows? Some liquid courage and you might want to say a few words about our dearly departed. They don't all have to be nice words. I know you and Joey were long done. But you're still family."

She smiled at that. It wasn't often Tony made her feel warm and fuzzy. Might be the first time. "Laura was trying to make some plans with old friends. If they're free, I'll drop her off and think about joining you."

"Good," Tony gave her hand a squeeze and stood, making his way back to the front to be with his mother who had just re-entered.

Laura's plans were already confirmed. Melissa didn't know if she could bring herself to meet up and talk about Joey. What if she had nothing to say? Would people think she was cold, like Victoria? Worse yet, what if she had plenty to say? One drink could break her seal of silence. She could say things she'd only shared with her girlfriends after an entire bottle of wine. Even they hadn't heard everything.

She wasn't mad at Vanessa, but Vanessa was a super-conductor for her anger. Had she killed Joey because he was a violent and terrifying man? It only takes one time to see the darkness inside of him. The black eyes that revealed no soul. He and Vanessa weren't married so she would only have received a taste of it. The rest he would save until they were married and she was trapped... in the first trimester of her second pregnancy.

Vanessa would never have to face that now.

If anyone had earned the right to pull that trigger, it was Melissa. She couldn't blame Vanessa for Joey's misdeeds. But it was easier to hate her, to shun her, to keep her at a distance. She did not want to acknowledge Vanessa's likely experience with Joey. Then she would have to acknowledge her own.

Most importantly, she would have to tell her daughter. But if she made Vanessa the villain, Laura would never have to know. That she was made up of one-half monster.

Melissa just prayed that Laura only inherited those blue eyes and none of what was behind them.

24

Old Saoirse's Pub was dead except for our group at the back of the bar. The sad little club of Joey's friends and family.

I almost didn't come. My foot cut had turned out to be worse than I thought. I spent last Saturday morning crying over Joey. By Saturday afternoon Courtney had dragged me to urgent care where I got some stitches. They cleaned my eye and gave me a patch for the corneal abrasion Joey left me as a final goodbye. My left sole throbbed and wearing heels to the funeral didn't help, but at least my eye recovered enough so I didn't have to show up looking like a pirate.

After Joey's funeral I tried to make myself cry. I figure if I can force myself to pee at home to avoid a nasty bar toilet, certainly I can make myself cry at home and avoid the embarrassment of doing it in front of these people. Aside from Collin and Tony, I didn't know anyone at the funeral. I recognized some, but I couldn't pick them out of a line-up. Maybe Joey introduced us once. But I left the service feeling out of place. Television made me believe that the widow would greet people at the funeral. People would come up to her and say kind things about the deceased. Then, inevitably, when she fell apart, a room full of people would uplift her. Depending on the type of show, perhaps an attractive widower would escort her home so they could 'grieve' together.

Instead, I sat there feeling like the *other woman*. I half expected his real wife to burst through the doors when I approached his body. Then everyone would boo and jeer, forcing me to leave...

No other woman came. I wish she had though, before I had the chance to look at him cold and lifeless in those sunglasses. Sunglasses! Was he secretly one of the Men in Black? Wouldn't surprise me after everything. When Tony came to me and comforted me, the shock almost made me reject him. I never would have guessed that through this Tony would be my biggest support.

All of this to explain why I had to change outfits after the funeral. If I was going to meet up with a group of people who might know my fiancé better than me, I needed to bring my 'A' game. A silky red shirt, jeans, and a pop of red lipstick. Normally I'd throw on some heels and use height to my advantage, but my slowly healing foot complained loudly at the thought. And the infused gummies I've been taking can only do so much.

When I walked in, all eyes were on me. I almost turned around to see who they were looking at. But seeing a slight wave from both Collin and Tony, I realized that was my group.

On the bartender's recommendation, I got a whiskey sour. I took my cocktail to the only remaining seat. Next to Melissa. The group consisted of all men, except for me and *Melissa*. Either they had all beat me by several drinks or they had zero social awareness. Melissa and I knew these jackasses were going to make things awkward, forcing us to sit together. As I settled, a man I may have met once finished his Joey story.

"So they ban us. Take a polaroid and stick it up in the back office," he took a long drink. "And Joey, he calls up Tony's buddy Irving. You know, with the city?" He looked to Tony for confirmation. "Next day, Irving goes in, does his Magic, and just like that—" he slapped the table, "—no more liquor permit." He started laughing. "You remember that, Tony?"

"I can assure you, it was all above board." Tony chuckled like an amused father whose son had done his party trick. "Joey had a way of leaving me out of the fun stuff. Somehow, he always found me when he needed to call in a favor." He laughed harder, everyone joining in.

The group laughed for so long, I almost ruined it by asking what was so funny. I arrived too late for this joke, fifteen years too late. Even Melissa belted out laughter.

When it died down for a moment, Tony looked my direction.

"Lissa, how about you. Any good stories?"

"Oh sure, plenty," I started.

At the same time Melissa said, "I've got some bad ones."

We looked at each other. I finally registered what Tony had said. *Lissa* not *Nessa*. These edibles made my head foggy, but not enough to numb my white-hot embarrassment.

"Go ahead," I said. Of course she should go first. She had Joey first. For fuck's sake, even my nickname was secondhand. Had Joey called me Lissa the first time we had sex and covered it up pretending he'd said Nessa? Was that the first lie? I may never know. The only person who knew was burning up right now. Being cremated, I mean. Not that he's in hell. Although...

Half-listening to *Lissa* and the others tell stories about Joey, I sipped my drink. Much better than an Old Fashioned. Joey's Old Fashioned. I hadn't had many others. Up until I met Joey, the emphasis on my cocktails had been dollar to buzz ratio. He always appreciated the finer things.

I should say something. Maybe I could talk about his bougie taste. The gap between stories drew on. Just before I felt like I would jump in, Joey's neighbor, Todd I think, started sharing his story. I sat back and let it wash over me.

With the nine of us sitting comfortably in a circle, uncomfortably sharing the single low table in the middle of us, I felt like I'd be interrupting if I spoke. They were a group of adults arranged around the table like a campfire while they all told ghost stories about the same dead man. Except unlike campfire ghost stories which always wound up being the same three stories, I didn't know any of these. And that actually frightened me.

They had a million stories about this strange man. My fiancé — no, not my fiancé, because that meant someone I was going to marry in the future. Joey had no future.

I may have mumbled "excuse me," as I stood, though no one noticed when I left the circle. I need another drink.

I asked the bartender for another and pointed at my glass forgetting the drink's name. She stared at me blankly. Our group was the only one in here, had she forgotten me so easily? Squinting under the dim lighting, I thought this may be a different beautiful, blonde, and otherwise nondescript bartender. I almost ordered an Old Fashioned out of embarrassed desperation when I heard a voice from behind me.

"I think she wants another Whiskey Sour." My heart fluttered, Tony to my rescue. I looked towards him eagerly. It's just Collin. "And I'll have another."

"Ginger beer with lime?" she said cheerily. She turned to gather her ingredients and began preparing them.

"Sure, you she remembers." I nudged Collin with my elbow. "How did you know what my drink was?"

He picked up my empty glass and examined it like a would-be Sherlock Holmes. "Frothy egg white drink with a strong citrus scent, in an Irish bar," Collin said, "Topped with a cocktail cherry. Nothing gets past an alcohol expert like me."

"Alcoholic?" I asked jokingly.

"Same difference," he shrugged. "Besides the gorgeous blonde behind the bar tried to push the same on me."

"How'd you wind up with a ginger beer then?"

He looked mildly irritated. "I told you. I quit drinking."

"You're serious?" I laughed. "Are you in a twelve-step program? When do you get to the making amends part?" I asked. I regretted it the moment it slipped out.

"Ginger beer with lime," the bartender announced loudly, setting it on the bar.

"Thanks," Collin picked it up as the bartender started my drink. "I *am* sorry for how I've been, Vanessa. It's been difficult."

"I didn't mean—"

"You did," Collin cut me off. "And you're right. I'm working on my apologies, sorry you're not first in line. I'm serious about quitting this time. If you were ever my friend, you'd support that."

"Coll—" I started, but he was already walking away. I thought about going after him, but now was not the time. My drink wasn't ready.

I saw Melissa stand and head my way with an empty glass. I whipped around staring at the bartender.

Shake faster I willed. In her defense, if she shook any faster her boobs might pop out of the top of her scoop neck tank top. By the time she was pouring it, Melissa was at the counter.

"What can I get you?" she asked as Melissa set down her glass. Melissa was stunning. She had opted to change too. She was wearing dark jeans and a white scoop neck t-shirt. Seeing her next to the bartender, they could be mother and daughter. Or sorority sisters because Melissa looked great for her age. Any age.

"I'll have what she's having," Melissa said. Goddam it, can't I just have one thing to myself?

"Whiskey Sour?" the bartender confirmed.

Melissa looked at me. "You're a real basic bitch huh?" She nodded at the bartender who got started on the drink.

I looked at Melissa, immediately on the defensive.

"Relax!" she said. "I'm messing with you. I ordered the same thing." She sat down at the bar, pulling out a second red velvet backed bar stool and patting the seat. I slid my drink in front of it.

"You're a basic bitch, too?" I said as I sat.

"Maybe," she shrugged. "But I stopped caring when I hit forty."

"I'll look forward to that in a decade or so," I bluffed.

"Okay, hot stuff. Being young ain't the flex you think it is." Melissa stared at the bartender wistfully. "I was seventeen when I met Joey. Laura's age. But, if some man in *his* twenties showed up saying he was her boyfriend," she turned to look at me, dead serious, "I'd run him over with my car."

My age gap with Joey had never seemed egregious to me. Nor had Melissa's seven-year difference. But I didn't know she was in high school when they met, that felt different.

"Funny, thing is," she continued. "Joey would kill the guy too. Hypocrite. When he picked you up, I thought he was just screwing around. To mess with me."

"Is this what you want to talk about? How I was nothing but a pawn to him?" I swirled the cocktail pick, which was stabbed through a cherry, around my glass. "I don't need your help to feel shitty about myself."

"Sorry," she said nonchalantly, while I almost fell out of my chair in shock at the apology. "I didn't mean it to come across like that. I'll skip the middle part. I was going to end by saying, he really loved you. He pled your case to Laura a dozen times. Told her all the things you would do together once you were married. What a great stepmom you would make. How you were his soulmate, and she would love you. She hated you. The idea of you. Thinking that the only reason her parents weren't together was because Dad had another woman. I let her think it because the alternative was telling her what a piece of shit he was. And having to explain how I could love such a dirt bag. He was a good father when he was around, you know," I heard her sniffle. "But I always wondered if that was because I kept her away from him. Like he wanted to be good just to spite me." The bartender set

Melissa's drink down in front of her. She picked it up and stared at it, holding it still, she asked, "Can I ask you *one* question?"

Her intensity made me afraid to say anything other than, "Yes."

"Did you kill him?"

I could've just said 'no' and let it be. But I only had the strength to say it once. I needed her to hear me. Against my better judgement, I reached out to her unoccupied left hand, awkwardly far from me since I was on her right. She set her drink down and I grabbed her right hand too. I looked straight into her eyes. The only thing I said was, "No." But I said everything.

She teared up and averted eye contact. "Then I hope they find the son of a bitch who did soon so we can move on with our lives."

I nodded. We picked up our glasses and clinked them together. I took in some liquid courage. My cheeks are damp and I'm ready to not be sad. I want to escape this moment. "Can I ask *you* one question?"

"Shoot."

"Did you really think my ass looked great in that dress?"

Melissa's face cracked into a smile. I laughed and she laughed harder. And I'm not sure when or if we stopped.

"Ready: three, two, one," the bartender, who I now know as Sydnie, counted down. The three of us tilted the shots into our mouths and swallowed, in what was either our third or forth round. I'd lost count. Sydnie wasn't ringing them in anymore.

She was getting plenty of cash from the men who kept coming back up to the bar, but Sydnie had proclaimed them 'old and boring'. They were only ordering the same top shelf whiskeys, and the occasional ginger beer. Which is why she'd insisted on making us delightful, layered shots she called

Beam me up Scotty which tasted of bananas and cream. I could only manage one cream-based shot for risk of becoming queasy. She switched us to Washington Apples which were fruity and *not* made with top shelf whiskey. They went down easy and Sydnie was having fun making them.

Melissa wisely took a long drink of water and continued. "That watch was *my* grandfather's. He refused to give it back."

"No!" I said, my volume out of my control, smacking my hand down on the bar. "But he didn't even wear it."

"I know! He got that expensive one. Ten thousand, I think. Said he liked Grandpa's too much to risk wearing and damaging it," Melissa said. "But I know it's because it was cheap. He thought other men were talking about it and judging him!"

"No one would do that," I said.

"I don't know," Sydnie slowly shook her head. "I know exactly how much your purse costs. And I have judged *you* to be the one who's paying."

We all giggled. The alcohol helped but sometimes there's something so relaxed about talking with women and knowing you understand them. I understood why Melissa married Joey, Sydnie understood why I bought that purse. The experiences were all unique yet connected. Peaceful.

Then a man came and ruined it all. "I'd like to close out," Tony said. Collin was with him, arm around Tony, leaning on him. "Gotta get this big guy home," looking at Collin's eyes I could see he was long gone. It had been a hard week, I couldn't blame him for drinking. My guilt over doubting his resolve earlier faded away. My hands are clean. He was an alcoholic and it wasn't my fault for knowing it.

"What happened to him?" Melissa asked, half gone herself. She was rocking in her chair. Or I was? One of us was moving.

"Too much to drink," Tony said.

"No-I-didn't," Collin shook his head insistently, his words soldering together into one solid objection.

Melissa blew a raspberry, "Ha! When did you become a lightweight?"

Collin didn't answer. Tony paid and, based on Sydnie's reaction, left an unforgettable tip.

Melissa watched them leave. "Collin and I fucked." I almost choked on my water.

"You what!?!" I said.

Despite having no context, Sydnie played along, "Good for you girl!"

"Spill it," I demanded.

"Joey and I were divorced. Collin wasn't with Becky yet. It was once, it was hot. That's it," Melissa shrugged.

"He *is* the younger brother, of course he'd want to play with Joey's things," I mused, reminiscing about the hot tub in Vegas. And the thousand times before Vegas Collin and I had flirted.

"The opposite actually," Melissa corrected. Sydnie started making another round of shots while eavesdropping expertly. She wasn't discreet, but we didn't care because she'd been invited into the conversation at least an hour ago. "Collin and I are the same age. I was dating *him* first. We never got around to 'hooking up'." She added in air quotes. "After the divorce it was all this pent up raw sexual energy, and I pounced."

"Amazing!" I laughed. "Collin is always such a mess. At least Joey had his life together. I think you picked the right brother to marry."

"I don't know about that…" Melissa looked longingly through the door as if Collin would come back. "Too late now though anyway. Better I just keep all the Caldarelli boys at a distance."

Sydnie cleared her throat and picked up her shot glass. "Can I just say something to you two crazy bitches?" she slurred. "I don't know who that Joey guy is… but he sucks." Melissa and I shared a look. "And you ladies are awesome. You should stop fighting over him and forget about that loser."

Who knew the bartender could give such a rousing speech while half sauced? Melissa looked inspired. She raised her shot glass. "To forgetting Joey."

Sydnie and I raised our glasses: "To forgetting Joey," we echoed.

Here's to the start of a new chapter.

25

Courtney is lucky I owe her a favor after this last week. Otherwise, I would not be up. It was one in the afternoon. After last night, I thought I might sleep through the whole day. But my grief and my hangover will have to wait.

I rang the doorbell.

It was the loudest damn doorbell on the face of the planet. Like Joey, Collin had opted for a large open concept house, it was even on the same block. It was *also* decorated like a rich man's bachelor pad. Expensive but sparse and boring furniture. Collin's was only that way *after* Becky took the boys and their kid friendlier furniture.

Now it was a big, echoey house. Standing on the porch I heard the doorbell twenty separate times as it bounced off the walls and around my skull. Sunglasses couldn't protect me from the noise and I twinged in pain. No reply so I knocked. No way Collin slept through this *and* all the calls from Courtney. He couldn't have had that much to drink last night. That bartender, Melody I think, was pouring *us* shots, not the men.

Maybe the bar wasn't where Collin ended things. Knowing him, whiskey was just the start.

Or Courtney wasn't just paranoid and Collin *was* avoiding her. He hadn't replied to her request to move in... Courtney is hysterical, convinced he wants to break up. Not wanting to live together didn't mean he wanted to end things. But she only took five missed calls to make that leap.

She was always the rational one. A wild party girl, yes, but also very logical. She talked me off the ledge this week after my police interview. They tested me for gunshot residue, fingerprinted me, and questioned me for hours. I was convinced I was their suspect. But she said they just had to rule me out. And she was right. I gave them whatever they asked for, then they let me go.

I did owe her. One more knock maximum. Then bed.

I listened carefully for any movements in the house. Nothing. Although there was a faint... barking? That's right. Collin had gotten Becky a Pomeranian as a 'please don't leave me' gift. She left him *and* the dog. But if the dog *were* here, he'd certainly be at the door barking his little head off.

It clicked. The yard!

I ran around the side of the house. Well, I walked briskly. Not an emergency worth jostling my queasy stomach over.

Sure enough, I got to the fence and the little beast was yapping his head off.

"Collin!" I called. "Collin, I know you're here!" Nothing. Even the dog quieted as I stuck my fingers though the wood slats to let him sniff them. "Collin!" I yelled. "Don't worry, Courthey isn't here with me. I told her you're just a big stupid coward who..." I doubled over suddenly. Nope. I am not throwing up. *I am not throwing up.* I am a big girl. "I'm going to climb this fence if you don't come over here." It was an empty threat. I have never climbed over a fence. Peering through the gate I saw the latch was just out of reach. "I'm going to open your gate and you're going to feel so silly you didn't just let me in!" I climbed up the gate a small amount, standing on the lowest vertical support. I stepped up one more and then hung on with all my weight, leaning forward into the gate. I reached over the other side and pulled up on the black lock release. It unlocked easily.

This fence is terrible security. I scrambled back down and pulled the gate open. The dog immediately jumped on my leg, begging for attention. "Where's your idiot daddy?" I asked.

I find him immediately. He is in the pool, floating face down. He isn't moving. He does not look right. I do not run to him or try to rescue him. I start crying. The screams for help follow. Alerted by my breaking and entering, Collin's nosy neighbors come running. It is a quiet Sunday and my screams disturb their peace. The angry look on the older man's face distorts to confusion when I point at Collin and say "There."

The woman jumps into action, pulling out her cell phone and calling 911. *But there is no emergency.* He is dead.

I could have turned around and never opened that gate. I could have gotten the news second hand like I did with Joey. I could have had one more Sunday that Collin was alive. But no.

I had to open that gate. And now he is dead.

26

I t's over, Nessa," Tony said.

I should refuse to believe it. This past month, since Joey's funeral, I started to question everything I thought I had known. The police interrogation had me doubting myself. *Did I hate Joey enough to kill him?* I had forgotten most of what happened that last night together. Blacked out at one point. I remember fighting and cutting myself and I can still see his eyes when he hit me. But by the next morning, I didn't remember why. Which doesn't matter because there's never a good reason. I didn't tell the cops about that part anyway. So they pressed on. *Had I loved Joey enough to kill Frank to get him the job? Had I been jealous enough of Joey's possible affair to kill Tiffany?* Of course not! But you're asked the same question enough times and your sharp answers start to dull and you doubt the one you've circled with your number two pencil. Because sometimes that answer does change.

The answer to at least one question *had* changed. Was Tony Caldarelli my friend? *Yes.*

I know. It's impossible to imagine but here he was. I had been so silly with our rivalry, but he had been there for me from day one. He had helped get the staff on board with me and guided Peter in my absence. He had backed me up with Phil. He was here now when no one else was. It was always Collin and Joey's dislike of him that had guided my feelings about Tony. Now that they were gone, I knew I wasn't going to let men manipulate my emotions like that again.

It was a relief to be able to lean on Tony when things had felt impossible. He held my hand every step of the way. Tony's connection to the legal world and the police was vital. He knew getting a lawyer would just make me look guilty. I didn't and it paid off. After less than a week they stopped interrogating me. They started treating me like Tony, like a victim.

"Are you sure?" I asked tentatively. My coffee cup shook in my hands and I remind myself that I am safe with Tony. This general anxiety follows me. I tried a daily ten milligram edible to calm me which I increased to thirty. It stopped working after two weeks. What, at first, had provided a quick path to a relaxed state then peaceful drift off had changed. I started to sink into the bed at night, the anxiety latching onto me like a hungry infant whose need to feed increased daily. I'd have to shake it off in the morning, lifting the weight and my heavy head. It *had* guaranteed a minimum sleep though. Which I had not gotten last night since I decided to stop self-medicating.

The Morning Boost was becoming a second home. It was difficult to go back to my house to be alone with the memories. For ten business days, I couldn't drag myself into the office, and even then, only after hours when I wouldn't have to face anyone. Tony agreed to meet me here often to discuss work but mostly the investigation.

Now he was telling me this all-consuming thing was over. My muddled mind struggled to comprehend. He said his friends on the inside had kept details from us while it was active... they finally filled him in. And it was my turn to know what happened months before they would be ready to share it with the public.

"Nessa, it *is* over," Tony repeated, breathing in deeply. He held a blue folder in front of him. Copies of evidence he was expected to shred. Why blue? It was an odd choice to *hide* anything in a cerulean folder. Gray or beige or black makes more sense to me... I snatched my wandering focus and forced it to sit and listen to Tony. "Some of what I'm going to tell you will be hard to hear. Hell, it's hard for me to say. But I'd rather you find out now, from me, than sensationalized online."

"You sound like you're about to confess to me," I laughed uncomfortably. Smiling, it turns out, is something that doesn't come naturally after tragedy. You really have to work on it.

He threw me a half-hearted chuckle. "Nothing like that." His face turned serious again. "I'm sorry if this is upsetting but the only way I know how to tell you is directly." He breathed in through his nose and sat up even more straight. The rigid chairs at the coffee shop always forced good posture, but his pose became exaggeratedly stiff. My heart started pounding. "This has been going on for longer than we knew. The detectives have connected the deaths of all five people to one person."

"Five?" I asked, doing the math in my head. I've run through what I know about those four deaths every day for a month. My mantra had become: First Frank then Tiffany then Joey then Collin. So many deaths.

"Joe didn't kill himself. He was the first victim," he said. I sucked in air, deeply. I don't know when I breathed out and in again but it was long enough that my head started spinning, my brain begging for oxygen. Maybe this should not have been a surprise. Joe's suicide came out of nowhere. It was less alarming to think someone might kill the stubborn grumpy old man. "You all right?" Tony asked, I just nodded. "I was bewildered too. They reopened his case when Frank turned up dead. I was asked to keep it close to my chest, but I've known since they reopened it. I didn't think it had anything to do with this. As it turns out, they had already run his death through toxicology. They originally ruled it a suicide because of the opioid overdose. But when they tested that cannabis tincture that killed Frank, it had a drug used for gout treatment. Joe had the same drug in his testing. They'd each gotten a lethal dose. Gout runs in our family, but according to his wife, Frank didn't have it."

"I knew about the tincture," I confessed. Tony furrowed his brow. "I knew that it was poisoned, by Tiffany, before she brought it to him. But I don't know who killed her. Or why she would kill Joe."

"Tiff was… Tiffany was just another victim. Strangled by the same person who killed Frank and Joe. And then Joey."

I nodded. "And then Collin. But why? And how?" I implored. I wanted to pull the answers straight from his mouth, but it would be like grabbing on the ends of pasta from an extruder and pulling. The words would be misshapen. Fusilli stretched into spaghetti; macaroni with no elbows. So I waited.

He looked at me with remorse and pity in his eyes, cranking the words out. "Oh Nessa. It was Collin. The whole time, it was my own brother." I shook my head, my tongue gluing to the bottom of my mouth. "It was. Collin killed them."

"No!" I shouted, muscling my mouth open. The people at the tables next to us looked at me. I whispered, "Collin didn't do this."

Tony looked around at the attention we were drawing. "You need to keep your voice down," he snapped. Then softer, "I know it's hard; remember this isn't public information yet. They haven't officially closed it. Can you handle this?" I didn't appreciate his lecture-like tone, but his point was fair.

I swallowed, "Yes," then took a sip of my coffee to prove how composed I am.

"Because if you can't," he pulled the blue folder towards his lap. "I'll just have to—"

"I can. Please," I begged, reaching my hand out.

He pushed the folder towards me. "Good." I eagerly flipped it open. "I'm glad I have someone who can share this secret. Who understands how painful it is." The first picture was the one of Joey's car parked at Tiffany's house; the one Detective Hernandez showed me what felt like a lifetime ago. "Ah yes," Tony peered at the picture. "It turns out that was *Collin* in the car. Daniel, my mechanic, confirmed it. He thought it *was* Collin's car, so he let him take it. Only realized how odd that was when he brought it back to the shop before Joey picked it up a few days later."

I guess that makes sense. I flipped the pages, more pictures of the car and Tiffany getting into it. After that was a picture of *my* car, in Joey's driveway. "This is my car," I said.

"It's from a neighbor's front door camera. The view to Joey's door is obscured by your car. But, see there," he pointed at a dark gray blob behind it. "That's Collin walking to his front door at two in the morning. His house was at most a ten-minute walk away."

I stared at the blob. *Could be Collin. Could be Bigfoot.*

I nodded. I flipped to the next page, pictures of Joey's front door, these taken in the daylight. I worried the next picture would be terrible. But it was just a picture of several tincture bottles, one by a mug with the small dosage dropper pulled out. From what I had heard about Frank, he had taken to skipping the dropper and pouring in whatever amount he saw fit. It was probably easy to get him enough of the — what was it? — *gout* medication to kill him in one fell swoop.

The next photo made my heart jump into my throat. A pool. *The* pool. I closed my eyes.

"Hey, it's okay. There are no bodies in these pictures," Tony assured me.

No bodies? No Collin, he means.

"You don't have to look at this one." He grabbed the next photo and put it on top. "See this?" I trusted and opened my eyes. It was envelopes with names written on them. Tony, Vanessa, Joey, Victoria, and Becky and 'the boys'. We all had one addressed to us. "Suicide notes found locked in his house."

"Whose?"

"Collin's," Tony looked at me in disbelief, as if it was obvious. I stared at the picture.

"Collin's death was an accident."

"That's what they thought at first," he acknowledged. "But it turns out he over-dosed."

"They told me he fell in the pool and drowned," I recalled.

"Nope. He took a bunch of pills and jumped in."

"To the dirty pool with half the cover on? Wouldn't the pills have been enough?"

"You saw him that night. He was wasted before he even got home. He couldn't have been doing much logical thinking."

"I guess," I conceded. "But he was sober enough to write those notes that night? And one to Joey. Why would he do that if he killed him?"

"He could've written them weeks before. Maybe he didn't plan to kill Joey. Collin wasn't much of a planner."

I had a thousand questions, but they all started with the same word. "Why?"

"Why?" Tony shrugged. "We can't understand *why* really. But the most logical reason is money."

"Money? Collin was never money hungry."

"I know you like to think of yourself as a friend of his, but Collin kept a lot from you. Did you know about Becky?"

"Yes, I did," I said, unsure if Tony knew I was Courtney's best friend. "Collin was always with another woman. I don't blame Becky for leaving."

"He never cheated on her," Tony defended. "Those *others* only came around when Collin and Becky were separated."

That was what Courtney always claimed. "Why would Becky leave then?"

"Money. Collin was in mountains of debt. Becky wanted the good life. Hell, Collin wanted the good life. He killed Dad to speed up his inheritance."

"But Victoria would get that before Collin would. They were still married."

"Exactly," Tony drank his coffee and followed it with a sip of his ice water, as if his mouth was suddenly parched. "Which is why he moved on to his backup plan. Thanks to the tip you gave me about Collin and Frank, I was finally able... the police figured out his connection. Collin killed his other Daddy hoping to get something out of that. Apparently, Collin *was* originally in Frank's will. But Frank changed it, removed him completely. Left everything to his current wife and his estranged *granddaughter*."

"So, he thought he could take out Tiffany and get her inheritance," I added. I looked down at my hands. "But she was killed so soon after Frank. When did he have time to learn about the will changing? And Tiffany was strangled. That's nothing like dosing someone with pills. Collin wasn't a violent man."

"You know he was out of control. He didn't make logical conclusions. He was drunk or high every day of the week."

I felt the need to defend Collin. "He was quitting. He and I talked; he was serious about it. He had no reason to lie to me."

Tony suddenly sounded aggressive, "Oh you talked? Before or after he strangled a woman? You think you know everything about him?" I sat up straighter, pulling away from him. Tony sighed, "Sorry, I know you want to see the best in him, I do too. He was my brother. But you need to understand, he was lying to you. To all of us. Except Joey."

"But you said he killed Joey."

"The police think Joey was in on it." I remembered the message Frank had left for me before he died. I remembered how scary Joey had been the last time I saw him. "Joey might have threatened to turn him in or blackmailed him for his cut. He might have helped with the murders. We can't know the specifics since the suspects are all dead. But I do know that Joey wasn't completely innocent. And he wasn't doing well financially either."

That was true. Temporarily. "Joey had an active contract," I objected. "With Angelo Giaimo."

Tony's eyes widened. "Are you referring to W.E.E.D's loan with Mr. Giaimo?"

I suddenly felt like I had done something wrong. "Yeah, I guess. But I don't think that was it. There were other deals, Joey... always had a plan."

"Hmm," Tony contemplated: I didn't want to interrupt him. I watched his mouth waiting for the words. He had a faint smile when he continued, "Does anyone else know about this?"

"I... I..." I stuttered, "I don't think so."

"You should keep it that way, for your protection."

"Protection?" I was taken aback. "From who-m? Whom?" I never know when it's 'who' or 'whom'.

"The board, for starters."

"Can't you talk to Victoria for me?"

"I can try," Tony looked unsure. "But I can't protect you from the police."

"The po-*lice*!" I whispered, but the end of the word seemed to catch hold and spread through the air, the other tables were staring again.

Tony looked around and raised an eyebrow at me. I looked down. *I'll be good.*

"Yes. Remember, the investigation might be done, but it's not a closed case until they put their final stamp of approval. You keep your head down."

"I haven't done anything wrong." My words were an oven baked meringue. Firm on the outside, basically marshmallow on the inside. Since when did doing nothing wrong protect you from punishment?

"Do not forget," Tony-scolded me, "aside from Collin; you are the only other suspect." *Me?* I nodded, trying not to react. My mouth went dry and I licked my lips. "Get me Angelo's contact info," I pulled out my phone, and he pointed at the folder. "Write it down here, don't text it." He slid the folder to me and I pulled a pen from my purse. "Mother and I will call him and figure out what needs to be done. No one will question why the treasurer and COO would reach out to him. You let me worry about this."

I don't like him treating me like a little girl, but I do appreciate everything he does for me. I've hardly worked this past month, but somehow everything kept in order.

Not somehow: Tony. My co-pilot had taken over and kept the plane on course. He had done so seamlessly and without any hesitation, even though I hadn't been the best pilot for him.

I wrote Angelo's number down. Just one more thing he had happily taken on his plate without even being asked. What would I do without him? I'm glad I don't have to worry about that.

My stomach gurgled. My head pounded. My heart drummed. *There is no way Collin killed these people.* But I can't question the police. Tony thinks they're right. Maybe I'm too close, too emotional. And who else was connected to all these people? Who else was left standing with a trail of bodies behind them?

Though, Collin wasn't standing anymore...

I don't want to think about it. I want to leave it behind and get back to my life. Get back to work. I am the CEO and this company needs me.

27

This is my fresh start. This time the way it always should have been; me as the CEO and Tony as my COO. My friend? That part was nice. Nice enough that I didn't want to complain about the other parts.

He was handling me like a child; a delicate, innocent little thing wandering through the world. Walking, for the first time. In his defense, I am brittle. One more argument, one more lie, one more loss; might just kill me. Is it so bad to have someone around to bubble wrap me? I am lucky that I have anyone who wants to take care of me. If Tony thinks it's best to escort me around he has his reasons. Everyone needs to see we are on the same page. *That makes sense.*

We had only made it to the first floor. The employees I never interacted with. Tony knew them all by name; knew some of their *spouse's* and *pet's* names. Their freaking hobbies. It reminded me of watching Collin work a room.

Tony was more meticulous. He was one of those robot vacuums who knew the floor plan but only from its own perspective. He seemed to awkwardly bump into walls and redirect. But in the end, every inch of the floor was sterilely clean. For Tony, this was a job.

Collin's interactions had been natural and everyone seemed to like him. Tony rubbed them all slightly wrong. Collin made people feel the warm fuzzies while people didn't like Tony's clinical approach. Collin was just so damn likeable.

And a murderer.

It hurts to think it. It hasn't even been an hour since Tony told me about Collin. It's a new and raw wound. I need to treat it and let it heal before I can be ready to move on. I can't take another month to 'recover'; popping in and out of the office at odd hours to avoid others, staying out late at bars, crashing on Courtney's couch after a microdose. I will not start the cycle again. I need to be strong.

Walking up the stairs, I held the railing like a frail old lady. We made it to the landing with me staring down at my feet the whole time. A new pair of shoes came into view. I looked up.

Victoria?

The older woman had her thick dark hair in a stern looking bun. She wore shiny black flats, and a polished black suit with red embellishments, clearly tailored. She had on a natural makeup look aside from her dark red lipstick. A smile formed on her lips.

"Vanessa!" she exclaimed, embracing me. "Welcome back." She whispered in my ear, "You can do this!" She squeezed me while my arms dangled at my side because *of course they did!* She had been polite, friendly, maybe even motherly to me, in the handful of times I had seen her; aside from Joey's funeral. We cried together at Collin's. But she had never hugged me until now, in front of an office full of people that reported to me. She patted the back of my head and let me go.

I greeted her to the best of my ability. "Good morning, Victoria. Do we have a meeting scheduled?" It was meeting day. Wednesday. Something could have been scheduled without me knowing.

"Oh no!" Tony interjected, stepping between and facing us both. "No Mother and I - I decided it was best that Mrs. Caldarelli take this office." He gestured to the office next to us.

"Collin's office?" I asked.

"The Chief Revenue Officer's office, yes," Tony corrected. Of course. Offices belong to positions, not people. "Since she has stepped in as Treasurer and we have the vacancy for CFO after Phil's—" he cleared his throat "—termination. I figured it was better to put offices to use while she's more hands on." Victoria nodded encouragingly.

"Yes." *That makes sense.* "Just like we discussed," I announced for anyone trying to eavesdrop. We hadn't discussed this specifically, but Tony and I had agreed that we needed to be a united front for all decisions he made in my absence. That way, no one would question *my* authority. If anything needed undone, we could do it together now that I'm back. There was no harm in giving an empty office to a member of the board.

"We'll get to work together more often," Victoria added enthusiastically.

Where did she get all her energy from? I had assumed she'd be in her eighties; like Joe was when he passed. But she seemed much more youthful than that. Even harder to understand when you consider her experience in the past several months. Losing a husband, an ex-lover, two sons; it would break most people. The events which had drained me seemed to have given her new life and energy. She was glowing. One day I hope to be as put together as she is.

Tony continued the guided tour, leading me through offices and cubicles hastily. A parade to announce: 'See everyone? Our ruler is alive and well.'

Finally, we got to Peter's little desk, just outside my office door.

"Peter, Vanessa's here," Tony announced.

Peter, who had been lost behind his monitor, stepped out to greet me.

"Welcome back, Ms. Sorella," Peter said. That was oddly formal. Had everyone been calling me by my last name and I've only just noticed it?

"Um, thanks, Peter," I said uncertainly. "I didn't exactly go anywhere."

Tony jumped in, "Of course not! Peter is just referring to having you back as a fixture, keeping to a more regular routine."

In Peter's defense, I hadn't seen *him* at all. He was kept busy. I had agreed that he was best used for Tony's special projects when I didn't need immediate assistance.

"That's fair," I acquiesced. Peter released a sigh. "Is that a new suit? Looks great." *Looks expensive too.* Peter had always been a professional dresser, but this was next level. Tailored, sharp, nice fabric. Looked exactly like some Joey had.

"Thank you." Peter straightened his jacket. "Tony helped me get a few." *They went shopping together?*

"Glad to help!" He moved on quickly. "Peter, can you make sure to look after anything Ms. Sorella needs?"

"Absolutely!" Peter exclaimed, looking at Tony. "Coffee?" Peter turned to me.

"Please," I said. Peter looked to Tony, who nodded, then headed to the break room.

"Peter has been great while you've been gone. I pushed through a raise for him last week. I assumed you would agree since he's been picking up so much of the slack," I nodded slowly at Tony's words. A raise already? Peter had just started working here. But I suppose my time off has put unanticipated stress on his role. If Tony thought it was best... "He'll be coming to me every morning and I'll give him some direction."

But... he's *my* assistant. He should come to *me*.

Tony pulled his keys out of his pocket and unlocked my office door.

"I'll set my purse down and we can go to the meeting," I said.

Tony put his hand up as if to say 'whoa girl.' Calming me like a spooked horse. "Oh, that's not necessary."

"We can't keep canceling the meetings," I protested. I had canceled all of them this past month, sometimes at the last minute, unable to bring myself to the draining meetings days.

"No, of course not! Luckily, we've been able to salvage most of them without you. But you've got a lot of work to do to catch back up," Tony was guiding me by placing one hand on the small of my back. I set my purse on my desk. "I promise, I've got you covered with the team. You should focus on more important things."

True. As CEO I can't spend my first full day back sitting in a conference room. *That makes sense.*

"I'll debrief you after the meetings," Tony said.

"Okay," I said to the door, since Tony had already left and closed it behind him.

I checked my emails.

I drank my coffee.

I tidied my desk.

I tried to enjoy the view, but it was far too industrial to be *enjoy*-able. I cleaned out my purse where I found I'd been hauling Joe's book around. I set it on my desk. What a heavy weight to carry for no reason. I considered reading it. Maybe trying to finish the damn thing. But I hadn't touched it since Joey died. Knowing it was for him ruined it. Not my fun little sneak peek into how to become a millionaire directly from the horse's mouth. No. It was a book to a dead man from a dead man whose real secrets died with him. I was a pathetic morbid observer.

Besides, I'm the boss and I have important things to do. I sent out an email to each department head, asking for an initiative update so they could bring me up to speed.

Time passed by so slowly I considered walking in on the meetings. Tony wanted to give me time to work, but the meetings were where all the work was being done. But if I join suddenly, if I interrupt, that will undermine Tony in front of everyone.

I called Courtney and invited her to lunch. I regretted it immediately when we got seated at Meat and Veg, Courtney's favorite farm-to-table lunch place. When she took her sunglasses off her smudgy mascara betrayed that she had been crying. Again. Or still. Since Saturday.

"Hey," she sniffled, reaching across the table to pat my forearm. "How are we doing today?"

We sat opposite each other in the comfortable enough booth, by the window. The restaurant was busy, it always had been, even though it changed names / management at least twice in the past few years. The generic looking restaurant had added mint green tablecloths and painted the walls gray, reupholstered the booths as a black fabric rather than red pleather. A facelift performed by the most recent management. One that would droop in a few years until a new owner came through. Speaking of facelifts, Courtney's Botox was fighting for its life as she squished and contorted her expression into her crying face. It was the only face of hers I saw any more.

"I'm fine," I said firmly, trying to brush it off.

Courtney looked at me with pity. "Vanessa, it's okay to not be okay."

I buried my face in the menu. "I'm fine. You don't have to read into everything. I say I'm fine, and I'm fine."

"Are you sure?" Courtney pried. "Because I've been so lonely and I think you have too. No one else can understand, no one else knows what—"

"Can we not?" I snapped. Courtney's lower lip started shaking. I'm being too harsh. I sighed. "I want to talk about *anything* other than the men in our lives. Please." She pursed her lips but then nodded. "Have you heard from Lindsey?"

Courtney flipped her menu up, hiding her tearful eyes. "Yeah. She seems really good. She wants to do a girls' night soon. Says she has something to tell us."

"Oh good, I bet she's pregnant." I hope I didn't sound as disgusted as I felt at the idea. "Good for her. Just not for me. That's why I'm glad Joey already—" I stopped myself. The fact that Joey had a vasectomy was irrelevant considering his other status.

Courtney flopped her menu down and stared at me, giving me no choice but to do the same. As the tears welled in her pitiable eyes, I gave a permissive nod. "Collin wanted more kids," she wailed. "And his boys are young enough we would've been able to raise them all together. I couldn't wait to be a mom."

I spent the next hour and forty-five minutes eating an overpriced chimichurri steak salad and listening to Collin's mistress go on and on as if she were his widowed wife of forty years. I knew to expect this when I invited Courtney out. It was all she had talked about for a month. It hits different when we're sober. And after finding out that *hers* is the leading suspect in the murder of *mine*.

"It was nice catching up," I lied in the parking lot. Courtney grabbed my arm and squeezed. She was a toucher.

"It's nice to have someone who understands."

I don't want to get her started again. But her grief feels so different from mine and it's pissing me off. "They weren't that great. I think it's time you moved on."

Courtney chewed on her lip before smiling sadly, the smile not extending to her glaring eyes. "I know you're hurt, so I'm going to let that go."

"I'm not hurt. I'm angry and I'm done!" I spat. "I'm done with Collin and Joey and all the shit they dragged me into. I wish I never knew them. I don't want to think about them and I don't want to talk to you about them anymore!"

She looked so deflated. I know it's not her I should be yelling at. But the ones I should be can't hear me.

"How can you write them off so easily?" Tears were falling down her face now.

Because one of them is abusive and one is a murderer. But I wasn't allowed to tell her what Tony had said. And it didn't feel right to claim Melissa's abuse story as my own since he hadn't been that bad to me. I just shook my head in response.

She said indignantly, "You're not perfect either. You've hurt people."

"Sure," I allowed. "But I'm sorry for it. I apologize. I change. I do better."

"And neither of them will get the chance to do that. You don't know what they would have done with more time," Courtney insisted. I knew exactly what Joey would do with more time. "Collin wanted to apologize. He wanted to be better." She looked away from me.

"You don't know that!" I shouted.

She nodded her head aggressively. "I do! I do know that!" She was getting louder and people were looking. "I know you think of me as some kind of homewrecker but Collin and—"

"Stop," I hissed. "I don't want to do this in the parking lot."

"No," she said, quietly at least. "You can *listen to me* for once." Courtney was making intense eye contact. "Collin and I had real feelings for each other and we really talked. He told me how desperately he wanted to talk to you. But you always blew him off. You never heard his side. You make everything into some kind of personal affront to you."

"Gee, maybe because he got wasted on the job the first week I was his boss," I said. "He made it clear to everyone that I had no supporters. No friends in the office."

"See? You make that entire thing about you. Collin had a weak moment. He felt terrible. He called me crying about how he disappointed you. It's like his dad set him up before he died. Leaving behind an open bottle of whiskey to tempt him. He only had a little."

"You're so gullible."

"Am I? Or do I just know that people can make mistakes and still be good people?" I looked down, not eager to argue with an irrational person. "He swore to me, it was maybe a shot, shot and half. He shouldn't have passed out like that. He was doing so well with quitting he thought it might've been withdrawal symptoms. Not like being drunk, more like being drugged."

"Yeah right," I scoffed, but then thought: *Drugged?* "Drugged?" I uttered.

"Yes. And some friend you were. He worked so hard to quit. He never touched another drop after that," she insisted.

"Until the night he died," I reminded her.

"So you say."

I shook my head; *I never saw him with alcohol that night.* "So *Tony says.*" I hugged her, catching her off guard. But I felt her hug me back. "I love you, Court. But I gotta go now," I released the hug, and turned to my car. The fog lifting from my brain.

"Wait, just like that?" she called as I was walking away.

I called back, "I have work to do."

Because *Tony says* a lot of things. But they *don't* make sense.

28

I rushed back to the office. It was almost two. Everyone was still meeting. Without me. Perfect.

I stopped at Peter's desk. I looked around and saw no one, so I tapped the space bar on his keyboard to wake the screen up.

Enter pin

Damn.

I flipped through the papers on his desk. It was copies of previous meeting packets. Several weeks' worth. I quickly surmised there was nothing of value. No evidence of Tony's affair. I picked up his note pad and flipped through it. He had hardly any notes. Dates, attendees, and meetings were the headers of various pages. With the occasional "follow up on" or "date of next meeting" written through the otherwise empty pages. *Not taking notes*, obviously since he was in a meeting right now without his notebook. *Not filing. Not working for me.* What is Peter doing?

"Eh-em," she cleared her throat to announce herself, emerging from behind Peter's monitors.

"Victoria!" I slammed down the notebook. Which makes me look guilty. *Guilty of what?* Anything my assistant knows, I should know. Victoria stood there silently, prompting me to say, "Can I help you?"

"I'd like to talk," she cooed. I waited for her to continue. She flicked her eyes to my office door, the intent clear.

"Yes, sure." I grabbed my purse and took out my keys to unlock my door. "How are you today?" I said, filling the silence as I made my way in.

"Quite well, thank you," Victoria said warmly.

As I sat behind my desk in the large chair, I felt small. The desk dwarfed me, the chair threatened to swallow me, ass first, and Victoria stood, taller than me now that I was seated. It was only seconds, but it dragged on in my head. I couldn't help but offer... beg her to sit. "Please," I urged. "Have a seat."

"Thank you," she said, politely, calmly, professionally, confidently. She sat with her back straight. She looked different from how I had imagined when Joey spoke of her. For one, she was thinner. People told me I looked exactly like her but she wasn't quite as... filled out. She was still plump. I hate the way the word is sometimes used, but I see it as a compliment. Plump fruit is desirable. A shriveled apple doesn't make your mouth water. She also didn't look to be in her late seventies or eighties. Hopefully I'll look like her when I'm older, if I can afford regular spa treatments and a damn good tailored suit. The cinched waist may be making her look thinner. The red thread on the black suit outlining her silhouette. Her perfect posture showed her drive, ready to spring into action.

"How are you doing?" Her dark eyes bored into mine. "Anthony says he gave you the news."

"News?" I asked. I generally knew what she was referencing. But her casual choice of words is confusing. Maybe she was talking about something less personal. I'll let her say it.

"About Collin, dear. And Joey. His father, as well, I suppose." Victoria did seem concerned about how I was doing. Some emotion crept in when she spoke her sons' names. But there was no love lost between her and Joe, at least from her perspective. "It must be hard to accept. And what a relief to know it's over!"

A relief? I'm not a mother, but I doubt I'd feel *relieved* at the death of my children even when some conclusion is on the horizon.

"I don't..." I started, losing my nerve to say it outright. "I'm not sure that it *is* over."

"Of course it is. There won't be any trial," she said softly. "I'm afraid the only real closure we'll have is knowing what happened. Then the only thing to help you feel better will be time and distance from it."

That explains why she feels relieved. She's hoping this is the first step of healing. *It makes sense.* But she's wrong. I need her help to prove it. Or her reassurance. I need *my* mom, but *this* mother will do.

"You know Collin better than me. Do you really think he would do this?"

"Collin had his demons. His addictions drove him to be a man I didn't think my son could become. I never would have guessed he would do this," she clicked her tongue. "But he did. And what's happened has happened. The case is closed." This must be what she's had to tell herself. To live with the pain.

"It's *not* closed," I insisted. "That's just one possible theory. The main lead the police are tracking down. But I *know* Collin. It doesn't make any sense."

"Murder doesn't make sense to the *average* person," she said *average* with such distaste. Victoria was kind to me, but all the Caldarelli's had an elitist attitude. "I knew Collin. He must have had his reasons. For one, money can be a powerful motivation." She was right about that much.

"But Collin was no killer. He wasn't a violent man."

"The murders, they were mostly poisoning, drugging. That's harmful, but is it violent? And a gunshot. That's a quick, clean kill. Something a non-violent person might choose to avoid too much hands-on guilt," she said serenely. She was focusing on all the wrong things. Making every excuse why Collin *could have* done it. I need her to see the bigger picture.

"What about Tiffany?" I pressed.

"You mean the girl? She was a one-off. Hardly part of the whole thing." Victoria brushed Tiffany aside like a loose strand of hair, fallen from her perfect bun.

"She was strangled and then dumped somewhere. It's inconceivably violent. Not like a planned attack. More like a crime of passion. Like a boyfriend or a *lover* would do," I said.

"Collin had many lovers," Victoria pointed out. "But it seems like you have a point you'd like to make. Why don't you get to it then? We are both busy women."

I don't understand her tone. These are good points that might describe Collin's innocence. A mother would want that. Unless she knows already in her heart what I'm about to suggest. It would be devastating, your only remaining son: a murderer. But denial doesn't make it untrue. "There is no easy way to say this..." Victoria just stared at me as I spoke. There *was* no easy way to say it. I went the long hard way, hoping she would piece it together. "Were you aware that Tony was seeing... as in dating, Tiffany?"

She didn't react. "Why should I know of all my sons' dalliances? I didn't know *you* until after Joey died," she stated.

Dalliance? *How dare she...* no. This is not what we're discussing. Victoria is clearly hurting. Lashing out. I need to press on. "He was. Dating her, I mean. At the time of her death — her murder," I corrected. I stopped, hoping she would jump in. Acknowledge what that means. She didn't help me. I continued, "It seems possible he would have reason to—"

"And you have proof of this?"

I don't know what I expected her to say. Not that. "No... I guess not. But I could at least tell the police, let them look at it from a new angle." Again, she had no reaction to my words. "There's more. I found several bottles of prescription drugs, opioids, in this desk. They were all Tony's."

She took in what I said. "Can I see them?"

"I don't... I gave them back to him," I stumbled, suddenly feeling foolish.

"What else then? What other claims would you like to make against my only son?" Victoria pressed.

"Victoria, I'm not trying to upset you. I just think there are many things you don't know." I sighed. "If I reach out to the cops, we still have time before they close the case."

"You'll reach out to the cops, with what evidence exactly? Are you going to reach in that desk and magically pull out a murder weapon? Or are you going to make more baseless claims about my—" she stopped abruptly, staring at my desk. Specifically, the small leather book. "Where did you get that?" She snapped. Her aggression made a knot form in my stomach.

I quickly slid the book across my desk and pulled it onto my lap. "Online. I ordered it," I responded too slowly yet spoke too quickly.

"May I see it?" The venom in her voice was gone, or perhaps better hidden.

"It's my journal," I covered. "That's private."

"I see." Her eyes focused on my lap. "It sounds as though you are dead set on going to the police. And reopening some very painful wounds for an old widow who has tragically lost two sons." She looked into my eyes then. Her eyes had become glossy and wet. But she had no real sadness in them.

I looked at her, refusing to back down. "I am."

"What a shame." Her eyes narrowed, the glossy shine disappearing against the black backdrop. "I agree with some of what you're saying. Collin was never a violent man, but he was a *real man*, like his father. And we all know, poisoning is more of a *woman's* method of choice. If he didn't kill himself, Collin must have been poisoned too." She stood to leave. "If there's nothing else, Miss Sorella."

"I think we're done here," I said to her back. Those Caldarelli's really know how to storm off.

I froze. My heart thudded hard in my chest; slowing down but pumping more blood with each beat. I breathed in deeply, gathering my thoughts. I cannot afford time to freeze. I put myself firmly back in the moment. Thankfully, my briefly frozen time had paused the world for me.

I pulled out the card with Detective Hernandez's contact information and started plugging in the numbers before the door had even closed behind Victoria. I didn't want to lose my nerve. He picked up immediately. "Hello?"

"This is Vanessa Sorella. I'm calling about the Tiffany Miller case," I blurted out. There was a long silence. Too long. He hadn't been the one questioning me for the past month. What if he wasn't even on the case?

Finally, he asked, "How can I help you Ms. Sorella?"

"I have evidence for you to consider. It's new... I don't think you have the right suspect." I swallowed hard.

He clicked his tongue. "Actually, we've got two suspects." I knew it! Tony was a liar *and* a murderer, trying to throw me off his scent. I bet the case is far from closed. Wonderfully, Detective Hernandez was still on it. I have a leg up on Tony.

"Good. I want you to find the right person."

"And *you* know who that is?" the detective asked.

"I have new evidence."

"Which is?"

I wanted to blurt it all out to him. Lay out every point bit by bit. Explain every death the way I knew it had to have happened. But I needed time. Time to gather everything to organize my thoughts. I need a working theory for every murder. The hows and the whys are rough sketches. I hope he can't hear my rushed, panicked breathing. I kept my sentences short so I could breathe between them. "Two days. I need time. I'll give you everything in person."

"Two days?"

"Yes. Can I come to the station to see you then?"

He hesitated. "I'll come to your house. Friday morning. I'll be in touch." he hung up.

Thank God because I didn't think I could keep my voice from shaking. I was still trying to force all the separate ingredients together. The last one I've added is Tony. Now I'm stuck in that confusing stage of making dough where it looks too wet then too dry. The whiplash rocked my skull as Tony went from rival to friend to villain.

I played back her words, kneading them in my brain. How much did Victoria know? Our conversation still fresh. She had said there was a murder weapon in the desk.... did she know about.... I pulled the middle drawer open, the box sliding to me. It was unlocked — I flipped it open — empty.

A gun with my fingerprints was out in the world. I have to get ahead of this. I have to be smarter and better than Tony. Tiffany must have known something. She delivered the poison and Tony had her files shredded. But not the ones the auditor took. I stood and rushed out to Peter's desk to continue my search. In my hurry, I almost bumped into him.

"Oh, Peter!" I tried to cover my surprise at being caught. "I thought you were in meetings."

"Just finished," he said.

"Good. Good." I stood there, unmoving.

"Did you need something?"

I thought he'd never ask. "I need the contact information for the state auditor who took Tiffany's files. Do you know the name of the department he worked for?" I tried not to sound frantic, by the way he was looking at me, I wasn't doing a good job.

"He didn't say," Peter said unhelpfully.

"And you can't recall any of the files he took?"

He shook his head. "It's been a month." I started to plan a time I could come back to snoop when he wasn't here. There must be something on Tiffany's old computer about her relationship with Tony. Or something about Frank? "But I know how we can get ahold of him," he offered. *Lead with that next time.* "Saw him at golf last week. I subbed in for Tony; he was having some kind of foot flare up and couldn't walk. We're supposed to see him on Friday too," he blathered on while my heart raced. Golf with Tony. The state auditor was just another Tony Crony.

My heart failed the race and sank. "Who is he?"

"I don't remember exactly. But I can try to get his information from Tony. I think his name was something Hernandez."

My eyes widened. I practically shouted, "No!" *Fuck me.* Why didn't I talk to Peter two minutes earlier? "Don't worry about it."

"You sure? It's no problem at all," he offered.

"It's fine. Don't bother him. Or Tony," I threatened, not caring how weird that was to say. I turned back to my office. Peter kept talking but my head was underwater and I understood none of what he was saying. I closed my office door. The realization overtook me.

Realization that I understood nothing. I had handed the controls of the plane to my co-pilot but he was actually a hijacker. And I know we are about to crash but there is nothing I can do about it. Except brace myself for impact.

I sat down in my big stupid chair at my big stupid desk. There is no one to help me now. I put my head in my hands. I've just called Tony's friend to give him my only evidence. If I cancel that, I'll just make it worse.

W.W.J.D.

What would Joe do?

The same thing every rich person would do. He'd hire an expensive lawyer. Then he'd shut up. Well, I'm a rich person. But I don't have connections. Lawyers on retainer I can trust. I can't search for 'lawyers in my area'. The ones on billboards are for car accidents not murder defense. Joe would not Google search for 'hot single lawyers in my area', he'd use his contacts.

I lifted my head out of my hands. Joe's Rolodex. At the tip of my fingers. Flipping through it, I found he hadn't alphabetized by name. Rather by profession or function.

Typical. Wealthy men like Joe don't see you by who you are. Just what you'll do for them.

L should be for *lawyer* or *legal*. But it looks like Joe used it for *locksmith* and there was no contact card. Flipping through the rest, nothing else made sense. I started again. *A* was accountants. *B* was bankers. *C* was... *Consigliere*. Who did Joe think he was, the freaking Godfather? No wonder I breezed past it the first time.

I pulled the first card. *Keith Klein - Esq.* I typed the number in my phone.

Tony thinks he can beat me using his connections. Two can play at that game. Unlike him, I didn't get to where I am by having my Daddy hand me things. I took what I could and clawed my way to the top. And look at me now. No more autopilot. It's time to land this fucking plane.

29

Being exhausted and exhilarated makes you feel like a fraternal twin of yourself. One of me is confident, capable, and ready. The popular twin you want at your party. The other would rather nap or read through the party. They're the one the popular twin makes you invite and then they drag them along. Then no one enjoys themselves. But don't worry, that awkward me is at home asleep and is not invited to the party. Popular me is in control now because today is the day I take down Tony Caldarelli.

I don't exactly know *how*. At seven hundred fifty dollars an hour, that's what I'm paying Keith Klein for. What I *do* know is everything else. Every little thing Tony thought he could hide. Every murder he thought he would get away with. While pretending to be my friend.

It is fitting that I'm using Joe's lawyer to take Tony down. One of his many victims, dead but not forgotten. Though when Keith stopped getting paid by him he forgot Joe existed. I jogged his memory well enough. With the wad of cash I'll be paying him, he won't forget *me* anytime soon.

It's hard to sit quietly without begging to know what Keith is thinking as he reads the final pages of Joe's notebook. I'd spent all night finding any scrap of evidence I could. It was almost ten when I finally thought about looking at Joe's book.

Victoria asked about it knowing it was Joe's; possibly knowing what it said. The final pieces of the puzzle gently slid into place. I kicked myself for not reading the end sooner, thinking it would somehow spoil it. I had given up on the advice after Joey died. My current predicament was directly attributable to most of this advice. But the final pages might be my salvation. I read and re-read them all night. Careful to pick out every juicy bit. Like eating chicken wings and sucking the bone clean.

I have the words memorized now, right down to the marrow.

I watched Keith, trying to guess which part he was reading. His face was inscrutable. I recited the words back to myself.

————————————

I'm going to divorce Victoria and leave everything to you [Joey] and Collin. Your mother and Tony, though I love them dearly, are selfish people. They've spent all my fucking money and if I don't change something now, the only thing I'll leave to my sons and my grandchildren will be my life insurance policy.

Tony is super dangerous and untrustworthy. A complete snake in the grass loser whose head is too big for his body so he looks like one of those suckers filled with gum and his weak little body made of a paper stick barely supports it. I've started to believe he has been dosing me with something that makes my mind hazy. Which is why I have written you this book while my mind is still sharp. Once I deal with your mother and Tony, I will step down as CEO so you can step into the role.

-Caldarelli, Joe* (2027). *Joe's First Ninety Days*

*Found deceased by his (murdered) assistant who herself was the grandchild of his best friend (murdered) who had a love child (murdered) with the deceased's wife who is suspiciously alive and well.

————————————

Okay. More of a paraphrase… an adlib. But you get the gist. It was multiple pages, I can't learn them all by heart. The point is *that* is why this whole thing started. Joe was going to divorce Victoria and write Tony out of the will.

"Hmm," Keith was unimpressed as he set the book down.

"Finished?" I asked.

He said, "Yes," then leaned back and casually put his left leg over his right.

"And?" I tugged at him.

"What exactly does this mean to you?"

"Motive!" I shouted, and then remembered to be quieter, assuming Peter might be Tony's little spy. "Follow the money. Joe was going to divorce Victoria, after a decade of separation, and change his will to cut both she *and Tony* out."

"Even if that were true, he never did. His estate is going to be settled soon. There's no contest to it and Victoria will get everything. There's no proof they knew of this book. It's been in your possession."

"But what about the drugging? Tony was slipping something to Joe."

"Joe thought so. But he also admitted his mind was hazy. If anything, it weakens your position. You shouldn't mention it again."

"Right." I looked down, disappointed.

He moved to tuck the book into his expensive looking brown leather briefcase bag thing. "But I'll take it under consideration," he said.

I reached out my hand to say *stop*. "Can't you make a copy? I'd rather I keep the original."

"Copies are not evidence."

He was right. It's probably safer with him than with me.

"There's more!" I blurted eagerly. "Tony has a reason to kill all of them." I started to count them out on my fingers for him. "He killed Joe for his inheritance. Frank, he's the main person who fought against Tony getting the job of

CEO so that one was revenge. And like I told you, Tiffany and he were dating. She probably found out something because she brought Frank the poisoned tincture. Joey and Collin, same thing, they figured out what he did. And they were next in line for Joe's will... He hated them, he had lots of reasons to kill them."

"There's been a time or two I wanted to shoot my brother," Keith chuckled, catching me off guard. "But I never would. You sure do have a lot of theories about what Tony might do. Let me be clear: *if* I take on your case, it's not to prove Tony did something to my dear friend, Joe." He touched his palm to his chest. "It's about proving you didn't do it."

If he takes on my case? Not to sound desperate inside my own head... but I *need* Keith to believe me. "That's easy!" I laughed, trying to sound breezy and unbothered. "Because I didn't do it. I have no motive. I barely knew most of them."

"Motive. That's the easiest one. The prosecutor could provide a thousand spins on any motive. You knew Joe?"

"I did."

"From what you mentioned earlier, you knew he was going to make you the CEO when he retired."

"When I first got the job, yes, I thought that. But then later Joey told me—"

"Ah-ah-ah." Keith wagged his finger at me. "We must go on what you *thought* at the time Joe died. Motive to kill comes *before* killing. Joey and Collin would be an easy motive too. For the money Joe left behind. Joey left you everything in his will."

"Me and his daughter," I agreed. "But Joey had practically nothing."

"He would've had a lot more if Joe's estate and life insurance finally settled."

"It would have been Victoria's though," I protested.

"Not according to this book," he patted his leather bag. "Remember, your defense has to be on what you believed to be true. And you were the only person who read this book."

"But *I* gave you that book. I didn't have to," I said.

"But I would have to give it to the prosecutor. That's Brady evidence." He shook his head, regrettably. "It's also a great motive to kill Collin. One less person to share the spoils. Your very public outrage towards Collin and Tiffany in this office with all of these witnesses is reason enough." He'd learned all this since yesterday? He continued, interrupting my internal thoughts. "Then there's Frank."

"What about Frank?" I practically bit Keith's head off.

"He discovered a connection between *your fiancé* and Angelo Giaimo. Seems like a shady deal was going on there."

"Who told you—" I cut myself off. Peter had taken Frank's voicemail. That slimy snake. No wonder he's been so buddy-buddy with Tony. They're both slithering around together. "I didn't know anything about that. I knew Joey and he were friends, but that's all."

"Who will believe that, Ms. *Sorella*?" Keith put emphasis on my last name, giving it the weight I hadn't ever chosen to throw around. "No one will accept that the *CEO* of the company, the fiancé of the *criminal*, could be so easily manipulated. So oblivious and stupid—"

I pounded my fist on my desk. "Okay!" I pushed the word through my barely parted lips, forcing myself to remain quiet. "I get it. Not having a motive is not a particularly good defense.... for me. But I'm hiring you so you can tell me what is. I'm innocent. I just need someone to help me prove that." Desperate tears were on the verge of release but luckily my eyes were too dry after a night of no rest.

"As I have said," Keith began, unnaturally calm, "I have yet to decide whether I will be representing you. Until I have made up my mind, it is best you think of me as more of a devil's advocate."

It wasn't hard to picture. With his tiny frameless glasses and eyebrows so blond they disappeared, Keith's face didn't leave you a lot of places to focus. Thin lips covered most of his small stained teeth while he spoke. The stains I assume he got from smoking based on the faint whiff I caught when I greeted him. I couldn't look into his yellow green eyes either because those plus his pale skin made him seem jaundiced to me. Instead, my eyes wandered: watch; suit; tie; shoes, the left one dangerously close to touching *my* desk. Nothing matched, but I added up the costs of it all and agreed: yes, *this* was the devil's advocate and the devil paid well.

I need him on *my side*.

"I need your help, Mr. Klein. I don't know what's going on because I haven't done anything. But I feel like I'm working against a ticking time bomb. I have no idea how much time there is or what happens when it explodes." I put my hands on my desk, palms up. Someone told me once it makes you look sincere. I used the opportunity to squeeze my breasts together with my upper arms. "Anything I can do to convince you, so you can help me prove my innocence, I will do."

He played with his green tie. It worked well against the brown of his suit but its silky texture didn't go well with the corduroy suit. Not that I know everything about fashion; the clash was off-putting. Like he had bought many separate high-cost items without consideration of how they looked with each other. He finally broke the silence. "Everything we've discussed is circumstantial. What I'm after is evidence, proof. Because whether you are innocent or guilty—"

"I'm innocent!"

"—doesn't matter to me. All I need to know is if we can put up a good defense. Tell me *every* potentially incriminating thing and how you would defend against it."

"There is no incriminating evidence. There's no physical... anything. Because I didn't do it."

Keith was digging into his bag. "That is not true." He pulled out a stack of loose papers. It was large. "After you called me, I spoke to a connection I have with the police."

He looked me in the eye forcing me to return his sickly stare. "Nothing I say here leaves this room. Understood?" I nodded. "It seems they have an exorbitant amount of evidence against you." He paused but it wasn't so I could speak. "Joe Caldarelli. By your own admission you had a lot to gain from his death. The investigation determined that you did regularly come to his office for meetings giving you opportunity to access his private whiskey stock here. They do believe that is how he was drugged. And now they will have his journal, which was in your possession for some reason." He was flipping through the loose sheets and landed on a photo. "As for Frank Miller, this exit bag from your cannabis dispensary that delivered the tainted tincture came with this note." He slid the photo to me. A picture of the note that Peter had sent Frank's widow saying it was from me.

"That was after he died."

"Unfortunately, Frank's wife has a fuzzy memory on the timing of when the note was received. Though it is unusual you sent cannabis to his house *after* he died. If that's your claim." He slid the photo to his left. "The last message Tiffany Miller received from you was a request to meet up."

"I didn't meet up with her."

In a mocking tone he read from a paper in front of him, *"Hey, Tiff. I don't like how things went today. Can we talk? Woman to woman?"* I bit my lip as he pulled out another photo. "This photo shows Joey Caldarelli's car in front of Tiffany Miller's house."

I had my response ready, none of this was new. "Tony had access to that car, it was with his mechanic."

Keith clicked his tongue. "The mechanic's official statement was that he never would have released the car to anyone. But it was on an open lot. According to Joey before he died, *you* had the only other key. Joey's ex-wife confirmed he was down in LA at the time of Tiffany's murder."

"Tony could have gotten the car—"

"Facts only," he said. I closed my mouth as he slid the photo to the new stack to his left. He leafed through pages reading as he went. "As for Mr. Joey Caldarelli, you and he had a heated discussion the day he died. You left after sustaining an injury, but your car stayed in the driveway all night. When you returned for it the next morning you 'didn't notice' Joey's front door was ajar and he was dead in the entryway. Nor did you try to retrieve your shoes which were left in the house."

"I was trying to grab my car and go without seeing him."

"Your car, which was conveniently parked blocking any camera all night."

"I already showed the cops I paid for a ride home. And I didn't come back until late morning with a friend. She can vouch for me." Courtney had already provided her statement supporting me. That should be enough.

"But you only lived two miles away. A distance you could easily have walked. Since you were alone all night."

I racked my brain for my defense I had provided against this when I had been asked weeks ago. It felt like years. "My foot!" I recalled. "I was injured. There's no way I could have walked there and back. I have pictures of it, and a hospital bill."

"Hmm," his mouth stayed closed and he looked thoughtful. "But do you have proof of *when* you got the injury? We know it was in Joey's home." He did not wait for my reply and slid the picture of my car in Joey's driveway into his stack on the left. Still, no new evidence. If they wanted to arrest me for this, they would have already. The next picture *was* new. "And why would your fingerprints be on this gun?"

"Where did they find that?" I asked reflexively. They were still looking for it according to Tony.

"Why would your fingerprints be on this gun?" he repeated.

I stared him down, holding only moments before my gaze broke away, giving in, deciding to trust him. I pulled open the middle drawer of my desk and handed him the empty gun storage box. He flipped it open. "I see," he slid the picture onto the stack to his left. Was this the *Vanessa is Guilty* stack? He took the box and crammed it into his bag. "And who else knows this was your gun?"

"No one, it isn't mine," I protested weakly. "Why are you interrogating me?"

Keith blinked at me. Then calmly said, "If you cannot handle my process, you can find different representation. Interrogations are easy for the *innocent*."

I want to tell him to get out. That could be the biggest mistake of my life. If Joe trusted this man for himself, I'm in no position to question it. The wealthy have always done things in ways I don't understand. If I want to be like them, I have to do things their way.

I nodded to him permissively. He was right, if I couldn't handle this, a real interrogation would destroy me.

"I found the gun in Joe's drawer. But I never used it."

He continued. "And your fingerprints on these?" He slid me a picture. Two orange pill bottles with white lids. Labels missing. "These were found in the home of Mr. Collin Calderelli. The source of his overdose."

"They weren't mine," I began. "I found them... in this desk drawer." I trailed off sounding idiotic. Once again he moved the picture to the stack on his left. "They were Tony's. I gave them back."

"Right. And do you have proof of this?"

"That's a dumb question," I started strong. Then, defeated, "No. I don't."

"Your fingerprints were in lipstick on the lid. I don't suppose that was Tony's shade."

I shook my head and grabbed my purse. "It was lip gloss. It spilled in my purse. Here." I handed him the tube. "This is the new one. Same shade." He took it and examined it before putting it into his bag. "But obviously I wouldn't leave something covered in my lipstick and fingerprints by a body." I laughed uncomfortably for the millionth time, not sure I remembered what a real laugh sounded like.

"It was left in Collin's home, by this."

What he gave me next was a photocopy rather than a full-color photo. A letter.

Vanessa, I know I've hurt you with my recent actions and for that I am sorry. But the way I've hurt you the most you don't even know. From the very beginning, Joey and I were using you. It was wrong and I'll never forgive myself. It ate me up every time I saw you. I hope you can find a way to forgive me and Joey, but the first step is coming clean.
Let's talk.
Your friend, Collin.

When I'd had enough time to read it twice, Keith finally asked, "What was this about?"

"I don't know," I said in disbelief. "I never got this," I shook the paper at him, holding back tears.

"Hmmm," he hummed to himself. "And how about this?"

Again, it was a photocopy. This time of a note that had been torn, then pieced together. It was Peter's notes on the voicemail from Frank. All about Joey's connection to Angelo Giaimo.

"I don't know anything about this."

"Your assistant says he delivered this message to you *personally*. Should we go get him?" He half turned in his chair, as if to invite Peter in.

"No!" I said, even though I knew it was a performance. "I got the message. I just don't know what it's *really* about," I half-lied.

"Hmmm," he said annoyingly. He plucked the paper from my hand and put it onto his special stack. "Collin's house was locked. He had no keys on him. But *inside* the house, they found a spare key with *this* key chain." As he slowly slid the photo to me, I wanted to speed it along and grab it. What else? What new thing was he throwing in my face? Patiently, I waited for him to remove his hand from the photo. It was a picture of a white queen chess piece, that I knew to be ivory. A large letter *V* was carved into the bottom.

Victoria.

I swallowed but my throat was dry. A lump went down and the pain caught in my chest.

"I notice you have a similar chess piece there?"

I grabbed Joe's keyring and started to detach the piece immediately, my fingers shaking. "It's not mine," I croaked.

"No," Keith looked at the bottom. "This one says *JC*. This one—" he pointed to the picture "—says *V*." The small white king disappeared into his bag. He gathered the stacks of paper including the one in my hand and shoved them unceremoniously into his bag. "*Vanessa*, I think our time here is done."

He stood. I stood.

"But... Are you going to defend me or not?" I demanded to know.

He smirked. "You've only paid me for this hour." I immediately started searching my purse. "Sounds like you don't need a lawyer. According to you, you've never seen or heard anything. Things just appear around this magic desk. You can't be held accountable for that." He turned and my search became frantic. "I wouldn't worry. I hear they have a suspect."

"Wait!" I pulled out my checkbook and scribbled an absurd number, calling out to him again. "Wait!" I ripped the check out and hurried after him.

If I know anything at all, I know money will fix this.

I caught him just after Peter's desk and forced the check into his hand.

I looked him in the eyes. "You work for me now." I looked down at his hand to see if he accepted the check. It had disappeared, presumably into his bag. I looked down into it and saw the tip of a cerulean folder poking out of the top.

Why...

I sensed movement in my periphery and turned to see a man and a woman walking towards me. I recognized them. Detectives. I walked towards them, Keith, in lockstep. *My consigliere.*

"Detective Pierce, Detective Buan, nice to see you," I said in a voice intended to soothe. *I didn't do anything wrong.* And, I paid a lot of money to prove it. I have nothing to be worried about.

"Ms. Sorella," Detective Buan began. "I'm going to need you to come with us."

I shook my head. "No, not today. I've answered all your questions, but I really must get back to work." I looked towards the occupied meeting room.

Detective Buan was unimpressed. "This is not a courtesy call. And it isn't optional," she had said that part quietly, aware of the people suddenly loitering in our vicinity.

"In that case, I have to insist you go through my lawyer, Mr. Klein, to arrange a meeting." I used my right hand to gesture to Keith.

The Detectives looked at him.

Keith put up his left hand and brushed off the suggestion. "Oh no," he said jovially with a small chuckle. "There seems to be some confusion here. I'm not a defense lawyer. I'm a corporate attorney. Mr. Cardarelli retained me to represent W.E.E.D. in some legal matters." Tony stepped out of the meeting room then and Keith gave him a wave. "There he is now. Good luck, Ms. Sorella." He steered away towards Tony. "Mr. Cardarelli!" he called.

Impossible. I paid him. He has to help me.

I wanted to protest. But nothing came out. Who would I complain to? I never belonged in this world, in this role.

They knew it. They saw my vulnerability and everyone around me took advantage. Even Joe's advice, designed to lead his son to success, burned up and turned to ash in my hands. I looked down at my hands which so recently held a check that should have bought me everything I needed, but they were empty.

Detective Buan continued, "You have the right to remain silent..."

It was the only good advice I'd gotten since I became CEO. So I shut the fuck up.

30

Tony watched Vanessa scrupulously. She had glanced in his direction, but her line of sight soon fell to her own feet.

It was arousing; to see her now in this state of submission.

Nonetheless, this is not how he wanted things to go. She caused this. She was far too headstrong. His least favorite quality of hers.

Since his brother's death, Tony had begun to see all the reasons Joey had chosen Vanessa. He had always known she was physically remarkable, one of the sexiest women Tony had ever seen. He'd never looked deeper than that because Joey had found her first. Joey didn't want his younger brother playing with his things.

When he was finally out of the picture, Tony could see all of Vanessa's best qualities come to the surface. She was practically the opposite of how she had seemed all those years before. She was simple and naive, soft and malleable. She wanted to be guided, and she did what she was told.

He has presented her with the illusion of power, and she had lapped it up like a greedy bitch. She made for a great puppet until she started thinking she was a 'real boy' and forgot her place.

He tried to save her. Mother warned it couldn't be done. She was always right. Vanessa's stubbornness reared its ugly head, so he cut it off, only to watch it regrow like a hydra. He thought he had finally cut off the last one. She simply would not let it go. Fortunately, the Chief of Police, Hernandez, had warned him.

In the end it had been the same as the beginning: every man for themselves. When it was Tony or Vanessa who had to face the gallows, Tony would choose Vanessa. It was a matter of self-defense.

The femme fatale went behind Tony's back trying to convince people of his guilt. Vanessa's insistence that Collin couldn't have been the murderer because *he* wasn't violent was unfair! *Tony* wasn't violent. But when backed against a wall, every man would defend themselves. It's human nature. And Tiffany was even more headstrong than Vanessa.

Keith's presence on his left snapped him back to the moment. The man looked ridiculous in the suit, he was much thinner than Joey. But it was the only one that fit him. He was going to have to dry clean the damn thing if he didn't want it to reek of cigarettes. Keith handed him the leather bag and mumbled some words. Tony smiled and nodded, not hearing and not caring. His gout had flared up this morning. His foot painfully distracting as they stood around.

His back to the meeting room, Tony sensed the occupants as they stepped out. Phil clapped a hand on his shoulder. "Looks like the cunt got what she deserved," Phil whispered to him as Vanessa was led out.

What a dick. But a necessary evil. Tony turned to face him and smiled and nodded. He shook Angelo's hand and assured him, with Phil back, it was business as usual. Angelo agreed before he and Phil left.

When everyone else but Victoria and Tony dispersed, they shared a knowing look. Everything was wrapping up nicely.

He still hoped there might be a way to save Vanessa. It was too soon to suggest that to Mother. That did not stop him from planning in his head.

Perhaps after she learned her lesson he could rescue Vanessa with an expensive defense attorney, a real one. She would be grateful, indebted. She would learn her place. Then she could come back. Not as CEO, but if she was willing to be a better follower, Tony could see himself leading Vanessa by the collar to greatness.

But he would have to check with Mother first.

31

I lean back in my chair and sigh, looking around my new office. It is almost as big as the CEO's office. It took me a month to design it the way I wanted. I got a glass top desk, no drawers. I don't need any paperwork, I have a computer.

My white chair is outrageously comfortable and since my assistant ordered it, I have no idea how much it cost. For the finishing touch, I had her get plants and lights to hang and decorate. I read that it's important that my office feels *lived in.* The plants will be a lot of work, but my assistant has time.

With Tony's full support, the executive team hasn't given me any pushback as I transitioned to the role of COO. I outrank all of them except for Phil. Just like Tony when he was COO, I'm the right hand to the CEO. Everyone reports to me because he trusts me.

I almost jumped at the sudden knock. Knock. Knock.

"Hey Pete." Elyse let herself in. We would have to work on that. She needs to understand, *she reports to me* now, not the other way around.

"Hello Elyse..." I said hesitantly. I hadn't called her in. "I have asked you not to call me Pete."

"Okay, *Mr. Liao.*" Not what I meant, but I like the sound of that. "I was wondering if you could help me out with some of these categories for the contact thingy you wanted me to type up. I don't know what some of them are." I recognized a card she extended as being from the rotating cylinder that held Tony's key contacts. "Like what's a consijar... consijlar…" She showed me the card and I stifled a laugh, squashing it into a smile.

Silly girl. "That's consigliere. Means advisor."

"Well, why wouldn't he just say that?" Elyse folded her arms. Then she looked at me coyly. "Do you think you can come help at my desk?" She had crossed the room and was now in front of my desk.

"I'm busy."

"Oh." Elyse looked away. "Maybe just lunch together then?"

I couldn't hold back my laugh this time, though I did keep it brief. "I have plans," I could have left it there but I added, "with my girlfriend."

Unnecessary, perhaps. But the poor thing isn't getting the hint. I have moved on. And up. We were no longer on the same level.

"Oh," she said again, sadly. "Do you think Tony is free?" Elyse's smile was wicked. "These are *his* contacts."

"Don't!" I started, startling her. "Don't bother him with these petty things." I'm not confident she will listen to me. Something I'm working on with her. But Tony expressly told me *never* to put these contacts in the computer where they could be searched, for whatever reason. Probably because he is an old school man, doesn't know you can password protect a document and computer. I would still rather he not know. And that he never spends time alone with Elyse. Tony told me to tell the cops that Tiffany and he weren't seeing each other, but her notes said otherwise. Best Elyse not get involved with him, just in case.

Elyse stubbornly stood there in front of me, deciding whether to listen to me before finally uttering an "okay", and moving to leave.

I let her get most of the way to the door before saying, "I almost forgot, I've got something else for you." She stomped back to my desk. I'll destroy that moody little teenage girl inside of her soon enough. "I need you to run around and grab drink orders from the executive team. Go quick so you can make it to the Morning Boost before our first meeting.”

Elyse’s eyes shot open wider and her nostrils flared. She clenched her jaw then spoke through barely parted teeth, “When you hired me, you said I was going to be doing an important job here, not just data entry and coffee runs.”

I pretended to be offended. “Don’t you think I, as the COO, need assistance? You doing these tasks enables me to do much more important things.”

She averted her eyes, “Yes, but I never would have—”

“What? Quit your job at the Morning Boost? Never would have stopped begging for tips to make a half decent living? Never would have done something with your life?” I asked. It was harsh, but she needed the reality check. Her parents never pushed her to be great like mine pushed me. “It’s only your second week, Elyse. Don’t forget, I started in the exact same role as you. Look at me now,” I gestured around the office. The second biggest office in the whole company. For me: the youngest COO they had ever had. “So, do you think you can handle this simple task and free me up for more business-critical things?”

“Yes, Pete.” She left quickly before I could say anything else.

I don’t like the way she said my name. I’ve told her: it’s Peter. Always Peter. And there was an attitude to the way she said it. No... not attitude: *insubordination*. I have some work to do on her.

Alone now, I can finally get back to my important work. I stood and reached toward my third monitor. I slowly peeled back the thin plastic covering that had protected it in shipping. IT set my computer up, but I preferred to do that last step on my own. Satisfying.

With that settled, I opened my email again. I’ve been copied on tons of things. Memos and updates. The executive leaders informing me of what they were working on rather than asking me for permission. A lesser man would feel threatened by this, would wonder what he was even supposed to do. But I know this means they know how to handle things.

I had been concerned, initially, that I might have been promoted beyond my own competencies. I didn't understand anything being discussed at the meetings. I never had anything new to add. And no one asked for my input. I started to think the whole thing was a mistake. I got so desperate I almost called my father for advice.

On the fourth day, a calm washed over me. Tony did not make mistakes. He must have known something I did not know. I put the pieces together. He knew the executive team already knew what to do, I was just there for reassurance.

Like a conductor.

Not a train conductor, an orchestra conductor. In school, I was part of the honor orchestra. I played the French horn *and* the clarinet. I never really paid attention to the music teacher who was also the conductor. My parents got me private lessons, basically a requirement at my school in Palo Alto. We all learned how to play our own instruments and then we did it.

What did the conductor do? Not much probably. Although she did occasionally lecture students who got out of line. But if you played well enough, and never wanted first chair, she left you alone. Were we amazing? No. But if all of us individuals *had been* amazing, we *would have been* amazing together. It was on each of us to succeed or fail, not the conductor.

That was why Tony put me in the role. Not because of my (practically complete) MBA. But because everyone already knew how to do their jobs. All he needed from me was my loyalty. He trusted me to show him when people got out of line. Or to keep an eye on them when he wasn't around. Like I did with Vanessa.

My parents always pushed me in school, said the degree would make me successful. That might have been true back in their day, but everyone has their Bachelor's now. And since Mom and Dad *only* paid for my first four years of college, I don't know what they expected me to do. I found a way to pay for it. Ironically, the criminal charge for selling cannabis that got me expelled was now my perfectly legal job. And my new position meant no work at the facility, so I guess they forgot about the background check.

But to my parents, it was never enough that I got into Columbia's Business School. It always came back to my failures. Every week when I visited, they asked me when I was going to get a *real job*. I stopped visiting. When I called Mom up to tell her I got a job as an Executive Assistant, she was thrilled. Then Dad had to push and pry until I told them it was for a cannabis company.

I haven't called them all month. When I go to family dinner for Aunt Helen's birthday this Sunday, I'm going to tell them all my new title. I'm the Chief Operating Officer of a multi-state public cannabis company and I'm not even thirty yet. Aunt Helen can shut up about how one day my cousin Sean is going to be a doctor. She has no clue he's been buying ADD meds since day one in college to 'stay focused because everyone in med school does it'. I'm tired of hearing how perfect he is. And so is Mom. I'm giving her the chance to talk about anything other than that loser Sean. She gets to brag about *her* son for a change.

It'll be their first time meeting my girlfriend too. More bragging rights for Mom.

My girlfriend's stunning, successful, and mature. Since she's older than me I'm sure she's eager to have kids before she can't anymore. Mom will love that. She's been begging for grandbabies. There's a free babysitter in the bag.

There was a soft *knock, knock* on my door which was already opening on the second knock.

Maya walked in, toned legs heading straight for me. Her strides were long because her cream-colored skirt was short. Her pale blue button up was more than a few buttons shy of being *buttoned* up. Her long dark hair was tucked behind her right ear, cascading past her cleavage on her left side. Simple, elegant, sexy.

She had followed my simple instructions on how she can look her best. Every time I have seen her since then she has been perfect...

Because I am the conductor and she is like my little cellist. I tell her what to play; she knows how to make her cello sound best.

I considered telling her to tone it down since she was for my eyes, not Phil's. I can't tell him *not* to look at her.

"Hi." She looked at me with satisfaction. Maya knew when she pleased me. "When do you think you can *get off* for lunch?" I smirked at her not-so-subtle wordplay.

"Whenever I want," I said. "I *am* the boss. Where do you want to go?"

She came over to my desk and sat on the edge facing me. "There's this little Mexican place I know." She used her finger to draw on my chest, nails a short and appropriate length, in a flattering natural color. Not like when I met her.

"No," I shook my head. "I don't like Mexican. Too many things going on with it."

Maya looked unprepared for that, but, ever my bubbly optimist, she corrected her face in a smile, "Sushi?" I shook my head. "Sandwiches? Or is there something that sounds good to you?"

"Whatever you want. I'm easy," I assured her. She was always trying so hard. Probably because she was getting older and still wasn't married. But she didn't have to worry about that kind of stuff with me since I'm not judgmental.

"Okay, Indian?" I made a face, reminding her of what she already knew about me. *Too spicy.* "We can get burgers again... Maybe the lettuce wrap will be better this time."

"Good idea!" I jumped in. "We can take your car. I'm low on gas." ...And I haven't made it to the dealership yet. Waiting for my next pay stub to show my proof of income. Maya doesn't need to know I am still driving my mom's old car.

My phone buzzed once. Without looking at it, I stood. Maya stood too. Looks like she has downsized her heels like

I had suggested because now I am at least one and one half inches taller than her. "I better get back to work." I kissed her on the cheek, tapping the back of my phone.

She shook her head lightly and some of her silky hair came out from behind her ear. Her perfectly tidied appearance now disrupted. "I didn't just come in here to talk lunch," she objected. "I was hoping you'd help me clean up my proposal on the Puff Puff Pass. Timeline, MROI, everything Tony asked for. It's a lot of work."

I was already guiding her to the door. It's important to establish boundaries. I can't do everything for my team. Even the ones worthy of special treatment.

"This is *your* passion project, Maya. I don't want to step on your toes. I'll make sure Tony knows you have my buy in." At the door I encouraged her further, "You got this." I gave her arm a firm squeeze, a promise for later.

"Thanks, Pete," she said, voice low and sultry. I decided to let her have it for now. I'd remind her later that *that is not my name.*

I returned to my desk, satisfied that my talented Cellist was off to play her cello as only she knows how to do. When she presents to the group, I'll be sure they know it was under my instruction. That way, everyone will buy in to the Puff and Pass. I'm happy to help her succeed.

My phone showed one text message from Tony.

I need you on notes in the meetings.

Yes, perfect. Exactly as intended. Everyone will perform their parts in perfect harmony, exactly as I have planned. While I, the conductor, take notes.

Description of the person who wrote everything in this book, including this description.

Photograph by Didi von Boch

Jaide McGee has a way of finding the story in everything, even if she has to make it up. When she isn't regaling friends and family over an elaborate home-cooked meal, she's telling them jokes at inappropriate times or teaching them Excel formulas at inappropriate times. She loves to travel to Northern California beaches with her boyfriend because they have the dramatic cliffsides and foggy weather writers require for nourishment. Jaide's second greatest fear is her writing being taken too seriously AND not seriously enough. If you want to know her greatest fear, check out her website : jaidethewriter.com and her social media @jaidethewriter on Instagram and Bluesky (until another trendy one takes over).